America's Glasnost

** Democracy from the Ashes **

How the 2016 Presidential Election
Could Reshape American Freedom
& Make a More Peaceful World

a political novel

by

Ernest C. Smitten

especially for my friends on the Old Continent, who know little of American politics. and for my American friends, who know even less

First Edition 2008

ISBN: 978-0-6151-9922-1

Printed in the United States of America

Also see www.sonicpress.com/ecs – Everything is Art

Book and cover design by ECS.
Written by ECS. in Turin, Italy, Summer 2007

Contents

Chapter 1

A Cause for Hope

He couldn't seem to get all the little white cat hairs off his freshly pressed dark blue suit jacket. As soon as he thought he had the last one, like a Tetris game, another one always appeared from the corner of his eye. But he had no time for that now. He was already being introduced by the popular Concord mayor. And that was simply the cost of getting up close and personal with the good people of New Hampshire. No one ever said Presidential campaigning was easy or stain-free, especially in these small primary states, where the pressure is always on with every handshake. Every day, every event feels like a make or break. The next four years, or the rest of your career in politics could melt away with one ugly slip-up or even just a disappointing second-place finish. Roger Adams did not like second-place finishes, but with a historical name like Adams and a politically active upbringing, he felt a kind of obligation to take his place at the table, at least for the debates.

The country had finally seen what a non-white-male President could look like. A woman had taken the 2008 election, but only by the narrowest of margins, which was becoming the norm for all elections over the last few decades, as the money and the marketing glitz worked the same magic for both sides of the Republican-Democrat coin.

Nearly everyone was disappointed with the Madame President after her first few months. She was constantly on the defensive, spending seemingly all her time proving she was as tough as a man, could play hardball like a man, waffle in the middle of the hot-button issues and wade waist-deep into unnecessary scandals like a man. She even had to stack her cabinet with men to prove what a man she was. To say this made her ineffective as leader of the free world would be an understatement, but she seemed less concerned about that than did any of the people buzzing around her twenty hours a day. The people closest to her, her advisers and her family, could all see it in her face, that she had realized her lifelong dream. She was calm and confident, not because her policies were making a difference - it was enough that they weren't completely collapsing - she was simply, astonishingly proud that she would be forever known as, "The first female President of the United States of America."

She had secured her place in history alongside Margaret Thatcher, Benazzir Bhutto, Gloria Arroyo... Sure there were other woman leaders, but this was America, shining beacon at the top of the free world. It was damn hard for a woman to be taken seriously in America - at least at any level higher than city council - and she had done it. This was her Mission Accomplished. It didn't matter so much what came next. She would just ride the fence on the most divisive issues and most of the hard work would be handled by the professional staff and advisers, the dedicated party people who had been doing this their whole professional lives. But the irony of the first female President casting an even more macho image than that of the previous "cowboy" President was not lost on the voting public, and there was a sadly familiar sense of disillusionment in America.

Her own lack of enthusiasm for the job and her unending brokering of rudderless compromises led to a gradual slide felt quickly throughout Washington and the country, and carried over into a lackluster, and failed, campaign in 2012. She fought it bitterly in the final months, hurling reckless claims into the media one last time, as she realized that her air of inevitability, which she had tried so hard to avoid in 2008, had her under its spell this time, but it was too late, and in the end, she only came across as mean, and her negatives in the polls continued to climb.

Adams himself would not stand a chance to even speak to this audience, had Ross Perot not devoted so much time and so much of his personal fortune to electoral reform, under the guise of re-establishing his withered Reform Party, before he passed away peacefully one starry night at his Texas home, back in 2011. Adams reflected on this man again for a moment, as he often caught himself doing at odd times of the day. Adams shared almost nothing in common with Perot from a policy point of view. They were nearly polar opposites in politics, yet they had shared a deep respect for each other's frankness and had been in many ways, easy friends. Without Perot's organization coming back to life and his personal dedication to the issue, third party politics certainly would not be the kingmaker it had suddenly become. The 2008 election had seen a record 100 million eligible voters stay home on Election Day, and Perot argued convincingly that the credibility of American democracy was becoming too fragile. 100

million people not voting, he said, "is the largest boycott I've ever seen in my life." He always utilized that deep Texas twang, with an inflection of down-home wisdom, to make his opinion seem even more unquestionably correct. "And with that 10-gallon cowboy hat on his head, he was the closest thing we've ever had to a real life Yosemite Sam," Roger thought to himself briefly.

Adoption of the two-round popular vote, where if no one wins 50% of the popular vote, the top two candidates campaign for a two-week-long second round, was now casting multiple (more than two) actual issues and unscripted, even unscriptable, debates into the headlights of Presidential politics for the first time in a century. And Adams was often a highlight of those stories, whether pushing for states' rights in a weekly magazine or offering his controversial health care ideas in a town hall meeting. He had plenty of quick comebacks and zingers to keep the other candidates on their toes too, but his simplification, most said *oversimplification*, of the big issues, took most of the headlines.

As he stepped up to the podium now in Concord, New Hampshire, for his fifth speech of the day, Adams slouched to the right, holding the wooden podium with both hands at arm's length with his arms extended out straight. He was a stout man, five foot seven on a warm day. He was not out of shape - he rode a bicycle for an hour every day - but he had the natural build of one of those 19th century circus strongmen. His broad chest sloped downward and fused seamlessly into his wide, strong belly. You could be sure he had hair on his chest, just from the shape of him.

He knew his words well and his concentration went toward making eye contact with as many members of the audience as he could. It was an easier speech this time, one of the hopeful speeches, short on specifics, a speech to show leadership. He generally gave these speeches later in the day, as they did not require the mental alertness of citing statistics or trying to persuade the crowd of his controversial opinions. Adams harbored a personal reluctance for the inspirational optimism speech, but he did not betray this, for he had also realized early on, that the American people never tire of their hunger for both optimism and religion. Given the choice, he would choose optimism every time. While not anti-religious, he was relieved to be running for President in a time when America's religious taste was running low, relative to recent decades. The downswing in faith, or at least *talk* about faith, was, surprisingly, attributable to the leaders of Muslim, Middle Eastern nations. After the Triple-10 attacks, leaders across the Middle East were moved to revamp their approach to Al Qaeda, but not quite in the same way America was transformed by 9/11. The kings of Saudi Arabia and Jordan, along with the Egyptian president, agreed in Mecca less than a week later, that the most effective way to preserve their power and their nations, was gradual, but not glacial, democratic reform and above all, more secularization of government in the Turkish mold. Heads of state across the Muslim world, save Iran, soon spoke with one voice, decrying the wanton destruction caused by extremism and pressing for a cultural shift toward reason. It may not sound like news to the western world, but making a call for humanist enlightenment in the heart of the Muslim world was not even possible before the attacks that shook the foundations of the Middle East.

Triple-10 was the name given by the media to the simultaneous multiple suicide attacks that struck the center of Riyadh, Cairo and Kabul on October 10, 2010 (10/10/10). On that bright Sunday morning, four oil tankers filled with gasoline and one with liquid natural gas exploded at different corners of each city center around 9 in the morning, destroying buildings, bridges and railways, and killing more than 5,000 innocent people in total. No one was more outraged, of course, than those most directly affected - the people of Saudi Arabia, Egypt and Afghanistan.

It should be pointed out that on the Islamic (lunar) calendar, the day of the attack fell at the start of the "Month of Rest," during which fighting war is forbidden, and which is directly followed by the month of the Hajj, which also forbids fighting. The date also coincided with an end-of-times scenario that had become increasingly popular among evangelicals in the United States awaiting their rapture, thanks to a best-selling book by mega-preacher Wayne Silvest. Debunkers appeared on several television shows, unanimous in saying that if anything, Al-Qaeda had purposely chosen the date in order to motivate the deeply religious Christians to react irrationally.

Fortunately, these attacks had the opposite effect on nearly everyone around the world. Support for Al Qaeda, at least in words, had been fairly common, even among minorities in western nations. But after Triple-10, even the most disaffected immigrant youth could not find the sense in the indiscriminate killing of so many women, children, and fellow Muslims. Populations across the region realized that they were in just as much danger from the now seemingly indiscriminate violence as anyone in New York or London. The whole world finally came to grips with Al Qaeda, not as a simple voice against liberal Western ways, but agents of chaos, anarchists bent on destroying the fabric of all societies, families, everything. Muslim leaders now spoke more often on theological points, whereas few had previously dared to debate the pillars of their faith, leaving the radicals free to propagate their extreme interpretations. Fatigue with the religious extremism of Al-Qaeda – among Muslims - had reached the tipping point, and religion in general, became a less popular talking point in politics from East to West, right across the globe as Reason became the new popular antidote to the continuing problem of terrorism. Religion didn't go away, of course. The numbers of people attending religious services in the West actually increased slightly, for the first time in 50 years. But religion became more personal and private than it had been for decades, no longer seen as the easy character card play that politicians had considered essential for so long. While some of the vocal minorities in the Muslim nations blamed the government for inviting the attacks by cooperating too much with the U.S. and the West, Middle Eastern leaders soon found themselves well-supported by their populations in actually increasing cooperation with the West in a quest for balance. Al Qaeda had finally come to be seen as a universal common enemy, not an insurgency against Western foreign policy, but an enemy of all civilization, a cult stuck in a Middle Ages philosophy, and the whole world finally began to truly unite against them. Al Qaeda did not disappear entirely, but their numbers and effectiveness dwindled gradually as more ardent police work led to more frequent arrests in areas where they had previously roamed free and new recruits were no longer so easily convinced to pit themselves uselessly against the world as martyrs.

It was this more temperate religious climate, this pendulum swing in the direction of Reason and the common humanity of all the world's people, that allowed more practical leaders like Roger Adams to move naturally to the fore. He was now nearing the end of his twenty-minute "Cause for Hope" talk and moving into his more forceful speaking style.

"No matter what kind of enemies we must face, at home or abroad, I say, we can have cause for hope. I am not one to talk about blindly hoping for a miracle. I say to you today, we must have not only hope, but *cause* for hope - I mean an actual reason to believe, that what we want to obtain, what we *must* achieve, is possible. Young parents working hard to support their families must have *cause* to believe that they will not lose their jobs, that it is *realistic* to believe that they can earn enough money to provide everything their children need, and that includes a chance to go to college. When the next large scale natural disaster befalls the American people, we must know that there is a plan. Real hope is not a magical force that comes down from the sky by chance. Hope is based on the knowledge that we are prepared, that there is a plan. It's no big mystery. We know what types of challenges await us - hurricanes, earthquakes, economic downturns, runaway medical costs, diplomatic confrontations, criminal activities and terrorist attacks... We know what types of challenges await us. The question is, will those challenges, the priorities of the American people, become the top priorities in our federal government as well, or will the insider system of Washington favors and trade-offs prevent the American people from being capably prepared for those challenges? We can only have cause for hope if we build that hope together - with our own hands. With your vote, I am determined to make the business of the American people the only business in town, and to build the cause for hope that we all need."

His voice rose dramatically over the cheering through the last sentence and after saying "Thank you" three times into the microphone, he stepped back and waved his hand to the crowd multiple times. They stood and applauded loudly for several minutes as he walked through the room, shaking hands and graciously taking the usual comments, "great speech," and, "you have my vote next month."

At the back of the room, his meaty elbow met the flat, wide hand of his campaign manager, Dusty Bremer. They swept out of the noisy hall through double swinging doors. They took two steps and stopped. Immediately before them stood two businessmen whom Adams recognized immediately. Matthew Emmitt took Adams' hand quickly, holding it firmly while looking straight into his eyes. Emmit's import-export business wasn't glamorous, and his simple polo shirt and floppy brown hair showed that he wasn't too worried about glamour, but he did control a slice of the pie and with his support, Adams would certainly be taken seriously by other donors. He had been relying almost exclusively on donations under $100 up to this point, and spending only what he had to, not willing to overstep his support level. He knew he was running with a less than mainstream message, regardless of how sensible it may have been to him, and it would take time for people to come around. But with the field wide open and primaries slightly less critical than in past years, thanks to the two round election (although that didn't stop the states from zigzagging all over the calendar with new primary dates), many large donors were holding back significant portions of their funds and official support until the first few primaries sorted out. Adams would be lucky to get any solid big-time backers before the New Hampshire primary, but if he did, it certainly wouldn't be too late by any measure.

"Nice to see you. Strong speech tonight," said Emmit warmly, very nearly stepping on Bremer's hurried, business-like introduction, "This is Matthew Emmit." "Thank you," sighed Adams, clearly worn down from the long day, which had covered three different cities across the state. Emmit suddenly dropped Adams' hand and asked Dusty, "Which way are we going?" "We have a room over here," said Dusty, waving his arm toward the right. "Sergey, how have you been?" Roger asked, turning his head toward the other businessman, Google co-founder Sergey Brin, as they walked. "Fine. The whole family is doing fine. Thank you, Roger." he said, as they quickly shook hands, their arms accidentally brushing Dusty's chest as they hurried into the side room. Adams and Brin sat down in the brown leather chairs, while Dusty set a glass of water on the table next to Adams. There were seven chairs, but Emmit remained standing and crossed his arms, gazing firmly at Adams. "What can I get you to drink, gentlemen?" asked Dusty. Brin put his arms on his chair's armrests and said, "Nothing thanks." Emmit said nothing and only continued to stare at Adams. Dusty, confused by the silence, looked around as if he had heard a critter in the room and then took a seat. As soon as Dusty sat down, Matthew Emmit said in a voice loud enough to be heard through the heavy wooden door, "Roger, you have no major backers, no party machine and no experience in politics." He waited a few seconds to watch Roger's eyes widen with surprise. "So what are we doing here, Roger?" He leaned back now on the edge of a table and lowered his voice to a regular business executive roar. "We're here to change all that Roger, because we like you. We like your message and we like your style.

Mostly, we like your message. We believe you should have a real chance in this thing."

Roger's eyes were still wide. He turned to Brin.

"Sergey?"

"It's true, Roger. We've been watching you from the beginning and we want to support you because we believe you can make a positive difference in this election."

"Well, that's terrific," said Roger, sitting up straight in his chair and suddenly not feeling tired at all.

"You better have a drink of that water there, Roger." said Emmit. And then before Roger could lift the glass to his lips, Emmit continued, "You can announce immediately that you have one million in backing from each of us.... that's for starters."

Roger set the glass back down and instinctively stood up to shake their hands again. "Thank you, gentlemen. That's outstanding! ...and really unexpected."

"Just keep doing what you're doing," Sergey said cheerfully, holding Roger's arm with his left hand while shaking with his right. "Like Matthew said, we believe in your message and we want to help you be heard."

Roger shook Matthew Emmit's hand again and said two or three thank yous before turning to Dusty, who he noticed was leaning heavily against the counter, as if catching himself from falling. "Dusty," he smiled, "I believe we have some ad buys to make."

"Yes, I think we do," he stammered, shaken with disbelief.

Chapter 2
Concord Grapes

Thanks to Perot's electoral reform (and everyone called it, "Perot's electoral reform," despite the fact that many European countries had been using the same two-round election format for decades, or perhaps *because* our fancypants European allies, who we sometimes disdain with more vigor than we fear our enemies, had been using the same two-round format for decades), the state primaries started to become open-ended free-for-alls, with the major candidates both more worried about losing face to the message candidates, and more worried about saving their money for a longer race. Winning the Republican or Democratic nomination was still the road to the White House though, and as always, only a few candidates were capable of raising enough money to convince enough voters that they were indeed electable. Suddenly, Roger Adams was a serious candidate. All the politics pods started talking about him as soon as he announced his two million dollars in donations. Of course, they only talked about his two million dollars. His fifteen second ads blanketed New

Hampshire and New York's RealiVision and TrueLifeDef television networks, and all the important 3net sites. Adams' fifteen seconds featured him in a "casual guy" light brown business suit, which looked a bit more like an old TV liability claims lawyer suit, sitting on the edge of an oak desk, saying curtly, "Hi. I'm Roger Adams. I built the solar desalination turbines for America, but that was only a start. I believe the government needs to be focused on the important business of the American people, not the shady business of special interests. With your vote, I will represent you honestly and directly, in *your* interest. I'm Roger Adams and I approve this message." The most important part of the ad was actually just saying his name a couple times. Most people, when they did hear his name, remembered that he was the businessman who had built the first proof-of-concept solar desalination/steam turbine plants in 2008 that now provided nearly ten percent of the United States' electricity and one quarter of the fresh water while draining off 2mm per year of sea level worldwide. By the time the global warming frenzy had reached its peak during the 2008 election, Roger Adams had spent two years trying to find an investor for his invention, when one finally came through. It was actually by chance that he got to talking with an antique car salesman about his idea. After trying all the venture capital firms, all the banks and all the power companies he could find, it was a car salesman, David McCrory, who took an interest. To Roger's total shock and amazement, the car salesman, who specialized in restored European cars from the post-war era, gave up on trying to sell him the 1966 Aston Martin in which Roger was sitting and looking up at him uncomfortably.

The salesman stopped talking about the history of the car for a minute and then asked Roger bluntly, "What do you do, friend?"

"I manage funds at an international bank." He rubbed his thumb and middle fingertips on his right hand together nervously and cautiously added, "And I'm designing a new kind of energy plant."

"You do all that at the bank?" McCrory inquired, half naive and half joking.

"No, of course not," he said without laughing. "It's just an idea I've been working on."

By the time Roger stepped out of the tiny silver sports car, McCrory was asking if he could partner with him on his desalination steam turbine idea. Here was this sales guy, suddenly trying to make a *buy*. After a half hour of convincing, Roger agreed to meet with him for dinner the next night and discuss a partnership.

Roger had already filed for all the patents, but building these plants would be a very large investment. Even regular old-fashioned desalination plants were so expensive that no one ever wanted to build them.

7pm, the next night - Roger walked into The Velvet Turtle, a place he normally only went when he really felt like treating himself to the luxury of a perfectly prepared, high-class meal, which frankly, wasn't all that often. He was generally content with whatever dinner he could scrape together from what he had in the kitchen at the time. He saw McCrory already seated with a glass of wine at a table right in the middle of the front room. "I don't think I've ever sat right in the middle of the room like that," he thought to himself with a curious smirk before walking over. "Hello David. How are you? Still interested in putting all your money into a high-risk project?" he said, smiling and looking him right in the eye while pulling out his chair to sit down. McCrory rose slightly out of his chair, out of polite habit, and winked at him, as salesmen do, "I'm fine. Are you still interested in saving the world?" he responded with a chuckle. "I am," Roger stated matter of factly, "but first let's build a desalination plant." Over well-done steak and delicious juicy shrimp, Roger detailed how the desalination pumps would actually be several miles away from the steam turbines.

"The sea water is carried inland through pipelines to the hottest, lowest elevation and least populated areas, the deserts of southern California, for instance, where it would then be distributed through hundreds of small fiberglass pipes, where the sea water would be evaporated into steam by the heat of the sun during the day. As I'm sure you know, if you've taken a basic chemistry class, or just wanted to boil your eggs a little faster, the more salt you add to water, the faster it heats up. And these small fiberglass pipes are like forgetting to open your car windows on a hot day. The fiberglass traps the heat, like a greenhouse. We might even build a greenhouse around the pipes for double heat-trapping, and of course, the smaller the pipes, the smaller amounts of water in each one, for greater steam conversion efficiency."

Roger was getting a little excited now. This was the first person who had actually taken the time to listen to his whole plan, and he wanted to get the big picture across before this guy lost interest, even if his shrimp were getting cold.

"Obviously a small pot boils faster than a large one.

The low elevation sites are chosen so gravity can help pull the water down the pipelines, thus operating with a minimum expenditure of energy on pumping. Everything is designed for maximum efficiency, you see. Let me know if I lose you on any of this."

"I'm following you, Roger."

"Terrific. Now between these small sea water pipes are rows of small solar panels. During the day, they collect and store the sun's energy, again taking advantage of the desert location. But at night, this energy is used to maintain the high temperature in the pipes, to keep the water evaporating day and night. Any extra solar energy not needed for heating the pipes during the night can be transferred directly to the power grid. When the water turns to steam, it naturally travels upward, where we have a steam turbine waiting for it. Of course, the steam turns the turbine, creating electricity. None of this is new technology, you understand. That's the beauty of it. It's all been proven to work already, it just hasn't been all put together in this way before. Now, after the steam turns the turbine, it condenses, it turns back into water, and we catch it. Fortunately for us, the salt and most of the minerals stay down below when it evaporates, and after condensation, it runs down through filters through the magic of gravity, and the magic of us placing the right kinds of filters in the right spots of course, so we now have fresh water too. As you may know, both the southern and the western states are really starting to panic about where all their water will come from. Snow packs are down, rivers and reservoirs are drying up. Las Vegas and Los Angeles are suing each other for water, because there just isn't enough to go around. OK, so that's nothing new, but do you know how much rain L.A. and Las Vegas got last year? 4 inches and 2 inches, Dave. They've got 20 million people in L.A. being restricted to showers every other day. They're in crisis mode. And this is global too. Do you know the Prime Minister of Australia goes around telling his people, 'Pray for rain'? What century is this, right? Governments don't know how to take action. Only a business can do this."

"You better take a few bites of your food there, Roger. It's gonna go cold on ya and yer gonna hafta put it in your hot pipes there." said the salesman, practically slapping his knee with a showman's laughter.

"Good idea," Roger agreed quickly. "It does look delicious."

After three bites, he returned to his sales pitch. "So there are three major problems that this project would solve. One: rising sea levels due to global warming - sea water is pumped out of the sea, lowering the sea level back to normal, assuming we have enough of these plants - I figure with a couple hundred, we'll start to see an impact. Two: electricity generation - we always need electricity. Three: the drinking water shortages that I just mentioned. Now these plants are expensive to build, which is why we don't have them everywhere already. But all three of these problems, global warming, energy and water supplies, are all coming critical right now. Listen David, you don't have to believe all the end of the world stories about global warming. The media always has some end of the world story to sell. Before it was global warming, it was the next ice age. But regardless, a large number of people are seriously worried about global warming, and the biggest threat from global warming is, theoretically speaking, rising sea levels."

Roger hunched down and lowered the tone of his voice, now really believing he might have a financial backer for the project he'd been working on for the last two years. "Look around. Everyone is jumping off the roof about this global warming catastrophe, but no one, *I mean no one*, has any solutions, besides parking all our cars, shutting down commercial air travel and recycling our shopping bags. That's not feasible, David. Everyone knows that. Nobody knows what to do! This plan can work because it provides proven technology solutions combined to make a major dent in all three of these critical problems. Once we can show the payoff, it will sell, not just in the U.S., but worldwide, because these three problems are all reaching such a critical stage, that it's worth the investment cost. You have to have water, right? You can't just say, 'Oh water's too expensive now, I'm going to stop using water.' Right? Same with electricity. Governments are going crazy right now with this intense fear of global warming wrecking the whole planet for human life within twenty years... People really believe that we must do something immediately. Let's give them the solution - three solutions in one - that they're begging for, David. Let's build this."

And then, with a handshake over a cold sixteen-dollar steak, they agreed to build it. They signed a 50/50 partnership contract and in March 2007, they had their first measurements from their half-size solar desalination turbine plant. When they arrived at the utility trade show in Houston in June, two representatives from power companies and five Department of Energy officials were waiting for them. They all stood and waited while Roger and David put up their small banners on the simple white booth and then they all sat down and talked about joint public-private ventures to get full-scale plants built and the optimal locations to build them in. By Election Day 2008, four plants were being built, one north of San Diego, one with a pipeline from just south of Los Angeles reaching all the way to the outskirts of Las Vegas (a joint venture between the cities of Los Angeles and Las Vegas), one outside of Houston, and one near Gulfport, Mississippi. Even during the primaries, the Presidential candidates, Republicans and Democrats alike, tried to take credit for getting the plants started, coining irritating catchphrases like "new energy framework." Roger had initially been stunned, that all these politicians were trying to take credit for something they had nothing to do with. He was the one who had been inspired to solve these problems while daydreaming one afternoon at work, after seeing another crazy global warming disaster scenario "documentary" on BBC World the night before. It was he who had spent two years drawing up plans, begging for financing and finding potentially interested engineers in his spare time. Roger was not the kind of person to demand attention for himself, but he was damn proud of his accomplishment, and at this point, he accepted an invitation to appear on 60 Minutes to make sure people knew that it was a few dedicated, hard-working American engineers who made this happen, not any politician from any party. None of the candidates dared boast about it as their own invention again after his appearance on national television, and by the end of that week, there was talk of drafting Roger Adams for President. Of course, it was far too late to enter the race at that point, and Roger Adams had only just started overseeing the building of the solar desalination steam turbine plants, and making many millions of dollars in the process. Hillary Clinton was enjoying a twelve-point lead over Republican John McCain.

That had been in 2008. His determination to build the desalination project, and his confident, defiant appearance on national television calling out *all* the politicians on their bragging, near the end of a very long election cycle instantly made Roger Adams a popular Washington-outsider type, the type of leader the American public always longs for during a campaign, but can never believe in enough to actually vote for.

Now, eight years later in 2016, still defiant and more confident than ever, Roger Adams was determined to change the election formula. He sat now in his New Hampshire headquarters with his team of supporters, eating gooey cheese pizza with thick blankets of parm and oregano, which would become his trademark election results meal after this night, waiting for the primary results to come in. Behind the small cheap television, an army of television cameras and an array of RealiVision cams covered the wall from head to toe. The media had taken notice of his last-minute cash infusion and ad blitz coming out of nowhere, and were anticipating a surprise fifth or sixth place finish in the Democratic primary for the upstart independent candidate. Even if Adams wasn't on the road to the Presidency, he made for a good news story, the outsider bucking the system, taking on the big-time politicians, working for the little man, trying to make the system a bit more honest, and always with something brash to say.

Dusty came over and put his arm around Roger. "We've come a long way, my friend. And no matter what happens tonight, I think we still have a long road ahead of us."

"You're right, buddy," Roger replied, "I think you're right."

He turned and picked up another slice of pizza and a couple more napkins when the din of excited supporters and volunteers died down enough that he could actually hear the television. The volume on the TV fell noticeably, indicating that a commercial break had just ended. Roger looked up at the television at the same time that he held his slice of pizza to his face. Just then, he heard a news presenter's drab monotone voice through the dramatic election news jingle and focused his watery eyes on the screen. All he could see was his own name, and it startled him as if waking him from a dream in which he was falling. He reflexively let out a puff of a breath, accidentally blowing parmesan cheese and oregano off his pizza all over his Manchester regional volunteer organizer's back. He quickly brushed it off, apologizing embarrassedly. Four or five volunteers in the vicinity had a good laugh, but all jaws dropped as attention returned to the TV screen. Roger Adams' name was not just on the results list - it was in third place. An unbelievable third place finish, with 12%, for a guy with no party machine and no big donors until a week ago. He even beat out John Edwards by 4%, the same John Edwards who had nearly become VP in 2004 and had served as Attorney General for Clinton 44 after famously declining her offer to join the 2008 ticket. "Never again will I run for the Vice Presidency," he had declared, displaying the kind of maniacal ego most candidates' campaigns spend much of their time trying to keep a lid on.

The room was dead silent, save the television reporter's droning voice, for at least two minutes. Everyone was waiting for a correction, for the real results to come in. And then all at once, the room burst into wild cheering and jumping up and down. The disbelief had apparently been punctured and jubilation took over. Roger looked around, thinking this was what real Presidential campaigns look like when they're picking up their first wave of momentum. And then, once again, he didn't know how to register what he was looking at. He and then Dusty along with him, shushed the room for several seconds, and then turned back to the television. Now his name was appearing in fourth place, but just a few seconds ago, it had been third, with 98% of precincts reporting. His eyes darted around the screen, searching for an explanation, feeling distrustful of the reporter. He was thinking of changing to another channel when Dusty put a greasy pizza finger on the top of the screen and yelled, "Oh my god! This is the Republican primary! Look - Republican!", as if no one in the room knew how to read.

"Dusty," Roger asked in slow and calm astonishment,

"are you saying we placed in *both* the Republican and Democratic primaries? Third and fourth?!"

"I think we did!" Dusty said loudly for everyone to hear, and the room burst into a new wave of celebration. Sure enough, it was the Republican slate. (The President was not standing for re-election.)

The results were:

Vice President Jeb Bush 52%
Georgia Governor Sonny Perdue 16%
South Carolina Senator Lindsey Graham 15%
Roger Adams 8%.
Missouri Rep. Matt Blunt 7%

Shouting over the ear-splitting screaming and cheering, and putting a hand over his face sideways for a sliver of privacy from the wall of cameras, Roger asked Dusty in his ear, "Has this ever happened before?" Dusty strained his neck upward as he was carried a couple steps away from Roger by the ebullient crowd and shouted, "I don't know!"

Chapter 3
The Good Wife

He reveled in the simple pleasures - the comfort of being at home, the fresh air of the small town, and sliding out of his suit jacket like a snake shedding a dead skin. He kicked off his shoes, stretched his toes, and without even realizing it, let out a deep, "aaaahhhh." His shoulders, so tense so often, that he didn't remember what relaxed felt like, softened and sloughed a little when he entered the living room. There was Lenka, all five-foot-eight of her, standing tall, muscles tight like a race horse, mane flowing, absolutely nude and slowly brushing her teeth in total silence, turning gently in the sunbeams to allow her tired husband a good full look at her delicious body. The tooth brushing was coincidental. She just happened to be brushing her teeth when he came in the door, but she used the motion now to produce a small jiggling effect throughout her body. Her golden brown skin glistened with a few remaining streaks of shower water, her cheeks flush and her breathing deep, fresh from running. She glanced at him with her big brown eyes that seemed to emanate their own light from within, and then looked down again, as if she didn't know anyone was in the room with her. Roger fell back against the edge of the doorway and soaked in the show. Every time he came home to her, he felt like he couldn't believe his luck, even after six years. She always knew how to make him feel like he was the only man in the world - and he wouldn't mind if the rest of the world simply disappeared.

She was 37 and he was 52, but they were such a well-matched couple that no one seemed to notice the age difference. She enjoyed dressing up and making her husband look good by standing at his side, but there was no mistaking her for a trophy - she may have only gone to a state university, but she never held herself back when opinions were being offered. She was inquisitive from birth, and even fiery when she felt it would get the point across, but always, always elegant. She had a natural sophistication that poured out from her attitude, her posture, everything, that enchanted and intrigued Roger from the first time he laid eyes on her.

She disappeared now into the kitchen with a half look back at Roger, meaning "wait right there." Roger let his eyelids come down slowly, as they suddenly felt extremely heavy. On the edge of sleep after a few seconds, he returned to life with a start when he felt his wife's hand sliding into his. "Lenka," he whispered, "I need you." "I know," she said with a slow smile. "And don't ever forget it," she added with a chuckle. This raised a smile from Roger's slumping face and brought him fully back awake. She pressed him against the wall and dangled a large red ripe strawberry in front of his mouth, which he ate in two bites. She then gave him a full kiss on the mouth for a good thirty seconds. It wasn't every day they managed to enjoy this kind of alone time and they were both ready to take full advantage. He wrapped his arms around her and she peeled him off the wallpaper and started them spinning in a sort of chaotic ballroom dance around the living room, still kissing, and his hands sliding down to hold onto her full round ass. Just as Roger began to feel dizzy, Lenka pushed him away and darted up the stairs, giggling all the way. He managed to focus his eyes on her succulent flesh in motion just seconds before she reached the top. He moved quickly up the steps himself, and sat down on the bed next to Lenka. "In the bedroom? How old-fashioned," he quipped. "I'm not closing any curtains," she replied, fully aware that the nearest neighbors they had wouldn't be able to hear a missile launch from their property, much less get a view into a window. Being already completely naked herself, and sensing that Roger needed no more warm-up time, she began stripping off his clothes, starting with his socks and working her way up. They kissed and pressed tightly against each other for at least half an hour, taking nibbles out of each other's necks, until they were both moaning in agony/ecstasy. His chest now heaving, Roger put two fingers into Lenka's sopping wet pussy. Feeling the soft flesh of her hole, the shape of the labia and the tight, dripping walls inside her, turned him on more than anything. Straddling him, she pushed her left, full C-cup breast halfway into his mouth so he could barely breathe, and she gasped in orgasm. His hand was soaked in her juices and her screams went right into his ear, which made him totally lose control. He flipped her onto her back and laid his weight upon her hips. With one hand sliding up her right thigh, he slid forward, pushing gently inside her. They moaned together. He tilted his weight slowly back and forth, sliding up and down, until she screamed even louder than the first time. His entire body was tingling and his brain felt completely empty, like it had sailed right out of his head and left a helium balloon in its place. He shut his eyes about as hard as he could, and felt it all shooting out of him for what seemed like eternity. His heart was pounding so hard it hurt. He was practically screaming now too, his hand still gripping the top of her thigh, and finally, he rolled off of her, leaving his right arm draped over her. Panting and puffing, they lay there for a good ten minutes, their hair stuck to their foreheads and their whole bodies melting into the sheets. He felt her getting up to go to the shower, but only barely, as he passed into a deep slumber.

...

Roger came around slowly, not sure where he was, totally disoriented, in fact. It was still dark. His brain sorted automatically through the tasks he had ahead of him for the day, but he didn't have the focus to pay attention to the background thoughts in his own head. He felt a strong presence in the room. He turned over slowly and found his gorgeous wife sleeping like an Egyptian mummy, her slightly smiling face turned peacefully, directly upwards, to the sky. "Mmmmm," he murmured happily and rolled toward her, slowly landing an arm and a leg on top of her silky body, not really trying to wake her up. She made some indiscernible noise and wriggled a little, but did not wake up. Six A.M. He spotted the clock over Lenka's head and tried to calculate how long he'd slept. "Ten hours? No. Eleven? I don't know," he thought to himself. "The sun was still up when we went upstairs." Then the memory floated to the top and suddenly felt real. "Did I?..." he thought, hazily. "I stabbed those men?", he asked himself frantically before quickly realizing he was still mostly asleep and the knife fight in the picturesque mountain stream had been a very adventurous dream. Now, with the impossibly vivid green grasses, hard shadows and blue waters bubbling up to the front of his mind, he was intensely curious. "What was the rest of it? What was I doing before those bad guys showed up?" And then the images vanished, like a minor memory from 10 years ago, and he gave up thinking about it. He cuddled up even closer to Lenka to appreciate the opportunity to just lie in bed with her. No meetings to rush to, no dressing up to go out, just me and her, alone and quiet. He put the tip of his nose into her hair and fell back into a light sleep, although well aware of holding Lenka with his whole body, almost like a form of meditation on how much he loved her.

...

"Congratulations, honey." Her soft words woke him gently.

He smiled and grumbled incoherently.

"What honey?" she asked with a sinister smile. "I don't know what you're trying to say." She loved to tease him about what a deep sleeper he was, especially when he tried to mumble something that was totally impossible to understand.

"What is it, sugar muffin? What do you want to tell me? Bagel? Ladder? Fish sticks?! What?"

Through his squinted eyes, he could see her towering over him on the bed and giggling like crazy. He let out a giving up kind of laugh and rolled over, pulling the blanket up to his chin. "Go away," he finally blurted and squeezed his eyes firmly shut.

"Ohhh..." she said melodramatically, "Now you don't like me anymore? OK, I can leave, but don't think you'll get away with bringing any other bimbos in here. I'll be watching the house, dear." She bounced down onto her knees and then slithered across him, the both of them giggling quietly, as if trying not to let on.

"Uhh... Nevermind then, you can stay," said Roger dryly.

"Ah!" Lenka cried unexpectedly, sat up and burst into a rolling laugh. "You think it's that easy?"

"Yeah, I do," answered Roger coolly as he turned over and she fell into his arms.

He kissed her passionately several times and then let his head fall again, unable to collect his morning energy.

"Oh, you're gonna have to do better than that!" she exclaimed.

He finally sat up and gave her one more kiss on the lips and put his hand in her hair. "I've gotta get going, sweetie," he said.

"Don't you get a day off after winning a primary?"

"Honey, now you know I didn't win the primary..." he explained, still only hazily able to open his mouth halfway.

"You know what I mean," she interrupted.

"Yeah, OK. But you also know, that when I do well, it means I have more to do, not less. The losers are the ones that sit at home in their underwear browsing the Best of the DeadSites on the internet, like MyPlace, or whatever that old page was the kids used to have."

"MySpace," she corrected him, still proud that she had found a couple really cool bands that had remained "underground," meaning essentially that they had never found any success at all.

"Yeah, that's it. Thanks honey."

He stood up to get dressed and thought about how much he enjoyed making Lenka seem far more hip than himself. He had been a major record collector and maybe even qualified as a scenester in his day, but that was such old news to him now. Plus, he liked to remind himself of how young and in touch she was, because it made him feel younger. He knew it was a simple psychological trick he was playing with himself, but he considered himself wiser for it. He even saw it as a positive, healthy way to bond with his partner, to live vicariously through each other in certain ways. So long as it was clear to both of them what they were doing, he felt it was a sweet and natural gift they could give to each other - a way of adding something to each other's lives that they would not be able to experience directly - and one of the keys to the happiness they shared together.

"So anyway, we have to do a lot of PR and interview work today, to capitalize on yesterday's win. I mean, 'yesterday's surprise'. I think we're referring to it as 'yesterday's surprise.' We're having a celebration dinner tonight with Dusty and some of the other staff though, OK? Seven o'clock?"

"Of course, honey," she said. "I can't wait." She

pondered at the closet and then picked a dark blue tie with one white diagonal stripe, looped it over his head, and used it to pull him close and mash her lips on his. She was already dressed - in a slim, silky beige dress and her favorite heels.

"Have a great day, tiger. I'll be home by six just to be safe." She turned and walked out. He listened to her walk down the stairs, her hand squeaking on the banister, as he tied his tie and cinched his belt. "I love you!" he called out. "I love you too, honey," she said on her way out the door.

Roger thought again about how truly happy he felt, not just happy, but really satisfied. Politics was important to him, but Lenka made his whole life worthwhile to him; she made him feel capable of anything. He would never continue with it if he should lose her somehow. (Roger's morbid streak ran deep, a natural side-effect of losing a parent at an early age.) Lenka lifted his ego, not by purposely stroking it, but just by being her catty self, by giving him her attention and always treating him as an intelligent equal. It suddenly occurred to him that he provided her with the exact same thing, which put a big smile on his face as he put on his shiny black shoes and then walked out the door.

The day was filled with interviews, with Roger explaining twenty times in a row, that the "surprise" in New Hampshire was just the beginning of a new type of conversation in politics. It was on repetitive PR days like this that he longed for the campaign to be behind him so he could get back to actually doing something, anything, so long as it wasn't repeating catchphrases all day. The so-called celebration dinner was mostly business. Dusty updated him on all the polls and the strategies for the week ahead.

After dinner, Roger and Lenka took a walk down to the beach. She could actually see his whole body soaking in the calm, the quiet and the heavy, damp cool air, which always helped him breathe easier. He could feel the inside of his lungs being moisturized and he visualized his skin storing up the energy from the fresh air, a water-based version of the solar collectors on his desalination steam turbines.

It was hard for him to even look at the ocean anymore without seeing a fat, Magritte-like, painted-black pipeline reaching out into it and running past him, in a straight line, from one horizon before him, to the other behind him. He had loved the ocean all his life, and then spent years at coastlines across the southern United States, and around the world, installing these bizarre-looking pipes. The pumps and the power plants all looked like normal infrastructure, but he could never get used to that view from the shore, and of course the fact that it was all his idea made it seem even stranger to him. He thought of Frankenstein, and then of the plain, black monoliths in the *2001: A Space Odyssey* series.

He had not built any actual monoliths, but he *had* drawn some unwanted wacky-rich-guy stories about himself when he bought the island in the middle of an Oregon town, although it was no bigger than about two football fields, and the four-bedroom home he built there was quite modest, considering all he had accomplished and the many millions he'd earned with his grandiose sea water turbines. The island was called Mantel Island, situated in the middle of a small picturesque river, well, a bit muddy really, in a family vacation town called Seaside, at the Oregon end of the 4,000-mile Lewis and Clark trail. He was not arrogant enough to even consider renaming the island, just because he had purchased it from the county. The town, and the whole coastal region, had been in a total uproar, actually, until word got out that he was not planning to build any new access roads or bridges, nor a ten-story monstrosity, but would transfer everything he needed to the house by boat, and he would not bring a single car onto the island. At that point, the community was more curious about how he would go about living there on his own tiny version of Venice than anything else.

It wasn't far to the beach, just five blocks from the northern tip of the island, down Avenue K. Now with the campaign becoming serious, they weren't home very much. Old Mrs. Frischmuth, out on her porch, nearly fell out of her rocking chair when she recognized her famous neighbors coming out of the shadows of her poorly lit but well-forested street. "My goodness, is that you Mr. and Mrs. Adams? I thought you were in New Hampshire. They don't tape those primaries ahead of time, do they?" she asked, sincerely worried.

"No, Mrs. Frischmuth," Roger explained, "I flew home right away for a few days rest, just as soon as I could get back to my lovely wife. Have to recharge the ol' batteries once in a while."

"Oh, I imagine you do, running around, speaking all day and shaking the hand of everyone you see. It must be exhausting."

"It certainly is. But it's worth the effort, too."

"Of course it is. We're all rooting for you, Mr. Adams." she called to him, as they continued walking.

He craned his neck and twisted his shoulders to reply, "Thank you Mrs. Frischmuth. I appreciate that," and they slipped quietly out of sight, the sound of their footsteps buried by the crashing of waves.

Lenka unrolled a thick blanket and sat down, Roger still standing, hands on hips, staring at the sea. After a few seconds, he realized Lenka was sitting and sat down behind her, sliding his right arm over her slight stomach and pulling her in close.

"Let's lie down and look at the stars," suggested Lenka excitedly. The tops of their heads touched on the blanket, and Roger's left arm was quickly falling numb in the space between the sand and Lenka's lower back, but he only tried to turn his shoulder because he didn't want to take his arm out from under her.

"Being in the city where all the stars disappear from the sky, it's like living on another planet, isn't it?" Roger mused.

"It's like living inside a box!" she said, doing him one better.

"I love you, sweetie," he said admiringly.

"I adore you, honey," she offered back.

She slid the back side of her fingers slowly, but non-sexually, up and down the outside of his leg, and lay quietly with him, knowing full well that he was all talked out from campaigning. And their eyes swept across the stark, speckled sky, listening to the water push up the beach, slide back down, and build up to a crash again, in its unsteady but comforting, unending rhythm.

Chapter 4
The Florida Republican Debate

"It may sound incredible, but lying has become not only common practice for politicians, it is the gold standard for our times, the only way anything seems to get done in government, and often in business, in schools, and in families.

Despite religious fervors of any stripe, lying will always be an essential part of human nature. We lie to get what we want, to avoid hard questions, to make life easier. But the cost must always be paid sooner or later, and our country has paid many times, with periods of political and economic instability, astronomical rates of violent crimes and general fear, the squandering of the respect of our enemies and allies among nations, and a declining overall standard of living for the first time in our history, to name a few. America was founded to break free from imperialist Europe. But from our genocide of the Native American Indians, to the exploitations of slavery and child labor, to Nixon's infamous cover-up, to the Iran-Contra scandal, from the Vietnam War to the Iraq Wars, decades of proxy wars and games with the Soviet Union threatening total global annihilation, as if the world were a toy and the fate of all people, a bargaining chip. America has been an aggressor nation, at times purposely playing the part of a dangerous madman to frighten the others, collecting all the marbles, scrapping with the other big boys for every nickel of economic might like an ageing celebrity struggling to maintain some career momentum before it all flickers out.

America has had times of triumph too, of course. Abraham Lincoln, with direct, elegant words and an iron will, stood against slavery despite the economic damage to the southern states, and held the nation together through our darkest hour. He stood strong for what was right, and he spoke clearly to the American people about where we were going and why. In sharp contrast to the covert Bay of Pigs disaster, UN ambassador Adlai Stevenson angrily challenged the Soviet Union to admit they were placing nuclear weapons on Cuba, just a few miles off the coast of Florida. When they maintained their standard lie, he produced satellite photos for all the world to see, defeating the enemy on the world stage with clear evidence of the truth. And Ronald Reagan, in Berlin, delivered a simple challenge to the face of his so-called 'evil empire.' 'Mr. Gorbachev,' he said, 'tear down this wall.'

When America has stood on principle, when she has been able to break through the smokescreens and speak the truth with a straight face, the world has listened and even admired us for our example of candor and dedication to freedom. Perhaps it is because of this legacy, that when America does fall short of its ideals, the whole world is truly disappointed.

When America's prison population surpasses the entire population of Ireland, when it turns out that we have kidnapped not only terrorists, but also innocent people off the streets and tortured them in secret prisons around the world, when police drones chase down our own citizens without cause, when we give tens of millions of dollars to rebel groups and dictators who ruin their countries for decades to come, our talk of freedom for all loses its credibility, and we are seen as amoral hypocrites. When the world sees our soldiers stationed permanently in the Middle East, or the poor people of a flooded Houston begging for food and water on every internet channel for nearly a week, the American dream begins to seem like maybe it is only a dream, that we have hoped for too much. But when our elected officials later try to say that they are not to blame because no one could have imagined these things could happen, that is the last straw - no one can quite believe it anymore. The people's common sense finally overrules the illogical explanations they've been feeding us. It *must* be possible to prepare for disasters and to put our vast resources to better use. Even our political system has turned into a good cop/bad cop single-party system. Republicans, Democrats, Republicans who used to *be* Democrats. It has become terribly obvious, that our government is lying to us.

Whether it's millions of uninsured citizens, or quiet American support of dirty wars in faraway corners of the world, we must realize that each of us has signed off on these perversions of justice, and that, by our silence, we are each helping to break down the rule of law which holds our societies together, both around the world and right here at home. Aside from good people stepping up to run for office themselves, the best thing each of us can do is to be educated on the issues and demand the truth at every opportunity, to insist that our representatives perform the people's business in a transparent manner, to never accept the lies, to actively challenge the validity of convoluted and false statements, for the sake of America, the world, and our future generations. For when we demand it, and *only* when we demand it, we will indeed receive the truth that we seek. For too long, politicians have given us candy instead of reality – because they believe that's what the people of America really want.

The government needs to come clean with the American people, and with the world. When the Soviet Union stood on the edge of collapse, not in 1989, but several years earlier, it was most threatened by its own system of corruption and secretive, bureaucratic inefficiency. Gorbachev recognized that the only choice, for the good of his people, was openness, known by the Russian word 'Glasnost,' and that one policy idea changed the whole world. America today needs its own Glasnost, a revolution of transparency, for the good of our people. An honest, transparent approach, taken in any measure, even just a little bit more honesty, will improve America's standing across the board, in terms of goodwill abroad, the economy, our security and our quality of life. Increasing honesty in several areas of government will have a compound positive effect, launching a new era of accelerating growth and prosperity for all Americans, and put American back on top of the world."

Anderson Cooper: "Thank you Mr. Adams. That's the last of the opening statements. Our format tonight will be a question directed to one candidate, with one minute to answer, and then two minutes of open debate. We'd like all the candidates to please allow the others to speak. We're going to try this. If it gets too wild though, I will have to step in. The first question is to Senator Graham, from Tim Russert."

Tim Russert: "Thank you. Senator Graham, you have attacked other candidates' universal health care proposals as unsustainable, yet the issue remains one of the most important to the American people. We haven't heard your plan yet. How would you address America's out of control health care costs?"

Senator Lindsey Graham: "Tim, health care is, of course, too expensive, but we know from experience, that fostering competition is the only sustainable way to drive down costs. Implementing a socialist hospital system sets prices artificially and would force us to reduce the quality of our health care, because we would not be allowed to spend the money necessary for the best possible care. Do we really want to wait three weeks to get a cast on a broken leg like our friends in England do today? Our Canadian neighbors come to us when they need world-class treatment. If we convert to their low-quality blanket approach, where will we travel for our heart surgeries? Tokyo? Mr. Adams' plan especially, is a recipe for disaster. He wants the American government to pay for every doctor visit, for every bottle of vitamins. He's going to bankrupt the federal government."

Roger Adams: "The Senator from South Carolina is either purposely distorting my position, or he has badly failed to understand it. The health care plan I have put forward, for the first three years, provides only well-defined preventive care for everyone up to the age of eighteen who is not already covered. More segments of the uninsured population are added to the preventive health care program only after costs begin to come down while we break the health care monopolies and shift our focus to preventing health crises, instead of repairing them. When people are encouraged, instead of discouraged, to see their doctors and get tested regularly, we will see healthier lifestyles and fewer expensive operations. Our current system is simply bloated too far out of control to be turned off like a light switch at this point. Unlike the overly ambitious plans of the past two decades, my solution takes on the big picture, but one step at a time, each success providing a platform for the next, and reinforcing the overall plan, which includes lifestyle education and financial incentives and disincentives. I just do not see a comparison with any system in Canada or Europe or anywhere else. The only similarity is that under my proposal, the fundamental goal of health care would be to actually care for people's health, rather than make a profit. Our current system is actually making more money off of perpetuating unhealthy lifestyles! Unhealthy people die early, requiring fewer services over a shorter lifespan. The system is literally trying to kill us, in order to save money. I'm new to Washington, but I just can't understand how anyone can be in favor of that.

However, the Senator and I are in agreement, that one size does not fit all. We cannot just copy the Canadian system or the French system; we need a system designed for our needs. Complex systems function differently under different economic conditions and in different cultures - with different histories and different expectations. No public policy can be effective unless it is crafted for the specific needs of the people it is made to serve. Agreed, Senator?"

Senator Lindsey Graham: "Yes, I..."

Roger Adams: "So how can you explain your 20 years of unwavering support for a foreign policy that attempts to impose American-style governance on countries that could not be more different from America, crusading through the Middle East trying to re-colonize peoples who have been struggling by violence to break free of a string of colonial powers for the last hundred years? With different histories and different economic conditions, shouldn't the peoples of the Middle East be allowed to create the kinds of government that suit them best?"

Senator Lindsey Graham: "I believe we were on the topic of health care. Now I..."

Roger Adams: "It doesn't matter what topic we're on Senator - your logic is fundamentally full of holes. You want to say my solution for health care is too similar to systems in other countries, yet in the Middle East, you want to impose a carbon copy of our entire system of government. You can't have it both ways, Senator Graham."

Vice President Jeb Bush: "No one has imposed American government on the Middle East, Mr. Adams."

Roger Adams: "No, because it isn't possible. But that hasn't stopped you from trying, endlessly, at the cost of many thousands of lives, both civilian and military. There's a logical explanation for the chaos that follows us to every nation where we try to intervene. The United States has a long-standing policy of arbitrarily installing pro-Western leaders who have not earned any support from the citizens of the country; they've only bought their power from the US by selling out their country's resources. When you prop up these artificial leaders with guns and money against the will of the people, you're not building democracy, and you're not creating stability."

Senator Lindsey Graham: "May I speak now?"

Roger Adams: "Please do. I'm fascinated to hear an explanation."

Senator Lindsey Graham: "The people of Pakistan, Afghanistan and Iraq are far better off now than they were 15 years ago. I don't think any of us wants to imagine where those countries would be without our support over the last decade and a half. I will not hand over entire countries to Al Qaeda so they can build a network of terrorist nations in any region of the world, whether it's the Middle East or northern Africa or anywhere. It's a dangerous world out there, not like the business world. These are real and complex situations, and they would be in far worse shape without our stabilizing influence."

Roger Adams: "No one wants to hand anything over to terrorists, sir."

Senator Lindsey Graham: "But that's what you would effectively do."

Roger Adams: "Letting people design their own government is not..."

Senator Lindsey Graham: "As for health care, I will always prefer to work with market conditions to bring costs under control, rather than to introduce another unsustainable welfare-type program."

Roger Adams: "Market conditions, manipulated by the

behemoth drug and HMO industries, are the reason even middle class Americans cannot afford to catch a cold, much less a hospital stay. Maybe you would like to eliminate the food stamp system too? Is that one of your unsustainable communist programs that just happens to feed 35 million hungry Americans each month, and has been successfully doing so for the last 50 years? Does government not exist, in part, for the purpose of protecting those of our citizens who are under threat, be it from hunger or disease or foreign enemy? Or does the Republic only exist to swell the egos and pocketbooks of a privileged few corporate interests and let the people suffer and fall away, so long as they pay their taxes? Do we not have an obligation to our fellow Americans?"

Senator Lindsey Graham: "I will not take away anyone's food stamps. But what you're talking about is the United States government paying the bills for every person in America! It just isn't possible."

Georgia Governor Sonny Perdue was itching to jump in, but he wasn't sure how.

Roger Adams: "It is about providing the basics, only to

those who have nothing, not flushing millions of our citizens down the toilet because they're not wealthy enough. And I submit to you, that it is possible, within a free market framework, if we shift the priority to inexpensive prevention instead of expensive drugs and surgeries. We've been at this since Truman, for crying out loud. How long before we decide it might be worth trying it in a different way?"

Anderson Cooper: "OK, gentlemen. Fascinating conversation, but we need to move on and hear from all the candidates tonight. The next question is for Vice President Bush, from Vanessa Danilov."

...

His showing in both slates of the New Hampshire primary had qualified Adams to appear in all of the debates, Republican and Democrat, as well as those open to all candidates. He participated in as many as he could. Among party-affiliated candidates, only Alan Keyes and Al Sharpton were not viciously opposed to Adams' participation. But as Adams stressed in all his interviews following the New Hampshire surprise, "I do not believe that the people of New Hampshire voted for me to be President just yet. The people have voted to hear more of what I have to say about what kind of President we should have. So my job now is to talk about how we can bring the American people's priorities to Washington DC, to make the people's business the only business in town, and I believe we can do just that."

President Lieberman was, of course, eligible to run for re-election, and everyone in Washington had been genuinely shocked for the first time since Nixon resigned in disgrace. Lieberman had promised he would not seek re-election in 2016 if he could not get his social security and Medicare reforms through the Congress. Everyone in Washington expected that he wouldn't say that unless he only needed a few votes, and that he would then probably get them. Even after he lost the vote, they definitely did not expect him to actually honor the promise to step down. Skilled politicians like Lieberman can always spin any promise on its head. His advisers all said that the President had honestly believed he could muster the support he needed, having built his career on unlikely bipartisan agreements. They said he genuinely felt that he had lost his greatest strength, to build coalitions in Congress, and that without that, he could not be effective, could not be the kind of President that he wanted to be. And there was no reason to expect a Republican majority in Congress in the next election. Many bloggers wrote that he had simply hurt the Democrats too much when he betrayed the party to pursue and then win the Republican nomination. His credibility with the Republicans was hardly an issue, once he decided to jump ship. He'd been building relationships across the aisle his whole career in the Senate. He had backed George W's war in Iraq through the worst of times, with the picture of the President famously kissing him on the cheek to prove it. He had even been forced to run as an Independent in his 2006 Senate race when he lost the Democratic nomination, although he had been only a few thousand votes shy of becoming Vice President on the Democratic ticket with Al Gore just six years earlier. Of course, the Republicans were thrilled to gain a Democratic defector. The Middle East wars in Afghanistan, Lebanon, Iraq and now Pakistan had transformed political alliances in Washington to the point that they could have been renamed the Pro-War and Anti-War parties, rather than Republican and Democrat, and indeed, several sitting members of Congress had switched their affiliations on this basis alone.

Each Senator and Representative spent great deals of time and effort qualifying their positions, defining their particular shade, but after a decade of bloody chaos in the region, delicate position definitions meant little. The average American could see only hawks and doves - continued chaos, or enough of this mess already. In President Lieberman's case in particular, it was odd that he had come to be defined as a pro-war Republican, considering he'd launched his political career as an anti-war Democrat in the waning years of the Vietnam War. He was deeply disappointed too, that he hadn't been able to affect any measurable progress toward reducing the violence directed at Israel from its Arab neighbors, nor any of the violence in the Middle East.

Aside from that, Joe Lieberman had also been the oldest person to assume the Presidency in US history, exceeding Reagan's record by about a year. He was in good health, but he was also widely perceived as no longer possessing the energy necessary for the wide range of critical issues facing the nation now, especially the seemingly endless military entanglements and fruitless diplomacy.

As the sitting Vice President, Jeb Bush was therefore the heavy favorite for the Republican nomination, consistently polling above 70% among Republican voters nationally. He had been an obvious choice for Lieberman's running mate - a very popular Governor of a large southern state, with a Presidential name, some foreign policy experience, and unmatched support among Hispanic and Jewish groups. The only question had been whether he was willing to get back into politics after five years in the private sector. He had declined to enter the 2008 and 2012 races for President, despite his name being tossed around like a football on a Sunday afternoon. But when the call from Lieberman came in, he assured him that he had expected to return once he had a little distance from his brother's unpopular legacy. He reportedly asked Lieberman only one thing before joining the ticket. "Is this a 100% Republican party campaign? No Independent status or Democrat leaning?" With assurances received, Bush was in.

Vice President Bush's strategy for this debate today, in the state where he had been a very popular Governor, was to try and stay above the fray, to say as little as possible and "look Presidential" while the others, hopefully, tore each other apart. This was not going to work out quite as well as he had hoped.

...

Vanessa Danilov: "Vice President Bush, how do you plan to make up the numbers in military recruiting, which are again reaching critically low levels?"

Vice President Jeb Bush: "If you're asking me will there be a draft, the answer is no. The American people have made it clear that they do not want and will not support a military draft. We have the finest, most professional military in the world, and I assure you, it will remain entirely professional. We continue to increase the incentives for young people to sign up for the challenge of defending our proud nation, and any of the men and women of our armed forces can tell you that military experience makes them stronger and provides more skills, than just about any other experience a young person can find."

Roger Adams: "Incentives, Mr. Vice President? What about removing our troops from dangerous countries where they don't belong? Now that would be an incentive. Our young men and women have been ridiculously over-extended in a civil war in Iraq, and they don't see why it is their job to patch up Pakistan today. I understand perfectly, that this administration feels it is America's privilege to wield some influence over the government of every country on Earth, but is it worth it, Mr. Vice President? Is it worth the lives of thousands of our men and women in uniform, to try to control the internal political turmoil in Pakistan?"

Mayor Michael Bloomberg: "We're engaged in a very important global conflict, Mr. Adams, and I'm not sure you have the experience necessary to comprehend that."

Roger Adams: "Even when we have officially lost these proxy wars and interventions in the past, Mr. Bloomberg, we have not suffered nearly so much from the resulting undesirable new government, as we have from the destruction of our own hands. Vietnam today is an ally and important trading partner of the United States. Yet the longer we delayed our exit from that country, the longer we simply prolonged our own misery, both militarily and domestically. Our gravest problems are in the places where we kill and destroy day after day and refuse to lay down our arms. I have not served in the military, and neither have any of us on this stage save Senator Graham. But I have been a victim of violence more than once during my life, indeed, at the hands of my fellow citizens, whom I had not wronged in any way, and I have also met hundreds of victims of domestic abuse, and I need no further convincing, that is an awful thing for humans to live with violence, and it should be avoided whenever possible, at home, at work, anywhere. All of us have seen the hideous images of our soldiers dying, beamed home to us from our overseas wars. Unfortunately, these wars are not just on television, and this American government has been fighting wars and supporting dictators around the world without pause, ever since we were forced to enter World War II. Any students of history here today may recall that this was a nation proud to refrain from entering wars, until we discovered we might use them to draw political boundaries and acquire resources from weaker countries in the aftermath of our victory in 1945.

I may have played in one of those cool rock bands in college, rather than studying the most effective strategies for killing people or collecting connections with wealthy people, but I did thorough study in my history courses, sir, and I do comprehend the difference between wars for the survival of our civilization, such as the one against the global mechanized aggression of Nazi Germany and Imperial Japan, and wars for material and political gain, such as the Iraq wars for oil and the

Lebanon wars for the domination of a Christian minority, and it is the latter type to which I am compelled always to vehemently object."

...

It was obviously not to his advantage to mention that his "cool," rather gloomy, college rock band had been called *The Pussy Whips*, but the youth vote was well aware of this fact anyway, thanks to a clip from a squibbly old VHS tape posted to GoogleTV.

...

Vice President Jeb Bush: "If you don't believe, Mr. Adams, that the struggle for the future of the Middle East affects our security in this globally-connected world, then I'm afraid you are too buried in your history books. This is a new world we live in, and we need leadership that recognizes that."

Roger Adams: "A new world means we have to be at war all the time from now on? Is that your new world? Or maybe you can stop speaking in politician code and clarify what you want to say, because I'm not always sure what the focus-grouped marketing terms are supposed to really mean. But I do absolutely recognize that the violence in the Middle East affects us all, and that the extremists have only ever received popular support for their attacks on the West based on our military presence and our very real support for undemocratic governments, despite our talk of freedom for all. If we are not there, in their lands, they will not attack us. It may not be the reason they attack us, but it is certainly their most powerful recruiting tool. We have the power to remove their incentive and their motivation. And increasingly, we are tied up in internal conflicts that have nothing to do with us and really do nothing to promote our national interest. We still have boots on the ground in Iraq five years after they voted to manage their democracy on their own. And furthermore, I recognize that by attempting to force the outcome of the succession of power in Pakistan, that you are, today, right now, laying the groundwork for the Pakistani people to blame *us* for their next failed government and their looming civil war. How is that good for our security, Mr. Vice President?"

...

Bush shuffled the papers on his podium and looked down at his feet, gathering his thoughts for an uncomfortable several seconds.

...

Anderson Cooper: "Mr. Vice President?"

Vice President Jeb Bush (speaking very calmly and clearly): "If America abandons its allies in the fight against extremists, and allows the entire Middle East region to collapse into unchecked chaos, terrorist groups will gain strength and confidence, and will certainly be planning to come at us again as hard as they can. It seems to me Mr. Adams would be better suited to debating with the Democrats, who also see running for cover as their road to victory."

...

Roger decided to let up on the vicious attacks for a while, feeling he had drawn the appropriate level of attention at this point, and did not want to appear overly nasty. While the Republican candidates were reciting their prepared statements and lobbing the expected softballs to each other, Roger was thinking about how he could introduce more issues into the debate, as the whole process seemed bogged down in bickering back and forth over just two issues at this point - health care and Middle East policy. But then he remembered that Dusty had advised him not to try to disrupt the entire format, because it would make him seem more reckless than rebellious. He was excited and he'd pretty much used his fair share of talking time early in the debate, so the reporters were focusing on the other candidates more in the second half hour. Before he realized it, he was being asked a final question. He shook off the daze he had been lulled into by listening to the coached, scripted and rehearsed playacting of the other candidates just in time to hear his question.

...

Vanessa Danilov: "Thank you, Anderson. Mr. Adams, the *Sky Wall Street Journal* has dismissed you as a populist, but on *Meet the Press*, you described the Republican field as (reading from a piece of paper), 'mostly radicals, unless you consider through-the-roof spending and adventurous war-making around the globe, conservative.' How would you describe yourself? Radical or conservative... or populist? Thank you."

Roger Adams: "I understand. You want me to put myself in a category. Listen, my agenda is not really conservative nor radical nor liberal, but reformist - I want to replace the buying and selling of our government, by special interests and foreign elements, with the priorities of the American people, plain and simple. That's what our democracy was founded upon, by the people, for the people, of the people. This does not mean every person making their own rules, but our representatives making our rules based on the actual priorities of the people of this country, not on those of a few elite rich people, be it the King of England in 1776, or the CEOs of the oil and drug companies in 2016. But if you want to call me a populist, which literally means *of the people*, then you can, but I guess you might call me *the Conservative Populist*, because I want to cut the billions in wasteful spending with a line item veto, just as Ronald Reagan wanted to do 35 years ago, and I want to stop this country's policy of making war and undermining democracies in every corner of the globe, whether openly or secretly. Eternal war is not a priority of the American people, and neither is it in the interest of our nation."

Mayor Michael Bloomberg: "Admit it, Mr. Adams, you are a populist. You have no experience in office, and you constantly speak naively of simply doing everything the people want. Are you going to take a poll every time you have to make a decision?"

Roger Adams: "I have experience in *the* office, as well as in the field. I come from a business background, just as you do, Mr. Mayor. In case you've forgotten, I constructed the beginnings of our new energy and marine management infrastructure while this government was still clawing its eyes out about how to reduce emissions by 2% in 20 years. I have proven that I can find a new approach and put people to work making it happen, and you don't need a poll to figure out that the pharmaceutical industry lobbyists are not providing anything for the hard-working people of America but bankruptcy and misery. But I do admire your education reforms and immigration policies. (pause) I may have a place for you in my administration... (audience laughs loudly), but you'll have to let me know if you can make a decision about your party affiliation before we can complete the paperwork. You seem to use polls to choose your party every few years."

Mayor Michael Bloomberg: "I'm running as an Independent, thank you, and I'm not spending any public money."

The mayor smiled meagerly. And with that, the first major debate was over.

Lenka grinned warmly as she adjusted Roger's collar and flattened his sleeve with her hand, just behind the red curtain, stage left, in the cavernous university auditorium. Roger turned toward Senator Graham, who was walking quickly directly for him. Roger extended his hand gentlemanly, but Graham stepped right up in his face, and toe to toe. "How dare you come out here and tear me a new asshole on national television?!" Graham screamed, his face exploding in crimson, "You have a hell of a lot to learn about Washington, green bean. How do you expect to ever get a vote for anything after you completely *fuck over* the people you might be needing votes from in Congress? Get with the damn program!"

Roger stood silently, his eyes bulging with adrenaline and resigned disgust. The Senator waited for a response, but none was coming. He walked away across the raised stage, toward the light cascading across the black floor from the distant open doors, still glaring at the back of Roger's head, and impolitely snatched a binder from the hand of his tall, brunette assistant.

Adams swiveled on his heel now in the other direction and saw Vice President Bush's team of Secret Service officers going out the other door, Jeb's big ol' melon-shaped head bobbing in the center of the sea of black suits. "Let's get out of here, honey," Roger whispered to his wife. "I need a hot meal."

"You were really torching 'em out there."

"I know - I need to think about what that means though."

"What do you mean?" she asked, more than a little surprised.

"I just need to... ponder... how things might go from here, try to imagine the possible scenarios. You know, how I'm coming across, how the voters react to the things I say and my interactions with other candidates." In the shadows, he spotted Dusty flipping intently through a pile of papers, which he held precariously slumped over his left arm.

"Oh, of course," she agreed. "You should probably try to keep at least a couple of people on your side in all this." Lenka's sarcastic smile broke his glazed-over expression and he lifted the corner of his mouth in a sideways smile, half laughing.

"You think they'll let me take any of that back?" he asked in a faux naive voice.

"Yeah of course, honey. Live and let live. That's what they always say in Washington, right?" she said, playing along.

"Yeah, sure," he said sarcastically and gave her a quick kiss on the mouth. "C'mon. Let's go grab Dusty and find a decent restaurant."

Roger rested his arm on Dusty's shoulder and said, "Not too bad today, huh?"

"It was a little cheezy at the end there, I thought, inviting the Mayor into your administration."

"Hey, I needed a setup for the party-jumping jab," Roger said with a light-hearted defensiveness.

"Alright. Attacking his indecisiveness was definitely called for. You were really on the ball out there. How did it feel?"

"It felt vicious," Roger stated matter of factly.

"Is that good or bad?" Dusty pressed.

"I don't know yet.... Where do we eat?"

Chapter 5
Offense

The luxury bus rumbled up the old highway pavement of I-75 toward Atlanta amid a thick current of traffic. The young driver, a Mexican immigrant (a legal one), waited nervously for a wobbling feeling in his arms to signal that the tires were ready to melt into the road. The heat drew ripples in the air before him, although it was still only May, which alarmed him even more, although the inside of the bus was a crisp 66 degrees, like a cool salad bar sliding right through a hot pizza oven.

Roger and Dusty sat across from each other, both of them with arms stretched comfortably across the top of the booth seats. Lenka and Shauna were both napping in the back. The hot, muggy morning in Gainesville had sapped the life out of them all.

"Dusty, you know the other candidates are not going to sit around waiting for me to cut them down next time. They'll be coming after me as aggressively as they feel they can get away with, now that I've made an impression and they see that I have nothing to lose in this. Most of them probably want to shoot me... with a gun, I mean... You know what I'm about to ask, don't you?"

"How much money do we have?" Dusty guessed.

"Actually, I know we don't have enough to hire an economist and a couple of legislation experts, but we need them *now,* before I start getting burned on any 'inexperience' attacks."

"Sounds like you should put a call in to Sergey."

"Thanks, Dusty. That's the confirmation I was looking for."

"You got it, boss," Dusty said in his comforting just-another-day-at-the-office style.

"It's... 11:30 there..." Roger thought aloud. He slipped on his beige Google GlovePhone and said robotically into his pinky finger, "Call Sergey Brin." He turned his hand and glanced into his palm, never confident that the voice recognition would dial the right number. It was already old technology, but it would always feel "spooky" to him. Sure enough, the text, "calling Sergey Brin... ," floated in 3D over the lifelines of his right hand like a bunch of gleaming white teeth freshly knocked out of his mouth. As soon as he'd put his hand back to his cheek, there was Sergey's voice, mild-mannered but enthusiastic all at the same time.

"Hi Roger, how's everything?" he asked cheerily, like an old friend just wanting to chat.

"Better than expected, I'd say, thanks to your support, Sergey. We had 800 people show up in Gainesville this morning."

"I'm glad to hear it, Roger. As I wrote in my email after the last debate, I may not agree with you on every issue, but your voice really increases the quality of the debate. I like the way you push everyone. So what can I do for you today?"

"We need to hire some more people, and to do that, we need more big money support. Specifically, we need to hire expert advisers so I don't get burned on any statistics in the next debate."

"Understood. OK, have Dusty send me an email with your budget targets and the nearest dates you have available to come out to California for some events, and Matthew and I will put together the list of people to invite. Sound good?"

"That's perfect, Sergey. You're our guardian angel."

"Just keep holding the politicians to account, Roger. Matthew and I are behind you 100%."

"You have no idea what a boost you've been to our little campaign," Roger gushed, instantly fearing that he had flattered too much.

"We know what we're into here, Roger. Don't worry. And I never forget that Google came from just one small idea in a garage too. That's the way we do it here on the west coast, right?"

Allowing himself to laugh comfortably now, "Of course," Roger agreed. "We'll get you that email by end of day."

"Great. Say hi to Lenka for me."

"Will do. Thank you Sergey."

He peeled off the glove and tossed it carelessly into a briefcase. If it hadn't been a gift from Sergey, he probably would not have bothered trying to get used to a new kind of cell phone. As cool as it was, he just never got excited by small gadgets made to solve problems that had already been solved. There were too many big problems still unsolved, in his opinion.

Florida had moved their primary up in the schedule three times in the last 8 years. The campaign had not expected to leave the territory of the bellwether giant for the next three weeks, until the vote-counting had begun. Now a fund-raising trip to California and an extensive national, and also international, television appearance were taking them away from the crucial shaking of hands and delivering of speeches. At least the CNN spot would only take them out of the state for half a day. It was certainly worth it. After the Florida polls showed that Adams was still building on his New Hampshire numbers, they promised him a full wide-ranging, one-on-one, half-hour interview. This was Roger Adams' first chance to lay out his entire platform for a national audience. CNN had not been the only, or even the leading, political television platform for many years, but it was still the most international, and it was still taken more seriously than some of the others, even by the people that preferred not to watch it on a daily basis.

Heads turned in the offices as he and his team walked through the corridors of CNN's Atlanta headquarters, a building where heads do not turn for everyone. Only Lenka sat with him in makeup.
"How do you feel, tiger?"
"I'm good. Relaxed. Ready."

An assistant came in.
"What is this, tea?"
"English Breakfast, Mr. Adams."
"No no, send it back. I'll have a martini."

The assistant walked out quickly in search of a martini. Of course, Roger knew he couldn't get a martini, but he had gotten rid of the assistant.

"The lights will get hot after a while," Lenka advised.

"Yeah. It'll go fast though. I'll wash my hands in cold water before we go on to cool me down."

"Don't forget - it's taped. The contract says that they'll let you reshoot anything you don't like... You need any warm-up questions?"

"No thanks honey. I went over a lot of stuff on the trip up."

"OK." He could see in the mirror, that she was thinking hard, making sure she was doing all she could to support him at this crucial moment.

"Honey?"

"Yeah?" she asked.

"I adore you," he said simply, with a wide smile.

His calmness caught her off-guard and sparked her sarcastic humor response mechanism.

"You look that Money Honey too deep in her Money eyes, and I'll take it out of your hide," she scowled, believably enough to frighten the makeup assistant, who then pulled her hands up in the air as Roger's head jolted back in appreciative laughter.

...

Maria was half-standing over her chair when he walked into the studio. She was patting down her skirt while trying not to drop the papers in her right hand. "Mr. Adams," she smiled broadly, "So nice to meet you." "Please, you can call me Roger off camera. I'm glad it's you here today. I'm a fan of your work." Lenka's threats echoed through his head, but it was impossible not to flirt, just a little bit, with such a woman.

"Oh, how sweet. Thank you," she said. He was relieved to see that she took it as nothing more than a professional buttering up, hoping for a softball interview, which any normal politician would have done, and probably had done, to a much greater extent than he had done now, unintentionally. He recognized clearly the opportunity to keep his mouth shut at this point.

Lenka stepped into the wings now, next to Dusty, and blew Roger a kiss. He smiled at her, and then noticed that Maria was waiting politely to catch his attention.

"First we'll roll a prepared intro with graphics and a quick bio, you know, your hometown, your early career, the sea water turbines, and then a summary of your campaign success so far. Then it goes right to the interview. The camera directly in front of you there will be the angle we use most of the time, but you can just look at me. Let me know anytime you want to start a question over again." She flashed him another broad, friendly smile as she asked him, "Any questions?"

"You're supposed to have all the questions, aren't you?"

"Aha, very clever, Roger," she grinned.

Suddenly her overbearing charm seemed to him too rehearsed. He put it out of his mind and instead started mentally running through all the topics he wanted to cover.

"I'm ready when you are," he offered.

"OK. Good," she said, and gave a signal to the producer.

Little red lights came on all around the studio, and a large camera rolled slowly toward Maria. Roger leaned back comfortably in his chair.

Maria Bartiromo: "Good afternoon, Mr. Adams. Thank you for joining us."

Roger Adams: "Thank you. I'm happy to be here."

Maria Bartiromo: "You've said that politicians don't spend enough time on the issues that matter to the

American people, so let's get right to those issues. You favor a phased approach to bringing down health care costs. Why are you opposed to universal coverage, which most Americans say they want?"

Roger Adams: "I would love to give every American full health coverage. And that's been tried many times. Hillary Clinton put years of her best efforts into it with teams of 500 experts, not once but twice. Those plans were just too ambitious. Our health care system is too large and too messy to tear down and replace completely all at once. Universal coverage is the ultimate goal, ten years down the road, but I believe the best way to get there is to get one piece of it right, starting with preventive care for our children, and then apply that success to our seniors, and then universal preventive care. Once the priority is on prevention, we will see the costs come down and then we'll be able to work on total universal coverage. The key to every solution lies in managing our priorities. Our health care system doesn't work for nearly half of all Americans, and it's putting American business *out of* business, because our priorities are mixed up. We spend less than eight cents of every health care dollar today on prevention and the other 92 percent on extremely expensive drugs and risky major operations. We wouldn't pour sugar into our cars, never perform oil changes or other maintenance, and then wait for a critical malfunction before trying to rescue them. Yet this is how we treat our own bodies, which are irreplaceable! In the UK, they test for nicotine before performing any operation. If you've been smoking, they reschedule your surgery. They actually take care of their people, rather than sell operations like a product on a shelf. I don't want to deny anyone treatment, but I would say, if you're a heavy smoker, or if you're more than 100 pounds overweight, you need to pay more into the system than everyone else, because you're raising the cost for everyone in a way that's totally avoidable. Let's turn this around the other way. Give people financial incentives and maybe they'll get serious about taking care of themselves. Taxes on alcohol should be much higher too. Nearly half of all Americans have some level of alcohol dependency today. Just because it's legal doesn't mean it should be abused. People need to take care of *themselves*. At the same time, the government needs to break the big business extreme-profit model. All marketing of pharmaceuticals should be banned across the board, which would immediately cut the cost of all brand name drugs by 20%. The bureaucracy needs to be streamlined too. We can't have ten accountants and claim-filers in every doctor's office. We're spending ten times as much money managing the health bills as we are on managing our health, and that's not right.

Maria Bartiromo: "You want to charge people for being overweight?!"

Roger Adams: "Yes. Why not? You want to eat thirty hamburgers a day or smoke two packs a day, go ahead, but it'll cost you. It's already costing you your health, and it's driving up the cost of health care for everyone else. Call it progressive coverage. Those who use it the most, pay the most. Of course, the plan would include incentives too. As long as an overweight patient shows progress from one visit to the next, they don't pay the higher premium. If they stop making progress, they start paying the higher premium. We're talking about dangerously overweight here. The threshold weight is determined by the doctor, of course, within certain guidelines. You certainly will *not* be charged for putting on a couple pounds at Thanksgiving dinner. But listen, the number of obese people in this country was never more than 5% until the 1980's. Today it's more than half. Computers and cars started doing all our hard work for us, and the nation sat down to a huge pre-packaged microwaveable fast-food meal and never got up. The human species may one day evolve to the point where we can live a fast food lifestyle, but not in two generations, it certainly won't. People might not want to hear it, but they need to get off the couch and get busy, or alternatively, pay the higher cost of health care for that choice. Education will be included in my program. Diets don't work. We know that. A lifestyle change is required. The program is exercise and healthier food choices. 50% of food stamps will be replaced with new produce-only food stamps at a 10% higher value. Smokers too, knowing what we know today, have no excuse for what they're doing to their bodies and to everyone's health care costs, not just their own. Another secret to health in other cultures is that they go on vacation. They live a slower lifestyle. The machines are supposed to do all the work for us, but they're making us work harder and longer than ever, and we're literally letting ourselves be stressed to death. We simply have to get out of the office and move around. We must recognize that we're only human."

Maria Bartiromo (visibly surprised): "I don't know how *that's* gonna go down with voters. (Roger, satisfied with his answer, sat attentively awaiting the next question.) Aaaand... How would the pharmaceutical companies be able to recoup their enormous research and development investments? Don't you worry you'll be cutting off their ability to develop the cure for cancer?"

Roger Adams: "Absolutely not. I understand that the drug companies spend millions of dollars developing these products, but they're also breaking the bank of the American middle class to pitch us Viagra. They cannot continue to pass those unnecessary costs on to the American people. They will just have to find a way to make due with the 367 billion dollars in profits they have generated since their industry started going through the roof thirty years ago."

Maria Bartiromo: "You identify yourself as anti-war. Under what circumstances would you send American troops into harm's way, if any?"

Roger Adams: "I fully supported the George W. Bush administration when we went to Afghanistan to wipe out Al Qaeda and the Taliban in Afghanistan after 9/11. That was the right thing to do. I got a little worried when he appointed an American oil man as president of that country, and I knew for sure we had our eye off the ball when he pulled our whole team out of the game in the second inning. Look back at Afghanistan. (He became more animated, using his hands as he talked.) We were attacked by Al Qaeda and the Taliban. Without any measure of success whatsoever against *our true enemy*, Al Qaeda, without capturing any of its leaders or destroying their ability to attack, we simply abandoned that country and went to carelessly playing, 'let's redraw the maps again,' in Iraq, Palestine, Lebanon, and Pakistan. That is beyond incompetent, it is incomprehensible. We have been pushing these unwinnable proxy wars for decades to create permanent instability, desperation, and hopelessness. I guess the idea is to keep this cycle going until one day, we miraculously find leaders we like and then we'll stop promoting chaos. Here we are 15 years later, still debating what our influence even *is* in the Middle East, and whether it's worth it to keep trying. We should have stayed in Afghanistan until the job was done - captured Al Qaeda's leaders, engaged in actual nation-building, and we would have a strong ally there today, perhaps another Germany or Japan. Instead, the government lied to us and ignored the priorities of the people, so they could try to change the balance of power in the whole region, which is an elite politician's priority, not the American nation's priority. And the people of Afghanistan are still suffering from Taliban attempts to retake the country after all this time, because we never finished the job there! Is that what we call liberation? I haven't even mentioned that half of Americans don't even know we're fighting a war for oil in Ghana. That's a small, formerly prosperous nation between Ivory Coast and Nigeria, for anyone who doesn't know. All these African nations with any hint of natural resources have been in turmoil for decades too. We're out there ruining entire regions of the world and gaining nothing by it!"

But let me get back to the problem of the Middle East. Remember the Iran-Iraq War in the 1980's? We were supporting our man Saddam Hussein in Iraq with cash and weapons, which we spent the 1990's trying to get back from him. There was also a little operation called the Iran-Contra scandal, which provided material support to Iran and of course, also fomented revolution in Nicaragua. For the last decade in Iraq, we've been funding both Shiite and Sunni militias, until we decided to let the Sunnis dominate again. Where is the logic in this? Even in the Israeli-Palestinian situation, we've drawn up one peace treaty after another, and then we instructed our diplomats to ignore them and eventually tear them up while we pay for more wars of aggression against nations composed essentially of desperate refugees. Why? Because the insulated elite rich men in Washington are deluded and crazy enough to think they can win one of these monstrosities one day, and then the decades of chaos and destruction, the millions of lives completely ruined, will somehow all be worth it. And that is one of the most insane concepts I have ever attempted to consider.

Even the quickest glance at human history tells you that the violence only worsens and little is ever won. Unfortunately, we the people have been conditioned to believe everything the marketing wizards tell us through our televisions, and so for fifteen years, we have been debating whether we should, quote, let the terrorists win, or quote, fight for victory, as if the fate of the world depended on whether we were all too 'yella-bellied,' as if we were living in a John Wayne movie. The truth is, ever since World War II, the American government, regardless of who was President, has preached freedom and democracy, while supporting dictators such as Saddam Hussein and Pervez Musharraf, and undermining fairly elected governments via sanctions, and by directly funding Israel's wars against its neighbors, or even *using* Israel to march through the Middle East, with billions of dollars and thousands of American-made bombs. Yet with all our riches and fighter jets, decades later, what have we actually won?

Worst of all, when the United States does not like the outcome of a democratic election, we attack that nation and its people, and that is why America can count its friends in the world on one hand today. We should send our brave men and women into bloody, treacherous battle only if we are truly faced with an aggressive threat to our peace and safety, which is why I favored military action against Al Qaeda. That does not mean it is OK to send pilotless machines on missions to blow apart other nations either. Thank god the Iranian Supreme Council chose to support a moderate President in 2009 who spends less time baiting our government, or we might very well have been speaking today as survivors of World War III."

Maria Bartiromo: "Speaking of World War III, you want to ban all nuclear weapons, isn't that right?"

Roger Adams: "I do believe that nuclear weapons

provide a deterrent. At the same time, 20,000 nuclear weapons provides a real possibility of completely obliterating our entire globe. I have no idea why we, or any intelligent person, would want to keep that lying around. It's like keeping a truck bomb parked in the driveway. It's just unbelievably dangerous to have so many. We would never want to annihilate millions of innocent people and make the entire earth uninhabitable anyway, so why continue to harbor this monstrous possibility? I would write up a new non-proliferation treaty wherein every nation in the world can have exactly twenty nuclear weapons. I would work to reduce our own stockpile to this level immediately and challenge the world to follow our example. With the type of nuclear warheads we have today, no nation could possibly ever use more than twenty nuclear weapons without leaving the Earth useless for human life, and even the world's least competent government would be able to keep track of twenty missiles, making them far less likely to fall into terrorist hands. And if one did show up out there, it wouldn't take long to figure out who's only got nineteen left in their bunker."

Maria Bartiromo: "Are you saying you would trust Iran with nuclear missiles? You want to give nuclear weapons technology to all our enemies?"

Roger Adams: "If every nation on Earth has nuclear missiles, I don't have to trust Iran. They'll have nuclear missiles pointed at them from every nation on Earth." ·

Maria Bartiromo: "Interesting perspective. OK, back to the home front. How do you balance the conservative and liberal views on controversial domestic issues, such as gay marriage, for instance?"

Roger Adams: "I don't balance any demographics, Maria. I call 'em as I see 'em. The old-school politicians like to tiptoe around these religious-voter issues and try to sound like they're on everybody's side. Well I think it's a damn shame, that when two people want to build a family together, someone has the gall to march into their house, to stand between those two people and say, 'We forbid you to have a family.' What the hell kind of a *Land of the Free* is that? Please excuse me for raising my voice, but it does absolutely make me angry when people go out of their way to strip basic rights away from their fellow American citizens. In my opinion, the right to marry the person you want falls under the pursuit of happiness. Marrying someone certainly does no harm to anyone else, and in fact, I believe we need more family togetherness in our society, not less, and fewer edicts forbidding people from pursuing their American dream. Freedom for all means freedom for all, not freedom for the people we decide we like personally."

Maria Bartiromo: "In concrete terms, Mr. Adams, do you support civil unions?"

Roger Adams: "Civil unions are not 'just as good as marriage.' I think it's a step in the right direction toward allowing same-sex couples their freedoms, but a very poor substitute indeed. How would you like to go home to your husband tonight, and be told by a police officer as you walk through the door, 'You must address this man as your "civil partner." He is not your husband.'? Why don't we get a court order to change his name to 7399826 while we're at it?! The government has no place wrecking our personal lives."

Maria Bartiromo: "I'm certainly not going to call my husband 7399826!"

Roger Adams: "I hope not! My point is, that the

government should not tell you what kind of relationship you can have with the most important person in your life."

Maria Bartiromo: "OK, point taken. What is your plan for America's educational system, and when do you plan to present it?"

Roger Adams: "Actually I don't have a plan, and I'll tell you why. When I see someone else who's smarter or more experienced than I am on a certain issue, I want that person to be working on the problem, and I will always delegate responsibility to people like the former UN Ambassador, Secretary of Energy, and Governor of the good state of New Mexico, Bill Richardson, who has an excellent plan to make America's education system world-class once again.

The problem with some of the testing-based reforms we've tried in the past is that some schools and some students will always be better than others, and we don't want to take the best and leave the rest to wilt, because all of our children are important. What we want is a rising tide to lift all boats, to allow the achievers to achieve to the best of their ability, while also helping the more challenged to meet their challenges and do better than they have before. Contrary to popular opinion, our schools do have money - they're just not spending it right. Again, the problem is priorities. In Governor Richardson's plan, the way to a better education for all students is to attract better people into teaching. Schools are not underfunded, but teachers are notoriously underpaid. Children don't learn by putting stacks of books under their pillows at night. They need a bright, motivated person to *teach* them - that means creating a personal connection and transmitting a curiosity and motivation to learn, not just information. When children don't feel that, and many children today don't get anything like that at school or at home, then they have no hope for a real education.

Attracting better teachers means paying a competitive wage to those teachers. Forget about vouchers and choosing the best school. The teachers are the critical link in education. Forbid tenure at all public schools and let the market dictate teacher salaries and hiring and firing. Governor Richardson has proposed a Teacher's Minimum Wage of $45,000 per year. Give each public school principal the budget and the authority to hire the best teachers they can, to let go of teachers who are burnt out, to rehire teachers who have recovered from their burnout, to put the most talented and motivated teachers possible into each classroom, pay them what they're worth just like in any other job, and thus, provide the quality education that our youth deserve and are capable of. Teaching will become a desirable profession again, and the American education system will soon catch up to the rest of the world, just by putting the existing money in the right place. If you have any further questions on education reform, I would direct you to Governor Richardson, because I believe he is the man with the best solution on this one."

Maria Bartiromo: "So if you win the Presidency, Bill Richardson is your Secretary of Education?"

Roger Adams: "Absolutely. He's got the job... just as soon as I get the job."

(everyone in the studio can be heard chuckling in the background)

Maria Bartiromo: "Nice to see you have your sense of humor, but not everyone is laughing like they were before the New Hampshire primaries a few weeks ago,

Mr. Adams. You're the first candidate in history to place so well in both the Republican and Democratic primaries in that state, in any state, and your poll numbers have been rising steadily, although you've never held elected office before. Did you expect to be doing this well in your first campaign?"

Roger Adams: "Nobody expected to see my name come up on both sides of the primary. But I have believed from the start, that the American people have been waiting, longing to hear someone speak the truth about our great nation, that if our representatives in Washington DC can just put the people's priorities first, that we can build a cause for hope together, that we can face the challenges ahead of us. We have only despaired in the past, because the people's business was nowhere to be found in Washington. How can we solve our nation's problems, if our government refuses to address them? After Hurricane Gillian, citizens filled their SUVs with food and water, and they drove down to Houston while the President was having tea with Chinese businessmen at the beach in Maine. After Hurricane Katrina, the citizens of Alaska begged their representatives to give up funding for a bridge to an uninhabited island and earmark it for hurricane relief, but our government had other priorities. You don't have to go to an Ivy League university to figure this stuff out. Ordinary people know how to come together and solve problems. They do it every day in their own lives! Getting back to the other part of your question, I am not an elected politician, but I have executive experience in the private sector, where wasteful spending is totally unacceptable, and I come from a politically active family, so I have been thinking about how to serve our nation for many years. I am gaining momentum in this campaign as my message spreads, because I am campaigning for the priorities of the nation to replace the priorities of the special interests and foreign agents who have taken over our representative government."

Maria Bartiromo: "So how much do you plan to raise taxes to pay for all your populist programs, Mr. Adams?"

Roger Adams: "That's the beauty of it, Maria. I don't want to increase spending or raise taxes. They started calling me *The Conservative Populist* up in New Hampshire, which to me is a fancy way of saying that I'm a reformist, not a big spender. I just want the programs we have to make sense. Many programs have the money they need, but the money has been prioritized badly, and needs to be shifted. I want the President, whoever is in office, to have a line-item veto, so the billions of dollars wasted on repaying favors in Congress can be saved while good bills are still signed into law. Our state governments work that way, why can't the federal government do it? The answer is that it can, it just doesn't want to!

We need a President willing to stand up to the Congress on taxes. Some people think I'm only here to rock the boat, but much of our bureaucracy just needs to be simplified, not remade from scratch. We don't need a flat tax, riling everybody up about rich versus poor, or a national sales tax, which would slow consumer spending, the vital engine of our economy. The system we have for setting income tax rates is perfectly fine. Some folks may be surprised to discover that our system of taxation is not even very complicated. The problem is the 100,000 pages of corporate loopholes and exemptions *attached to* our tax system. Again, that is there not to serve the American people, but to pay favors to wealthy special interests and to keep American money overseas. Simply remove the decades of bad priorities, strike them from the tax code, and use a Presidential line-item veto to keep them from coming back. End of story."

Maria Bartiromo: "If the solutions to America's problems are so simple, why haven't they been implemented already?"

Roger Adams: "Because the elite few who sit atop our nation, holding 80% of the wealth, have a choice, whether they should pay favors to their wealthy family friends in exchange for more wealth and privilege, or instead, screw their rich friends and help out large masses of people in dirty work clothes, none of whom they've ever spoken to, because they don't meet those kind of people on the tennis court or in the palace library. Who do you think they'd rather burn?

Wealthy people generally do not use the public services provided by our government. They can, and they do, pay for the best health care available, top-notch private schools for their children, drive on toll roads in expensive cars, hire world-famous lawyers when they have legal troubles, and even generate their own water or electricity in some cases. For the rest of us, we can receive basic health care if we are lucky enough to have a health insurance plan through our employer, our children can try to prepare for college at the local high school, if they are highly-motivated and can survive the shootings, beatings and bullying. We can take the bus to work, if a bus happens to go that way and we have two hours to spend waiting each morning and evening. The court can appoint an attorney for us, but will not help us to sue the cops that wrecked our home or arrested us for the color of our skin. While regular people scrape and push to get by, the government is busy building us into a prison with the drones and laser demobilizers and security checkpoints everywhere, controlling us instead of supporting us. Ten years ago, these things were only set up in Baghdad! What does that tell you about how the elites look at the rest of America?

Politicians support public services just enough to avoid a public outcry and a bad image, no more, no less. And they have to lie to us, because they know that if they told the American people what they really want to do, we would never go along with it. These sectors have hovered for decades on the brink of disaster, always with the plaintive cry that something must be done, but the system just wasn't designed to help so many. Somehow the Pentagon always has plenty of money for overthrowing governments it doesn't like and inventing new weapons with all new ways of inflicting misery and suffering on the human race. So apparently there would be money to provide health care and education to our citizens, if that money wasn't needed so critically for ruining people's lives instead.

I think it's an absolute travesty that it took us *ten years* to rebuild the great city of New Orleans. I think it's ridiculous that our outdated electrical grid suffers regional outages about once a month now. It seems the war machine is the only part of American infrastructure still working these days, and even our military looks a bit overworked, if you ask me. I say, let's bring them home for some peacetime and family time and then let's get our house back in working order! American citizens deserve better than this from our government! Once again, it is a question of priorities, the priorities of the people, against the priorities of the money in Washington."

Maria Bartiromo: "You have some money in the bank, Mr. Adams."

Roger Adams: "So did John Lennon. I do not shy away from the fact that I have a very successful business and a very comfortable home. I also send 42% of my income to Washington DC, while large companies pay less than half that. McDonald's for instance, pays just 20% and

General Electric pays an astonishing 8% of their income in taxes. Big business is leaching off the hardworking American people, and they're doing it legally. The biggest step we can take to correct this situation right away is to cancel the exemption on foreign earnings. Every American company large enough to do so has been shifting its earnings overseas, taking its money out of the American economy, because they pay no tax on that income as long as it stays outside the country. We should simply tax *all* their income at the current rate, minus loopholes. I remember Warren Buffet used to say that it wasn't right that he paid half as much in taxes, as a percentage, as his cleaning lady did. In my mind, there's nothing patriotic, nor sensible, about *paying* our most successful businesses to keep their money away from the American economy. It's completely backwards, and it's been done for decades, because wealthy people like to give each other favors and smile and pat each other on the back, instead of doing what's best for America or even investing their enormous wealth in America to contribute toward making this a better nation.

Listen, I built my wealth from an idea of how to approach a solution to problems not being addressed, not because I desired money or influence, and not because I was a seventh spoiled great-grandson of some Kennedy or Bush. Money is only a resource, to be used wisely, or else wasted. Given that I now have some share of wealth and influence, I will use them, and my experience with using them wisely, to make life better for all Americans, and that is the only reason I am here, to help make our nation great again, for all of us. I could go on vacation, right now, for the rest of my life if I wanted to, but I cannot stand idly by and watch the wrong decisions being cast, to the detriment of our democracy, our health, our progress, and the destruction of innocent lives, be they the lives of our family and neighbors, or the citizens of any other nation, and that is why I am running for President."

Maria Bartiromo: "That's all the time we have. Thank you so much for your candid answers. I'm sure we'll be seeing more of you in this campaign."

Roger Adams: "Thank you. I'll see you next time."

"AND WE'RE OUT!"

Maria put out her hand and said to him, "You turn it up

when the lights are on, don't you?"

"Well, I didn't come all this way to lie down and be quiet," he said good-humoredly.

The producer walked up to them, held a pen up to his clipboard and asked, "So do we need to cut anything?"

"I'll be grateful if you're able to include everything I said, in its entirety," Roger said in his polite, managerial tone of voice.

"OK," said the producer, a little unsure. "It's definitely interesting." He turned to the left and then came back, "Even the part about charging fat people?"

"Everything," Roger confirmed, "100%."

He again resisted the temptation to make any lingering eye contact with Maria, but with his head tilted down to avoid her eyes, he realized he was leering at the silky curves of her business suit. His pulled his head up quickly, stretched his shoulders from the aggressive sitting position he'd instinctively taken, and said gently in Maria's ear as he walked away from her, "Thanks again. Thank you." And he walked directly into Lenka's outstretched arms for a congratulatory hug.

Dusty appeared with Shauna, who was travelling with them up until the Florida primary, from one of about twelve doors lurking behind all the bright lights of the crescent-shaped television studio, and slapped an arm around Roger. "That was fantastic! I bet you forgot for a minute that that went nationwide too, huh? Another big step, my friend."

"I feel good," was all Roger needed to say, smiling.

"We have to head to the airport. We have a flight in three hours. Atlanta to San Jose. Sergey wants to call you at the hotel tonight. Tomorrow we have fundraisers in San Jose and Oakland, and a meeting in Santa Clara. Thursday, more meetings and a fundraiser in San Francisco, and then we fly back here for the bus Thursday night for Friday's events in Tallahassee. Ready to go?"

"Let's do it."

Shauna was searching nervously through the stack of folders in her arm. She was always sorting some papers or fiddling with some kind of gadget.

"How are you holdin' up there, Lenka?" Dusty asked, tilting his head toward her.

"I'm fine, thanks. I have the advantage of being able to tune out and take a nap whenever I want. Poor Roger here has to be alert for every little thing."

"I can handle it," Roger remarked defiantly. And they walked out of the building into the bright muggy street, where the bus was already idling, waiting to take them to the airport.

Roger rested on the flight, probably slept for a while, because it seemed like they were getting off the plane again just as soon as they'd gotten on. At the downtown San Jose hotel, a shiny new Carlton a few blocks from the Adobe building, Lenka went straight for the shower, declaring, "I feel sticky." Roger laughed as he sat down on the edge of the bed and pulled out his laptop to check his email. It was an older laptop, and he had at least 30 seconds while it started up, which he used to peek in on Lenka's shower. "How's the sticky coming?" he asked coyly as he approached, not wanting to startle her. "It's coming," she answered wryly. He poked his head in for a smooch and then she put her hands on her sheeny hips.

"Well, did you get a good look, mister?"

"Well it certainly ain't bad, lady!" he retorted and gave her another quick kiss.

When Lenka came out of the shower, all bundled up in fluffy white hotel robes and towels like an abominable snowwoman, Roger was on the phone. He saw Lenka coming and bulged his eyes out melodramatically at the approaching mountain of linens.

"OK, Sergey, that sounds good," he said, patting his

left hand on the bed beside him and signaling for Lenka to come around to the other side. Lenka sat down and Roger put his left arm around her while he talked.

"Yeah, we're planning ad buys for Florida for next week... Yes. You'll put it all in an email. OK. Fine. Hey Sergey, about this GlovePhone... Do you have one with maybe... a headset? You know, with old-style phones, I used to cradle it on my shoulder. I was always holding things and writing while I talked... If I try to do that with the Glove on, you see what I mean?"

"OK, and you can name it after me, OK? How's that?"

He laughed loudly now into the phone and Lenka could hear Sergey laughing through the tip of Roger's thumb.

"Alright. We'll see you tomorrow morning. Thank you, sir. Yes, Lenka will be there too. Yes. Goodnight."

"Hey," he smiled at Lenka.
"Hey you," she said as she wrapped him up in her arms, nearly suffocating him with all the towels and robes.
"Uh! I can't breathe," he cried.
"Alright then," she said and stood up.
"Wait, come back!", he pleaded, but she was already

standing in front of her open suitcase, scanning it with her eyes and jutting out her lower lip, where she was bouncing her index finger, her own personal version of *The Thinker.*

He switched back to business mode and said, "Honey, I know it's late, but we have some prep work to do on these meetings tomorrow. The team is going out for a late dinner. Are you up for it?"

"In the hotel?"

"No, Dusty and I are hungry. He wants to go to a spot about ten blocks from here."

"That's fine. I'm gonna climb into bed and chill out with some music or something, OK?"

"Alright. Don't fall asleep before I get back though."

"Why? You got some big plans there, tiger?" she teased.

He stretched his neck and pulled on his collar, letting out a less than emphatic, "I might."

She broke into the giggles and crawled across the bed on her knees to grab his head and give him a big kiss. "I love you, baby."

"I love you, too," he said softly and stood up to leave.

He picked up his jacket off the back of the chair. "Two hours max, OK?"

"Alright, dear," she said casually while sprawling her legs across the bed seductively.

He smiled at her broadly as he opened the door. She heard the resonating bass of his footsteps trailing off down the hall, and the image of his face, smiling just for her, floated in her mind. "Those eyes...", she murmured, and the image of his face faded into darkness except for the watery blue eyes, coming closer, shining like open ocean under a bright, noonday sun.

...

"Let's actually focus on eating for the first part of this meeting," Dusty suggested.

"No argument here," said Roger.

Shauna ordered a chef salad. The men ate veal. Halfway through the meal, they were struggling to talk about anything other than business.

"How's the veal, guys?" Shauna offered, making an effort to include herself in the team a little more. Roger and Dusty had obviously had a lot more time to form a close relationship, and she didn't like the awkward outsider feeling she had experienced with them for the last few days.

"It's juicy!" exclaimed Dusty excitedly.

"It is in fact, as you say, juicy," said Roger jokingly.

The guy-banter they had so well established did not

actually help Shauna feel more included. There was nothing wrong with her work. She'd been doing a great job of organizing the Florida campaign. She just had a rather different personality from them. She stood nearly five feet ten inches and she was as slim as the crack of a door. She always wore odd-colored, exaggerated suits. She was only forty-something, but her skin was tired. She was probably not too familiar with sunscreen and upon close inspection, her cheeks hung from her eyes like deflated balloons. But taken at a glance, and in some more flattering attire, she would have been a regular knockout for most men. Her skinny body was not devoid of curves (although her breasts did sit unusually high) and her tussled blonde hair was not pumped up as large as that of most Southern women of the time.

When Roger looked up from his plate and saw the look on Shauna's face, it occurred to him that she might not be up to speed on their brand of humor.

"How about your salad, Shauna? Did they get it right?"

"Yeah, it's good," she said half-heartedly and kept eating.

"So tell me, how long have you been managing campaigns?"

This drew her finally into some conversation, naming state representatives she had worked for and telling some pretty seedy stories from the campaigns of Senator Bill Nelson.

"So that's how Florida politics operates..." Dusty mused. "I'd always kind of wondered about that."

As soon as he was done eating, Dusty ran through all the names expected at the next day's fundraisers and who they were meeting with in the afternoon, and then he bowed out early for the night. "If you don't need anything else tonight, Roger, I'm ready to turn in. Flying always saps my energy."

"Yeah. It's late enough for me too."

Shauna piped up a bit nervously, "I have a few items I'd like to get out of the way tonight, if you can stay a little longer, Roger."

"No problem, Shauna. If it's just a couple things."

"Yeah," she said.

"Alright, see you in the morning, Dusty. Good work."

"You too. Goodnight," he said, and strolled out past the waiter coming to the table with the check.

Shauna pulled out a list of Florida donors and suggested how much they might be able to give, but was only half paying attention to her own words. She looked down, her eyes darting from the page to Roger's arm, to his strong neck, to his tie, to his arm again. She sniffled once and then inhaled his scent while struggling interminably not to actually lean into him.

The restaurant was still open for another half hour, but it was the middle of the week and everyone else had gone. Only two employees even remained. They could only faintly be heard busily clanking around through the kitchen door on the far side of the room.

Finally, she could not contain herself, the words falling from her tongue from their own heft. "It's been a long week, Roger. We need to blow off some steam."

With a deep breath and then an even deeper sigh, Roger agreed, "You're right, we probably won't get much more done tonight. Let's call it a night and come back fresh tomorrow."

"I had something else in mind," she answered, attempting to come across casual.

"What do you mean?" asked Roger, naively, too worn out to catch her drift.

Suddenly, Shauna lurched into Roger's face, startling him good, and said in a loud whisper, "I want to blow you, Roger. I want to get down right here and give you a sweet wet blow job."

He could see from the intense look in her squinty

blue eyes, that she was not joking around. Her dirty language had, naturally, aroused him a little, but he ignored this, sat up straight in order to pull back a bit from her aggressive posture, and placed his hand on hers, on the tabletop. Her nervous face sank as he began to speak.

"Listen, Shauna. I can't let you do that. I'm sorry, but you know I love my wife." Never liking to leave people without at least some information about what he was thinking if he didn't have to, he succumbed to the urge to thank her in some subtle way for the compliment. He lowered his voice and said, "I can certainly see the thrill of oral sex in a public place, but really, I'm gonna leave that up to Lenka." She pulled her hand away from the table and held both arms close to her body, obviously embarrassed, not quite willing to just jump up and run out like a little girl with wounded pride, but also not able to think of anything to say, despite wanting deeply to interrupt Roger's embarrassing speech.

Craning his neck toward her now, trying to look her in the eye, he continued, "Shauna, I really am sorry if you've ever misinterpreted my friendliness toward you. I want to be totally clear with you, that I like you and respect you very much as a friend and a colleague, and I honestly enjoy working with you, but as a friend and as a colleague, understand?"

She nodded her head silently.

"I don't want this to have any effect on our working relationship. Let's forget about it and just get a good night's sleep tonight and come back fresh tomorrow, OK?" He thought for a second about giving her one of those "other fish in the sea" comments, but decided it would be both corny and condescending. They gathered their papers and walked back to the hotel in awkward silence. In the lobby, they both said simply, "See you tomorrow." For Shauna, the words loomed like sets of large alphabet blocks in the middle of the room that fell slowly to the floor with a thud and then lay there like shipwrecks.

Roger was not quite the saint that this episode would make him out to be. He had had a few flings in his day, before Lenka. He was neither proud of them nor did he allow himself to feel guilty about them. He was much younger then, and that's the way things tended to work out, when he had no family, no career, nothing anchoring him, only a normal human desire for new experiences. Quashing the almost silly college-style come-on from his Florida campaign chief however, was not hard. He was never tempted because she did not appeal to him physically. And he had never pursued completely meaningless sex nor understood why it would be interesting to anyone - that was not even an option he would consider. Shauna was an attractive woman, certainly. Most men his age, of any age actually, would have killed a man for a chance at what he had just refused. But Roger was not most men, and there was no temptation for him to resist. He had actually turned down several very confident and attractive women over the years. He chalked this up not to his extraordinary charm or Adonis-like figure, although he was proud of these too (in a wholly self-deprecating way), but to the simple fact that he knew a lot of women and spent a lot of time with confident and ambitious women, who were naturally more likely to make advances on a man when they saw fit.

Adams was not a "man's man." Even in kindergarten, he preferred the company of females. The boys always seemed to be fightin' and tusslin', making people cry and putting mud in their mouths. Even now, full-grown men seemed hardly changed from those crass five-year-old boys... except that the men were somehow worse, and certainly more violent. Sometimes it made him literally sick to his stomach when he realized he was stuffed in a small dank room, in a den of those bloated swine, their swelled bellies hanging down like overdue parasitic alien pods, their skin rank with some cologne from the 1950's, dark nasty hairs spindling out everywhere - nose, ears, fingers - like spiders crawling all over the body. And when they opened their mouths, their crude, neanderthal words steamrolled everything in their path, hateful of everyone and everything, tinged with false pride to hide their insecurities or abuses suffered in their youth, words militaristic as weapons and shields, accompanied by a breath as foul as a damp moldy towel covering five-day-old Taco Bell forgotten in the backseat of an old Honda on a hot summer day with the windows rolled up. Of course, he could not announce this deep dislike of the company of men to the world, nor should he want to, but he was well aware that it colored his perception, and conduct of, business, politics, of life in general, in a way that did not seem to affect other people, as far as he could tell. Everyone in his life noticed his preference for women and many internally accused him of going out of his way to show respect to women in an effort to be "more progressive than thou." But the truth was, he genuinely respected and liked women a thousand times more than he did most men. He was in no way ashamed of his own manliness - he openly enjoyed football and baseball, or a pint of Guinness, for example - but since his college days, he had always made an effort to smell clean (the opposite of musky) and talk clean and fair about other people. There were some exceptions, of course, but there were indeed few A-type personality men among his personal friends, although in politics, as in business, he was surrounded by the dirty animals.

He was aware too, that women behave toward each other much differently than they do toward men, but this only meant that he was happy to find himself quite often in a fortunate position - a man in the company of women - always complementary in his case. And even when they were cruel, women never seemed outright barbaric. To be cruel is human, he reasoned, but to be cruel and also crude, is stupid, is less than human. He had never quite worked out for himself why this base level of human behavior continues to haunt us, after all we've accomplished as a species.

Chapter 6
The Florida Democratic Debate

"**W**elcome to the 2016 Florida Democratic Debate, sponsored by ABC News and MicroNets. I'm Ted Rowlands, and this is our Democratic field."

Roger could see job titles and years scrolling on the right hand side of the stage monitor while the camera rolled in front of the stage, catching one beaming face after another. He decided he should lower the intensity of his own smile, although he was happy to be there. A dramatic voiceover boomed through the auditorium, pausing for several seconds between each name: "former Secretary of Defense, General Wesley Clark; Attorney General John Edwards; two-term Governor Bill Richardson; businessman Roger Adams; and Michigan Governor Jim Cauty."

Senator Barack Obama remained extremely popular, despite losing the nomination to Hillary Clinton in 2008. Sadly, he'd been diagnosed with leukemia just a week before the convention, erasing his Presidential hopes, although sympathy for him among voters ran deep. It was widely speculated that he had received high doses of radiation, accumulated during his many visits to weapons destruction facilities around the world. Some in the media noted that his mother had died of cancer and he may have been genetically predisposed toward cancer. Those taken to conspiracies blamed the Clinton attack machine. He remained generally healthy and active with treatment, however, and remained invaluable to the Democratic Party as a strong Senate Majority Leader.

At 73, Clinton's Vice President, Senator Chris Dodd, whose fluent Spanish had helped their campaign more than they'd realized in 2008, was now too old to run, not to mention that he had also been tarnished by an administration disappointingly short on substance and long on special interests. John Edwards, who had gradually become one of Hillary Clinton's fiercest rivals and critics, remained in the private sector until 2012, when he was called on by President Lieberman to serve as Attorney General, a position in which the former lawyer had served without controversy, and from which he was currently preparing to resign, in order to campaign full-time.

The debate began with a few standard warm-up questions, but quickly turned hot, with Edwards labeling the former Defense Secretary's record as pro-war, while simultaneously tying him to the unpopular Clinton 44 administration in which he had served.

AG John Edwards: "...I think any member of the Hillary Clinton administration should be ashamed of themselves for allowing the hawks in our government to draw a Democratic administration into yet another Middle East quagmire. I spoke loud and clear against the Pakistan entanglement from the day General Musharraf's junta collapsed."

Defense Sec. Wesley Clark: "I can't remember the last time anyone called *me* a hawk, Mr. Attorney General."

AG John Edwards: "You may not like the label, Mr. Secretary, but I don't know what else to call a General who charges in head first and decides to find a political solution later."

Defense Sec. Wesley Clark: "When an ally in a critical part of the world suddenly collapses into political turmoil, there's no time to draw up agreements. I favor diplomatic solutions if at all possible, but when faced with a revolution, you simply don't have that option. We had to move in to contain the situation, and I stand by that assessment, 100%. Perhaps Attorney Generals are not adequately trained in planning battle strategies."

A few laughs echoed through the chamber. Clark looked around bewildered, hunting for a clue to the joke he had missed.

Governor Jim Cauty: "They're called Attorneys General. They're not Generals, General. But maybe that was your point?"

Clark looked embarrassed, but Roger drew the attention off Clark by jumping into the argument, ignoring the simple word order gaffe.

Roger Adams: "The assessment is logical, Secretary Clark. The only problem with it is the location. Pakistan is not our nation. Many countries will face internal difficulties, but as they used to say when I was a youngster, we cannot be the world's policemen. We do not belong there, and our presence has only made the situation more chaotic. I favor supporting those in need to an extent, but the United States government is not a one-world government. We are one nation in a world of more than 200 nations and there is no reason we should have to do everything. It should be terribly clear by now that we do not have the resources, nor the mandate, to take care of every society on the planet. But while this government tries to take its place as the so-called only superpower of the world, our own people are suffering right here at home!"

Governor Bill Richardson: "I agree, Secretary Clark. We are asking too much of our military and of our nation. Our troops have been pushed to the breaking point for more than a decade. It shows in our lapses of professionalism, in isolated, yet recurring cases of torture and civilian murders, and thousands of our young men and women coming home to their families with deep psychological wounds. The political situation in Pakistan is still unresolved, and Iraq has been spinning hopelessly in circles for over a decade while we constantly prevent the other nations in the region from participating in a meaningful way. There's nothing more we, as outsiders, can do. It's time to bring all of our troops home, *now*."

Defense Sec. Wesley Clark: "I'm relieved that none of

my esteemed colleagues here tonight currently hold a government position with the power to carry out their unconditional surrender."

...

In February of 2009, just weeks after Hillary Clinton had been sworn into office, Pervez Musharraf had stripped an IPTV television network of its license after it reportedly started airing a one hour documentary every night, which included footage of recent protests, of Musharraf promising to step down from the Army in exchange for changes to the Constitution which kept him in office (a deal which he had never honored), and pardoning AQ Khan only weeks after he was caught selling nuclear technology to Iran, Libya and North Korea. At the same time, members of the new coalition Parliament stepped up their calls for Musharraf's resignation. The intermittent mass protests had been growing steadily larger since 2007, and the camel's back was nearly broken by the time the opposition parties won 2008's elections and united against him. In a last act of desperation, just days after closing the IPTV network, Musharraf suspended Parliament and quickly lost control to angry mobs all across the country. The internet went wild with speculation that the small six-month old IPTV service had been set up by the CIA, calling it *the first new media coup d'état*, although new networks had been popping up everywhere in Pakistan by that time, and the rumors were never confirmed.

After officially holding on to power for two weeks, Musharraf flew with his family to Hong Kong and it quickly became unclear who was in charge of Pakistan. The united opposition parties saw the game as re-opened and without the assassinated Benazir Bhutto to guide and inspire, they fractured once again. The United States military moved in five brigades from Afghanistan two days later, with the support of just two Pakistani generals, and quickly found themselves involved in fierce fighting with multiple factions.

Already facing her first crisis decision, President Clinton 44 had accepted her military leaders' frantic warnings of various doomsday scenarios as justification to intervene, that the whole Middle East could collapse, and that by entering Pakistan to quickly restore order, we might even be preventing a third world war, which they'd predicted for decades would begin in the volatile and highly weaponized region. In reality, the U.S. forces stepped directly into urban firefights as soon as they entered the country, which they had not been expecting. Of course, they had to return fire in self-defense, and upon discovering that the situation was worse than the anticipated protests and looting, the generals felt even further justified in attempting to restore order. Unfortunately, the long-suppressed political factions had no intention of cooling off, and rather than fill a power vacuum, the United States essentially stepped into the crossfire of another civil war. And just as in Iraq, everything got worse before it got better.

Most Americans had been surprised that Clinton had gradually increased the troop presence in Pakistan, bringing in several waves of redeployments from Iraq, as she had spent the previous two years campaigning on an Iraq troop withdrawal. But the greatest pressure on her Presidency, since before it even began, was to show her toughness on defense, forcing her to triangulate, as Clinton 42 was so well known for, even on her earlier support of the Iraq war. She also claimed to be going after Al Qaeda, despite having good intelligence that nearly all of them were now in Iraq, Somalia or Afghanistan again. Or at least they had been, until the Americans started flooding into Pakistan. Clinton had managed to repeat some of Bush's most disastrous failures. Now her position had shifted right so many times that it differed from the Republican position in name only - that if we leave now, we leave the region dangerously unstable, allowing the terrorists to take over. She argued repeatedly that this was a different danger, while few Americans saw it that way.

Less than a week after Musharraf's escape to Hong Kong, it was reported that he was flying toward Hawai'i and planned to request asylum upon arrival in California. The American people went ballistic. Within hours, every news station, web site, and politician was completely swamped with angry citizens, demanding he be refused entry to the country.

"And maybe Osama bin Laden would like to retire in Miami!" one popular blogger screamed. Musharraf became totally vilified. Americans everywhere panicked that he would be a target for terrorists and bring Pakistan's political turmoil to US soil. The web attacks became personal too. Some of the more inflammatory web sites hinted that Musharraf was not very bright, linking to stories that he had fallen on his head as a teenager, that he had flunked out of college five times, and that as a young general, he had re-ignited war with India in Kashmir completely by accident. It was a wild 180 from the happy book tour he had enjoyed just a few years earlier, appearing on TV shows like The Daily Show, laughing and telling jokes.

President Hillary Clinton addressed the nation less than an hour after the story broke, saying she had talked to Musharraf and that China had agreed to grant him temporary asylum in Hong Kong, and that his plane had already turned around. But as soon as that was resolved, those resourceful bloggers discovered that Musharraf's son, Bilal, had already been living in California for years, and the whole storm erupted all over again, complete with links to maps and satellite images of Bilal Musharraf's home in San Jose. Feeling he was no longer safe in the U.S., Bilal also flew to Hong Kong. But the new President's first hundred days were badly tarnished, American troops were moving into Pakistan in large numbers, and the domestic scare prompted her to talk even tougher rhetoric on homeland security and foreign policy, which she continued to do for four years.

...

Roger Adams: "The question nobody's asking is why we supported the military dictator in Pakistan for so long in the first place, even before 9/11, and who in our administration led General Musharraf to think he would be welcome to hide out in California when his junta fell? The United States government has been playing dice in the Middle East, and sooner or later, you're going to come up craps. It's a very dangerous game this government has been playing with our brave men and women in uniform, and that goes for the current President, the President before him, and the President before her, in my view. In fact, the last 10 Presidents have been dangerously wrong on what the fundamental goals of our foreign policy should be. At least Dwight Eisenhower had the good sense to bring our troops home as soon as a mission was completed. I don't agree with everything he did or said, but he did warn that leaving our troops in a foreign nation too long would make that nation dependent on us and that the citizens must be vigilant against a military machine that would collect unnecessary influence at every opportunity. Since then, it seems our government has been *trying* to make other nations dependent on us and influence every region of the world, which has entangled us in one disaster after the next. Why must these be our problems? The politicians claim we must spread our influence to remake the entire globe. I say those politicians only enjoy the idea that it might be within their powers to do so, the dream of all ambitious leaders throughout human history. That is not what the American nation represents. Let us not go back to the days of conquerors like Napoleon or Alexander. Let's get back to the business of taking care of our great democracy, and of our own people, who have been neglected too long. Let's be an example to the world again, instead of trying to be policemen of the world."

Governor Jim Cauty: "You would cut defense spending down to nothing, close military bases and leave us unprepared and vulnerable. You would drop all our shields and invite aggression from Iran, China, Russia, even North Korea! Al Qaeda is not the only threat we face, Mr. Adams. Your isolationist, hope-for-the-best policy is the surest way to bring this nation under attack."

Roger Adams: "Massive defense spending does not make the American people massively safer. What it really means is flooding the world's most unstable regions with more weapons than they know what to do with, and engaging American troops in never-ending wars and occupations. We have in this country, an overabundance of capacity for war, which leads directly to selling, and using, that capacity for war and brewing fear among nations, in a perpetuating circle of profit and death. We would be ready and able to defend ourselves with half of the defense budget we have today. The word 'defense' means when you are attacked first, such as when Al Qaeda attacked us on 9/11 and we fought back in Afghanistan. The wars in Iraq and Pakistan are not wars of defense, they are experimental interventions, attempts to gain influence and resources in a foreign region by violence. The American people want peace, and the American government should give it to them!"

Attorney General John Edwards: "I hate to break your stride, Mr. Adams, but General Musharraf was a moderate leader in the Muslim world, responsible for killing or capturing hundreds of Al Qaeda hiding in his country. I agree with you that it's time to bring our troops home from Pakistan and Iraq, but it's a mean world out there, tougher even than the business world, and in the highest levels of government, sometimes you do have to deal with people who utilize a lower ethical standard than we have here in America."

Roger Adams: "You know you're in politics when a lawyer starts lecturing you on ethics."

(The audience roared with laughter, and the other candidates were caught laughing too.)

Roger continued, "Now don't describe my position for me. I never said I wouldn't deal with people I don't agree with. I said I wouldn't support them. But the politicians in Washington have a long history of providing weapons and large piles of money to dictators, while undermining democracies, until they collapse into chaos that is, and then we throw our hands up and say, "Oh my goodness, we better go save those people," as if we had nothing to do with it. We've done it in Iraq, we've done it in Lebanon... Let's be straight with the American people. Why doesn't our government explain to the people that we have chosen to starve the entire nation of Palestine, a people already living in a virtual prison, because we didn't like the way they voted in their free and fair elections in 2006, 2008, and 2011?!
Can you imagine doing that in America? What if the Congress banned all economic activity and freedom of

movement in the red states because the Republicans won an election? That would be insane. But that's what the American government has been doing to the people of Palestine."

Attorney General John Edwards: "We were talking about Pakistan, Mr. Adams."

Roger Adams: "I believe these issues are inter-related, but let's focus on Pakistan, if you like. Please explain to the American people why our government was selling sophisticated weapons to Pakistan throughout the 90's, even while that nation declared itself the Taliban's closest ally, and while we also knew they were selling nuclear technology to Iran, Libya and North Korea. Was it to justify our high ticket military sales to their enemy India? When Al Qaeda's top leadership was in the South Waziristan region of Pakistan, Musharraf made peace with them. This is our great ally? The man who signs treaties with Al Qaeda? Let's tell the truth to the American people, and see if we still go to war. Did anyone ask the American people if *they* thought we should be weaponizing the whole Middle East, selling guns and rockets to both sides of every conflict? You can't tell the people that, because they would never agree to it. They have too much common sense, and too strong a desire for peace."

Attorney General John Edwards: "The President of the United States can't take a poll every time a decision needs to be made. Now these questions can get pretty complicated. I don't think our troops should have to fight every battle, but when certain factions are being weaponized by other unscrupulous nations, it makes sense to level the playing field, to give the good guys in the region a fighting chance."

Roger Adams: "And what's to stop our enemies from using the same reasoning to sell their arms? Like it or not, the world really does follow our example, and it's our responsibility to make that example exemplary. And just so long as we're clear, your quote good guys in the region, were the Taliban's closest ally, right up until the day our fighter jets bombed them off the map, as well as Iran's nuclear arms dealer."

Defense Sec. Wesley Clark: "Playing nice guy just doesn't cut it. We showed tough resolve against Iran, and they backed down. You go in there and ask them to play nice, you're gonna have a nuclear Iran in a hot minute."

Roger Adams: "Secretary Clark, you know very well that Iran had no choice. Going into their 2009 election, their most important world allies were lined up against their nuclear program, they had engaged in political purges of all their most skilled and educated people, and their economy was in tatters thanks mainly to their own incompetence. Internally, they were on a road to ruin. That is why the Supreme Council supported Hosseini, a former Finance Minister, against their own previous hardline choice. The swaggering toughness of the United States had nothing to do with the outcome of their election, any more than Kim Jong-Il's posturing can convince Americans to vote for a particular candidate. This brings up the one good thing to come out of the mess in Pakistan - Joe Lieberman wasn't militarily capable of carrying out his lifelong dream of bombing Iran. If this American government had its way, we'd be deep into an unimaginably horrific World War III."

Ted Rowlands: "OK, gentlemen, we only have a limited amount of time here. Let's move on to another topic. Amy?"

Amy Becker: "Governor Richardson, what new programs would you introduce in your first hundred days, and how would you pay for them?"

Governor Bill Richardson: "Thank you Amy. In my first hundred days, I would begin redeployments of our troops in the Middle East and start bringing them home. Our veterans have been pushed to the limit for more than a decade now, and they need to know that we're there for them when they come home. I would create a readjustment program for our troops, a team of trained professionals who will be a phone call away day or night, to answer questions, provide counseling upon request, or assist with any procedural problems. The last thing our veterans need is to come home from a war zone and have to battle red tape. I would seek to move funds from the Pentagon to the Department of Veterans' Affairs, not only to support this program, but to shore up the VA system from years of underfunding and increasing health services costs.

I would also seek legislation from the Congress guaranteeing the right of the states to make available medicinal marijuana for prescription by a doctor to patients who need it. I think it's wrong to force terminally ill people to suffer, if we have a medicine that can help them."

Governor Jim Cauty: "Governor, you stand on the edge of a slippery slope when you take marijuana off the schedule I. Whether you want to or not, you're going to send a message that marijuana makes people feel good and we're going to have to start the whole war on drugs all over again. You're going to send us back thirty years!"

Roger Adams: "Come on and tell us the truth, Governor. The war on drugs is a war on drug *users*, who are also American citizens. Why don't we legalize and regulate all recreational drugs like we do alcohol? We can tax them to high heavens too. Then we can start treating people who use drugs as people, oftentimes people who need serious help."

Governor Jim Cauty: "Mr. Adams, I think you've just demonstrated how far out of the mainstream you really are."

Roger Adams: "With the way this stream is flowing, I'm not sure I want to be in it. Think about what happens to the people in this country who try drugs for the first time. Yes, they start out as *people*, usually young, usually emotionally troubled. They may have suffered abuse or experienced a breakup of their family. Once they become hooked, they have no choice but to seek out criminals to keep getting their fix, and so they enter a world of thugs and dealers. Then when they're caught, instead of having a chance to reclaim their lives, they're sent to prison, where they are also not rehabilitated, but again surrounded by criminals and possibly hardened into criminals themselves. This already does not sound like a good formula to me.

(speaking louder and more rapidly now) So *then* we let them out because our prisons are at 350% capacity, filled with millions upon millions of citizens who present no danger to society, until of course, they've spent enough time locked away with a lot of criminals, living in close quarters with our most violent gangs and rapists and murderers. This, ladies and gentlemen, is how a person who tried to relieve their suffering and became physically addicted, gets sentenced to a lifetime of criminal behavior. And maybe that explains why each of our popular crackdowns over the decades has actually led to increased drug abuse. We've only been fighting this war since 1970. Shouldn't we have made some progress yet? But drug use has existed throughout history. Perhaps the United States government should not be in the ridiculous business of trying to change human nature."

Governor Jim Cauty: "I can't wait to see what you propose."

Roger Adams (not noticing the comment): "Now what if instead of breeding criminals in these horrific conditions, we made recreational drugs available under highly controlled conditions, eliminating the need for contact with criminal gangs and depriving those gangs of their income, and then used the tax receipts to offer users rehabilitation? This troubled person would be offered help every single time they went to buy their drug! No drug dealer is providing that service, that's for sure.

And I guarantee you the average hard-working American is not going to quit their office job for a life of hard drugs. I'm fully in favor of public service messages warning that recreational drugs are extremely dangerous and should not be used, ever. But if you are hell-bent on experimenting with your consciousness, your government should not declare war on you for it, for the rest of your life.

At the same time, our prison population would decline by 60% and we would be able to manage our prison system again. Imagine that! No more setting *violent* criminals free before their time is up. And we'd stop creating hardened criminals from every teenager that ever tried marijuana. I predict the violent crime rate would drop by 20% within 5 years. We would save so much money, we could hire half a million new police officers to do preventive community policing and make our neighborhoods safe again."

Governor Jim Cauty: "Mr. Adams, you are out of your mind if you think the American people are going to swing open the prison doors and hand out hard drugs for the weekend."

Defense Sec. Wesley Clark: "I have to agree."

Roger Adams: "I am a practical and realistic man, I assure you. I have no great expectation that America will be magically transformed overnight into the kind of modern society in which the government does not execute its own citizens, nor lead its less fortunate people toward a life of criminality. But I have cause for hope, that some brave Americans will see in my words the opportunity to do things a better way, and public opinion may slowly begin to change. I also do not put faith in decades of silly TV ads showing eggs in frying pans. I'm in touch enough to know that teenagers find those ads hilarious.

But seriously, let's start with decriminalizing and taxing only marijuana and see how it works. More than half of incarcerated drug offenders were charged only with possession of marijuana. Incidentally, Governor, do you know that our federal government, by its own estimate, now spends over 70 billion dollars every year incarcerating drug users, who have hurt no one but themselves? That's billion with a 'b.' And that's almost double what it was just ten years ago."

Governor Jim Cauty: "Money well spent, keeping drug dealers off the street, if you ask me."

Roger Adams: "Except that that's not drug dealers, Governor, it's only drug users. These people pose no danger to society! Let the millions of people who smoked a few go home and go back to work, and we'll finally have the bed space to keep the dealers in prison until their time is served."

The air was tasting stale and muggy in the Florida State auditorium, despite the air conditioning. The musky colognes and fruity hair sprays of the candidates, baking under the hot lights, were not contributing much to the atmosphere. Roger sorted through his index cards, letting the ones he had already used slide from his hand onto the podium. He scanned the audience and his eyes fell on Lenka, who was wearing a scorching red dress. He looked quickly back down at his cards in order to maintain his focus, but in the after-image on the inside of his eyelids, he saw a proud, gleaming smile on her gorgeous face.

Time was almost up, and the candidates went into lightning round mode. The Democrats united in their call for a federal civil partnership bill and universal health care, while Roger repeated his stances on marriage for all, his gradual preventive health care plan, and added that he would push for a Presidential line-item veto in his first hundred days.

Roger gave his closing statement.

Roger Adams: "We have 12 satellites, 27 drones and 4,000 security cameras tracking Grandma going to the store for milk and eggs, while our one and only hurricane satellite falls out of the sky! These are not the priorities of the American people.

We're searched inside and out every time we enter a plane, train, bus or toll road, while huge shipping containers come through our ports from all over the world unchecked. I don't feel safer, I feel like a citizen criminal!

It should not be the function of government to act as parents to 500 million people, to watch over us, check our pockets, take away our candy, and approve our boyfriends and girlfriends. This country was founded on the notion that grown men and women can take care of themselves and it's time the federal government return that responsibility to the people. And at the same time, I say to the people, take back your responsibility, and don't expect the government to do for you what you can do for yourself.

Securing the nation means little if our liberty is sacrificed. Without its freedom, America is lost. When freedom is lost for any American, America is lost. Back in 2001, we had a popular saying here in America, that, if we give up our freedoms or lock ourselves indoors, then the terrorists will already have won. Well, my friends, we have slowly handed them that victory. I am here to say however, that it is not too late. Together, we can demand from our representatives in Washington that our liberty be returned to us.

I want to be clear however, that it is not my wish to ring the bells of freedom only to make a lot of noise. Liberty is a responsibility and a challenge. Each of us must individually desire to control our own destinies, to take charge of our freedoms. Unfortunately, if too many of us decide this is too much effort, that liberty is a burden too great, and we lay our freedoms down, the government will surely come and pick them up and lock them away again, and it will be our own fault. I believe the American people do love freedom, but we only need to be reminded from time to time, that our lives belong to us, that we must not ask a system to handle our responsibilities for us."

Ted Rowlands: "And that's all the time we have. Thank you gentlemen for being here tonight..."

Governor Bill Richardson: "Ted, if I could, I'd just like to add that I also favor the line-item veto. I have used it effectively as Governor, and I believe it's the only way to eliminate the billions of dollars in wasteful spending in Washington."

Attorney General John Edwards: "I would also support a Presidential line-item veto."

Roger, who had been energetic and focused throughout the debate, looked weak in the knees and completely astonished as the evening ended with several of the other candidates voicing their support for the line-item veto. It was not that it was among his controversial issues, but the tone amazed him. The finishing note of the debate entailed everyone grudgingly following his lead. Or perhaps they were only trying to deflate his outsider position. But the sound of all those politicians saying they agreed with him, on anything, shocked him.

Chapter 7

Defense

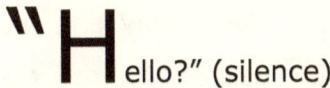"Hello?" (silence)

"Hello?..."

(finally crackling through, with urgency) "Hello. Is Roger Adams available please?"

"Yes, this is Roger."

"Please hold for former President Clinton."

Roger scritched his chin curiously as he waited.

...

"Hello, Roger? It's Hillary Clinton," her voice came through, the connection now loud and crisp.

"Hello Mrs. President. To what do I owe the pleasure?"

"I want to congratulate you on a terrific debate last night. It was the most fiery display I've seen in a while."

"Thank you, Mrs. President," he said politely, while he waited for her to move past the pleasantries.

"You know, Roger, you've made quite an impact on this election so far, and you should be proud of yourself for that. But I wonder if you've thought about what impact you might have further on down the line."

"I'm not sure quite what you're getting at..."

"I'm worried that you're going to sap the life out of the Democratic Party and the Republican Party may end up the benefactor, Mr. Adams. I realize you're an Independent, but I think you have more in common with the Democrats, and I'd hate to see you weaken the Democratic field, just to fall away and let the Republicans walk home with the Presidency. I think you know how I feel about Presidents named Bush."

"I'm a firm believer in Perot's runoff reform, Mrs. President, and I'm sure the big money machine the Democrats have in place can withstand a little healthy criticism, especially if it leads to a stronger America."

"I hope you'll spend some more time considering the effect you might have before next week's primary vote, Roger. You know, Florida is a critical state; it's Jeb's state, and I don't think you want Jeb and his machine in the White House any more than I do."

"Are you asking me to drop out of the race, Mrs. President?" he asked, mildly shocked.

"I'm asking you to consider the effect you might have, Roger," she said with an audible smile.

"Thank you for your time, Mrs. President," he answered

angrily.

"Nice talking to you, Roger," she said, in a way so friendly, it gave Roger the creeps.

...

Roger gave speech after speech, travelling up and down the state, drawing large crowds everywhere. Many of them were probably just curious what wild stuff he might come up with next, he figured, as the media relentlessly portrayed him as an 'eccentric,' which is, of course, code for 'nut.' It was the standard treatment they gave to anyone who threatened the traditional closed-door system. They had done it to Howard Dean. They had done it to Ross Perot... Ross Perot. Now here was a guy who had been a friend to Presidents, known them personally, and then stood up in front of the nation and called their policies crazy. Images of Perot's debate performances, complete with pie charts, floated through Roger's head like a corny television show montage. Perot floated out of one of the scenes, took a step closer, and spoke directly to Roger. "Government is always being reformed," Perot advised him. "Just sometimes it re-forms more quickly than others... You can do anything, so long as you can explain it to the people..."

"Anything..." Roger snapped his head up, his eyes half shut and his mouth half open. He took a deep breath and reacted as he felt a shooting pain in his right arm. Groggily, he sat up straight and looked around. He was alone in the front section of the bus, directly behind his driver, Manuel and the noise-reducing partition that separated them. He had fallen asleep with his head on his right arm, slouched over the booth seat and pinching his shoulder. He dropped his right arm into his lap to let the blood flow again and struggled to lift his heavy head. A faint image of Ross Perot smiling directly at him reminded him of his dream.

"Oh my god," Roger said, bemused and startled, "Ross Perot has become my Elvis! ...my own personal symbol of reform 'cool.' Maybe I really am becoming a nut!" he joked to himself, stumbling through his slumber toward the bunks in the back, sniffing his way toward Lenka via a small comforting trace of her perfume.

...

As soon as Roger walked into the Florida headquarters in Tallahassee on Saturday morning, Shauna met him at the doorway, looking like a doctor about to report to the family that a patient had been lost.

"We've got a major problem this morning, Roger."

"What is it, Shauna?"

"Less than an hour ago, we found that a video and some snapshots have been floating around. It's supposedly Lenka in her college days, 'going wild,' you might say. It's pretty nasty."

"Let me see it," said Roger, sitting down to the nearest computer with a grim determination.

"This is obviously doctored," he declared after Lenka's face came into view, the shadows and quality of color not exactly matching.

"That's what we assumed, Roger," said Shauna, comporting herself as seriously as Roger had ever seen her. "But I think the insinuation is just as bad. We need to agree on the wording of a statement and get it out to the media ASAP."

"Is Dusty here?" Roger asked.

"He should be here any minute," said Shauna.

"OK. I'm gonna call Lenka. What time is it? 7:45? OK, let's get this done by 8:30. If Dusty isn't here in five minutes, we start without him. In my office."

"Yes sir," Shauna said, still dead serious.

"I assume you've contacted the web hosts already to get

this shit removed?" he asked as he stood up.

"Absolutely."

"Good work, Shauna. Thank you."

He turned his head, got Lenka on the phone, and began pacing. "Honey, I'm sorry if you're busy, but it looks like one of the candidates has put out a smear attack on you early this morning. Shauna is getting it pulled off all the major sites, but we'll have to do some damage control too. We have no way of knowing how many people have seen or downloaded this..."

"Yeah, it's a smutty video and some photos," Roger explained. "Obviously doctored. We won't have any problem proving that it's fake, but we need to formulate our first reaction in the next half hour or so. Of course, I'd like you to be here for that."

Eight minutes later, Lenka walked through the glass double doors of Adams Florida HQ, wearing one of her typically swooshy knee-length dresses, her deep brown hair tied loosely on top of her head, and large Audrey Hepburn sunglasses hiding her expression behind maximum elegance. She set the sunglasses down on Roger's desk and sat down next to Shauna in one of the chairs, arranged in a circle in Roger's office. She looked up just as Dusty rushed into the room. Roger came in behind him, holding the large coffee mug Lenka had made him for his last birthday, which had a flash photo of her on the shore, smiling happily, with dark twilight ocean waves wrapping all the way around the mug. It was filled to the brim with his milky beige, thin-as-water coffee and said, "OK, ideas. Shauna, you've had the most time to think it over. What do you think?"

"The first statement should be short, only the most essential message. This is a fake, and it's dirty politics. But we can't sound too devastated."

"Dusty?" asked Roger, going around the room.

"I agree. One sentence. We state that it's fake, and we imply that it's an out-of-bounds attack from another candidate."

"Lenka, any thoughts?", Roger asked, knowing that she would never let herself be intimidated by politics, least of all dirty politics.

"We should say the guy getting the lap dance in the video is Michael Bloomberg," Lenka offered, laughing hysterically and defusing the tension in everyone's furrowed brows. Roger had to set down his coffee so as not to spill.

"Oh, I feel better now," said Lenka, as the laughter died

down. "I haven't even seen it yet - I don't know if there even is a lap dance. Seriously though, what if we say, 'Lenka Adams will speak out this afternoon regarding the disgusting lies being spread by her political enemies on the internet,' or something like that? So we say that it's a lie, but we make it sound like there's more to it, so people will be interested in the press conference or whatever it is later today?"

"I like the idea," said Roger, "but not that wording. We don't want to say 'enemies,' for instance."

Lenka leaned back in her chair, happy that her clever idea was deemed useful.

"Dusty, you think that could work, with different wording?"

"Sure, but I'd like to set up an interview, rather than a press conference. We don't want you squinting in the sunlight, looking sweaty and flustered."

"OK. But we need to get the statement out before the morning shows end."

"We don't have to say exactly when and where the interview will be in the first statement. We'll have all day to get that information out," Shauna said.

"You're right," Dusty agreed, "In fact, it'll sound *too* prepared if we already have the time and place. We should save that 'til lunchtime."

"OK, so... Are we writing this down?"

"I am," Shauna said.

"Lenka Adams, wife of Presidential candidate Roger Adams, to speak out, no - to respond this evening to the sleazy political attacks against her... online political attacks against her," Roger suggested.

"It might be too long with the, 'wife of' part in there," Dusty mused.

"And sleazy is not the same as 'untrue,' "Shauna reminded them.

"Maybe if we move that to the end...," Dusty continued his thought out loud.

"OK, take a few minutes to write that up and we'll look at it again," Roger ordered, and then turned to his wife. "Lenka, do you want to see what all the controversy is about?"

"Yeah, I guess I should," Lenka shrugged, not feeling nearly as offended as everyone else, only because she was doing her best not to take it personally.

Roger walked with Lenka into the front room, the cubicled volunteer staff area, where only two early birds in the back corner rubbed their morning eyes.

At 8:12am EST, the Roger Adams campaign released the following statement to the media:

"Later today, Lenka Adams will respond in detail to the disgusting fabrications made against her for political gain against her husband's Presidential campaign."

...

Dusty leaned forward in his chair, elbows on his knees, and squinted from the brazen shouting of the announcer's voice booming through the studio. Shauna stood behind him, tucked a long strand of her blonde hair behind her right ear, and crossed her arms expectantly.

"AND NEXT, stay tuned for an exclusive LIVE Fox News interview with ONLINE SIMULCAST. Lenka Adams, wife of Presidential candidate Roger Adams, responds to the SCANDALOUS VIDEOS that have recently surfaced FROM HER DEVIANT PAST."

As soon as the commercials had wrapped, Lenka began speaking. The interviewer never had a chance to form an introduction. Lenka and Roger had agreed to go on Fox only because Fox had agreed to go live and uncensored. The network had assumed this would be to their advantage, but Lenka was determined to control the tempo. She jumped right in -

Lenka Adams: "I can assure you, 100%, that those materials are faked. This is not *my* deviant past. I have never worked in a nightclub, and I have never been in the sort of position in which I am purportedly shown in these offensive hit pieces. The scandalous deviant that you mentioned in the intro is not me, but some tactless person, who is unfortunately, supporting one of the other candidates for President of the United States."

Mary Entwistle: "So the doctored photos and videos that have been spreading online - you're sure this was a politically motivated attack?"

Lenka Adams: "Well of course it was. Roger's been moving steadily upwards in the polls and both major parties and all the candidates are hoping we might somehow go away quietly. Listen," she said more slowly and more quietly, and leaning forward, "when I was twelve years old, I was raped, by a person I knew. When I was older, I discovered that many of my friends had suffered similar traumatic experiences. This is not new information. I speak regularly about this in my work for WaGAF, and I have no doubt that the people who did this were aiming for the most painful place they could find on us. Congratulations to them. They found it, they hit it, but we are still here. I want to say to anyone feeling like a victim tonight, young boys, girls, women, anyone, you don't have to take it. You can hold your head up high and be tougher for the experience. Find good people to support you and stand tall."

Mary Entwistle: "That's a great message, and I know that, sadly, there is always someone out there who needs to hear it. So what *did* you do before your charity work, Mrs. Adams?"

Lenka Adams: "I have certainly never worked in any segment of the entertainment industry. My background is in geology. I took an internship while I was still in school, and I was working as a geologist until I met Roger and decided to devote myself to providing better opportunities to girls and women in need."

Mary Entwistle: "Tell us the story of how you and Roger met. I'm interested."

Lenka Adams: "It's no movie of the week, I'm afraid. I was managing the soil survey team at the environmental qualification firm that Roger hired when he was building the first desalination turbines. I was wearing a ravishing plain white hard hat and safety glasses, holding a beautiful manila folder, and Roger simply had to have me. What can I say?"

(Roger laughed appreciatively while Lenka, sitting next to him, maintained a straight face. The interviewer appeared confused, then laughed awkwardly.)

Mary Entwistle: "How are *you* dealing with this situation, Mr. Adams? You haven't spoken about this matter yet."

Roger Adams: "There's very little for *me* to deal with here, Mary. As you can see, my beautiful wife is perfectly capable of handling whatever gets thrown her way, and I'm only here today to stand by her side. But I'll tell you what my reaction was. I was outraged, as was *everyone* that knows Lenka. And whichever of the candidates is responsible for this disgusting innuendo, and I am sure that it *was* approved by one of the candidates, although it may never come to light which one it was, that candidate is not fit to serve as a postal carrier, much less President of these great United States. It's time for the old boys' clubs to do some merit badges in respecting women."

Mary Entwistle (eyes wide with excitement): "Would you call yourself a feminist, Mr. Adams?"

Roger Adams: "As I said, I'm here to support my wife today. I'll be happy to answer all your questions about my campaign at a later time."

Lenka Adams: "Roger refuses to agree with me on this, but I feel the word 'feminist' lost its meaning a long time ago. Some people who don't like to see women leaving their traditional roles for more fulfilling lives like to use the word 'feminist' as some kind of dirty word, to conjure up ancient images of bra burning and man-hating. I think you'll find that Roger does agree with me, however, that women have the right to seek out their independence, freedom and pursuit of happiness, in whatever form that might take, be it traditional or not, as guaranteed by the Constitution for *all* our citizens."

Roger Adams: "Sounds good to me, honey."

Mary Entwistle (eyes opening even wider than before): "I'm amazed, Mr. Adams! It sounds like your wife is establishing new campaign issues for you. Will you be a power couple in the White House?"

Roger Adams: "Lenka has worked extremely hard for girls and women who have been victimized and traumatized in various ways, which I know to be a full-time job. Whether she would have time to devote to any other issues while in the White House, should we take up residence there next year, I don't know. You'll have to ask her."

Lenka Adams (jumping right in): "I have no plans to reduce my level of commitment to the Women and Girls Assistance Foundation. If I decide I have time to take on any other important responsibilities, I'll let you know. As for the campaign, Roger and his team are doing a superb job. If they start asking for *my* advice on political issues, I'd say we're in trouble."

Mary Entwistle: "Thank you, Mrs. Adams, Mr. Adams."

The monitor showed a quick cut to graphics with a voiceover, "You get more real, balanced information first on Fox News." And then it was instantly to more commercials.

...

The dirty tricks and negative ads from the career politicians had continued to increase Roger's numbers. Roger's ads, always 15 seconds long, simply called for a more transparent and reasonable government to put the priorities of the people first. In his speeches, he concentrated on the corruption built into the system, challenging the voters to be more active, and "to make the people's business the only business in town. The slimy tricks they pull only demonstrate how desperate they are to keep the status quo in Washington," he said to cheers and applause several times a day.

Leading into the final stretch, he was running nearly 20% in Florida, according to the polls. Back at Florida headquarters now, Roger stood near the front door, greeting every member of his Florida team as they arrived to watch the results come in, thanking them for all the hard work they'd put in and declaring the campaign a success, regardless of the outcome. Although he'd been gaining progressively more national attention, he expected the field to narrow after tonight's results, and for the voters to focus more on the two major parties. Tonight was likely to be the last big celebratory function of the campaign, as well as the end of the campaign in Florida.

"Hi! Thank you for all your hard work!" Roger yelled cheerfully but loudly across the room, causing the chatter to fall a notch, as a figure in a red uniform walked toward him up the sidewalk, a stack of white cardboard pizza boxes blocking the person's face and torso from view. Roger continued yelling excitedly, "I know it's not easy carrying PIZZA for an entire campaign team!" Roger beamed, both hungry for pizza and content with the accomplishments of his team. A contingent of volunteers hurried over to disassemble the tower of pizza boxes and spread them across the tables, a few old papers being pushed dramatically onto the floor. Dusty handed a credit card to the fresh-faced delivery boy, who barely looked old enough to drive, let alone vote. While Dusty signed the credit card slip, Roger produced a fifty dollar bill from his wallet and said to the kid, "We're gonna have a good night tonight. Thank you for starting us off on the right foot with this here delicious pizza." He folded the bill in half and handed it to the pizza boy, who looked like he didn't know what to say. Roger waited, and then said pleasantly, "I would invite you to stay for the party, but I'm sure you have more pizzas waiting to be delivered, don't you?" He smiled as the boy slowly put the money in his pocket and stammered, "Y-Yes, I do. Th-Thank you sir."

"It's no problem, son." As the boy turned and walked away, Roger suddenly felt a twinge of the responsibility of his position and, still smiling, called out after him, "Use it wisely!"

Only a few cold, lonely slices of pizza remained on their cardboard landscape, and the office was filled with personal conversations, steadily becoming nervous in anticipation of some kind of news, which had been expected as soon as polls closed. Shauna picked up the remote and pressed a button, and finally an election update was on the screen. Everyone quickly stopped talking and turned toward the TV. The four television cameras against the wall all zoomed in on Roger's face, awaiting a reaction, with Lenka going out of focus next to him.

"Preliminary results show Vice President Bush easily winning the Republican primary tonight in his home state of Florida," the reporter announced triumphantly, as if the victory had been his. "With 47% of precincts reporting, the former Governor is being given 64% of the vote..." In a flash, the reporter's head jumped to one side, and a graphic swished across the right-hand side of the screen, with names distorted in a graphical waterfall, dripping in the form of large water drops into a bucket and becoming legible as the absurd computer animation rippled and settled at the bottom of the screen. Alan Keyes dripped in first, to a majestic soundtrack, with a "2%" next to his name. Then Adams, with 8%. "The interesting thing to watch here is the nail-biter going on right now for third place," the commentator added urgently, as Bloomberg's name came in, also with 8%. The room was hushed, everyone knowing full well, that there were five main candidates and only two had been shown. Then the shouting began, as Senator Lindsey Graham's name came into focus, also with 8%. The television cameras panned around at the pandemonium, nearly colliding in the process. "The way it looks right now," the TV reporter could barely be heard to say, "it's anybody's guess who comes up with a potentially very important third-place finish here tonight. Even second place is not assured for Governor Sonny Perdue!" he added dramatically. "Senator Lindsey Graham, Mayor Michael Bloomberg, and independent businessman Roger Adams are all looking at 8% right now, but those numbers are likely to change throughout the night."

...

Florida Republican Primary Early Results (47% of
precincts reporting)

Vice Pres. Jeb Bush - FL 64%

Gov. Sonny Perdue - GA 10%

Sen. Lindsey Graham - SC 8%

Mayor Michael Bloomberg - NY 8%

Roger Adams - OR 8%

Alan Keyes - MD 2%

...

Dusty was chattering furiously about the myriad
possibilities, to which Roger was nodding and smiling.
This office had been campaign HQ for more than a
month, but it had never been so busy and noisy as it
was tonight. Lenka was wrapped up in his left arm and
his fingers danced lightly, happily across the edge of her
tummy. His hand slid up to her lowest rib when he
leaned forward to hear someone talking to him, and
returned to her stomach again when talking to Dusty,
who was standing directly in his right ear.

Shauna stepped in front of Dusty and held up her cell

phone to indicate she'd received updated info. She leaned in toward Roger's ear and said, "I just talked to Zogby. They've got Bloomberg lower than this."

"Thank you, Shauna," Roger said breezily.

Shauna switched to a different news channel and continued, shouting, "I think it's between you and Graham for third place, Roger, and you know Perdue has nothing outside the South."

"That's true," Roger agreed, completely unable to remove the silly smile from his face. He stopped to appreciate the overwhelmingly giddy mood that he now realized was accompanying each election night so far, and then he thanked Shauna again. "You've done a fantastic job for us here, Shauna. Thank you so much for everything. We might have been able to do it without you, but not nearly as well!"

"Thank you, Roger. It's been a really exciting campaign!" she beamed.

Graham's number inched up to 10% on the next update, and Perdue went to 11, putting second place in doubt. Then twenty minutes later, Perdue was up to 12%, and Graham was back down to 9. The office burst into another round of cheers. At this point, champagne started flowing as if they had won the whole thing.

Shauna changed the channel again and found the preliminary Democratic primary results. A full listing was already on the screen.

...

Florida Democratic Primary Early Results (65% of precincts reporting)

AG John Edwards - NC 41%
Gov. Bill Richardson - NM 30%
Roger Adams - OR 21%
Def. Sec. Wesley Clark - AR 4%
Gov. Jim Cauty - MI 3%

...

"Twenty-one!?" Dusty screamed, hardly believing that they had exceeded their aggressively optimistic goal of 20%. "We did it! Twenty-one percent!" An hour and a half later, the final results did nothing to dampen their mood, and Roger was giving interview after interview to the cameras about his stunning 23% finish and his third place tie with the Senator from South Carolina in the Republican primary, although Adams had officially received 439 fewer votes than Graham. It was a stunning rebuke to the man who had screamed so wretchedly in Roger's face in New Hampshire. And it occurred to him in that moment, that it had been Graham's campaign that had made the fake porn tape of Lenka. He hadn't thought about it much. He'd quickly decided the most productive way to deal with it was to let it slip quietly into the past. But with all the reporters asking about the virtual tie with Lindsey Graham, which they painted as a huge victory for Adams, the seemingly constant repetition of that name recalling the day when he had seen the man's ugliest qualities unleashed unapologetically before him, it seemed to descend on him from the rafters. He didn't really know, but he felt as if he knew - it had been Graham.

...

Florida Republican Primary Final Results (100% of precincts reporting)

	# of votes
Vice Pres. Jeb Bush - FL 60%	2,630,535
Gov. Sonny Perdue - GA 12%	526,108
Sen. Lindsey Graham - SC 9%	394,566
Roger Adams - OR 9%	394,127
Mayor Michael Bloomberg - NY 8%	350,735
Alan Keyes - MD 2%	85,684

...

Within a week, Defense Secretary Clark dropped out of the race, followed by Bloomberg and Cauty. Nevada's primary came next, where Perdue proved incapable of expanding his regional candidacy into a national one. Aside from Roger, it came down to Edwards and the quieter but straight-shooting Richardson on the Democratic side, and Bush on the Republican side, with Lindsey Graham struggling to draw donations for his limping effort, but not giving up yet. Bloomberg had plenty of money, but not a lot of support. Coming from a neighboring state, Bill Richardson pulled even with

Edwards in Nevada, and clearly had the momentum. Roger pulled in a respectable 16% in Nevada, but clearly the voters were tiring of the wild debates and the flurry of issues. They had begun to line up behind the most electable candidates, perhaps subconsciously drifting as a nation, toward a more orderly process, as they had been doing in elections all their lives. Adams had been spending his campaign funds judiciously, running final-week 15-second ad blitzes in each primary state and speaking forcefully on the same issues, but his campaign was no longer gathering steam and his poll numbers had stalled out. Meanwhile, Edwards continued to lose momentum as Richardson's campaign highlighted his broad array of foreign policy experience, as well as his excellent record as Governor, while subtly portraying Edwards as an insincere blow-dried lawyer.

Two weeks before the Oregon primary, the Adams campaign decided, but did not announce, that if he didn't win his home state, there was no point in continuing the candidacy. The day after the primary, Roger announced in an online broadcast from his home, that he was done. Surprisingly, John Edwards dropped out of the campaign a week later, admitting that he had lost all momentum and that his numbers did not look good in the upcoming states of Texas, Oklahoma and Illinois. He put on a plastic smile for the cameras and fully endorsed Bill Richardson for the Democratic nomination. He did not reveal that his wife's cancer had returned aggressively a week before the Florida primary. On the Republican side, Senator Graham and Mayor Bloomberg continued to press on, hopeful that Bush might somehow stumble or that things might still turn around somehow, or perhaps, like an old rock band facing the end of a long tour, just weren't ready to go home yet.

...

On a lazy July evening, Roger and Lenka were settled in to the couch with a bucket of ice cream, ready to buy an online movie (There was no renting any more, just purchasing in digital format for eight dollars, the same price movies had dropped to at the theater), when the phone rang.

"Don't get up, honey," Roger said.

"Don't worry. I won't," she countered, sitting motionless.

Roger smirked, stood up, and walked into the kitchen.

"Hello, Roger?"

"Yes. This is Roger."

"Hi. This is Bill Richardson. How would you like to be my running mate?"

Slowly, Roger turned slightly and asked, "Is that an offer, or are you just feeling me out?"

Lenka turned toward Roger where she sat and a confused expression flashed across her face. A hearty laugh came through the telephone line.

"That's an offer, Roger. I know you just started to unwind from the campaign, but would you please consider running on the ticket with me?"

Roger stared blankly at the wall, as if his subconscious mind required all available mental energy to consider the weighty question. Finally he responded, "You do realize, that I have to remain Independent, don't you Governor?"

There was a dead silence wafting out of the phone, and then Richardson asked cautiously, "Independent of what, exactly?"

"Of the two party system. If I don't have a capital 'I' in the parentheses after my name, my base will call me a sell-out, and they'll be right. I'm not worth anything as a regular politician. Certainly you see that."

"I understand what you're saying, Roger. So you would

like to join the ticket, but not the party."

"Honestly, I don't know. If the offer is still good, I'll need 24 hours to discuss it with my wife and my team."

"The offer is still good, Roger," he said warmly. Roger could hear him smiling through the telephone. "Call me as soon as you have an answer."

"OK. I'll talk to you tomorrow. And Bill, thank you for taking a chance on me. You're a good man."

"Thanks, Roger. Same to you."

Roger's first thought as he hung up the glove was that the Democratic Party had some kind of sinister strategy, and he, and possibly Bill, were going to end up being played the fool.

Chapter 8
Us vs. Them

"You want to announce the ticket two months before the convention?" Roger asked, stunned.

"We're hoping that by announcing so early, we might make Jeb scramble a little. Whether he actually makes himself look silly is up to him of course, but we wanna definitely provide him that opportunity," Richardson said, his smile showing off the trademark dents in his cheeks.

"Alright," Roger said agreeably. "Let's see how it plays out."

The Republicans certainly were stunned by the early announcement. As were the Democrats. The Republican media networks (All the most popular net writers, the "bloggers," as they had been called, were hired into the mainstream media shortly after the 2008 election) began celebrating a new Republican dynasty, assured that the Democrats had shot themselves in the foot once again.

Democrats were split on the choice. Some were

confused that the running mate was not a Democrat and did not even want to be. Others were mortified by the criticisms Adams had leveled at Democrats during his campaign. There were calls for a reversal at the convention. But by the time the convention came around, most Democrats had come around to the idea that Adams' campaign had been about cleaning up the whole government, not just kicking out the bums from the other party for a new set of bums. In hindsight, it was doubly-wise to start talking as early as possible about Adams joining the ticket, as it allowed the Democratic Party to unite behind him after the shock and controversy settled down.

Richardson, for his part, stood firm in his support of Adams, calling him a "man of action" (which is how the Republicans always liked to refer to Bloomberg), and a "daring leader." Daring was the euphemistic response to those that would call him "dangerous." Adams again became the talk of the campaign. While there was little other campaign news to report, the media spent weeks talking about the viability of the Democrat/Independent ticket, the historical precedent it set, and asking every elected official, and even the man on the street, their opinion of the Richardson/Adams ticket. All poor Bush could do was fly around the country "looking

Presidential," which wasn't exactly news.

"So what's on the agenda today, ladies and gentlemen?" Roger asked cheerfully at the start of the daily campaign meeting.

One of the advisers in attendance chimed in, "Bush has been off the front page for a while now, and we'd like to keep it that way if we can."

Roger had the funny feeling that everyone was looking at him. Dusty and Roger looked at each other. Then they both looked at Richardson.

"You're designating me the attack dog, Bill?"

"I'm sure you understand, the President can't always be the one casting stones," said Richardson's California campaign manager.

"I understand that perfectly," Roger said as he turned toward her. "I'm just asking, is this a one-time deal, or have I involuntarily volunteered for a recurring role as the attack dog?"

"There is an open position."

"I'm seeing more clearly every day the reasons I was offered this job," Roger grumbled sardonically.

"Oh now, it's not so bad, Roger," Richardson offered, sensing that Adams was not truly upset to have an even broader national platform for his naturally rebellious character. "Think of how exciting life will be with a whole new raft of enemies to confound."

"There is that," Roger agreed whimsically.

Although he'd expected a good-natured response to his defusing remark, Richardson was slightly surprised by the depth of humor and calm with which Adams deflected the stress of the situation. He tilted his head to one side with a quizzical look on his face, as if he still couldn't quite make out what kind of man Adams was, beneath it all.

"So where do we start?" Roger asked, suddenly switching into planning mode.

Everyone grinned mischievously.

...

The Richardson campaign didn't like nasty tricks any more than Adams' had, but they were a little more media savvy, meaning they did try to produce some well-placed comments to keep the Republicans off balance and to highlight their advantages. Simple sound bites were constructed for Roger to offer up like hanging curveballs to reporters. He delivered them casually, while shaking hands with voters at a campaign rally, or while walking to his car from a restaurant, and it was conveyed through the media almost like celebrity gossip.

"Of course, I understand that Senator Graham is still officially seeking the nomination of his party, but if I didn't know better, I'd say the Republican candidate is purposely delaying the selection of a running mate because he doesn't like to see me winning debates."

Putting a spotlight on the indestructible egos on the Republican side, while also making the Democrats appear better organized, was a major reversal from the perception they'd suffered for the last few decades. The difference showed in the polls.

"I heard the Republicans might like to nominate President Lieberman for the Vice President's running mate. They seem to be running out of options."

"The Republicans haven't ruled out bringing George Dubya back out of retirement for a big brother / little brother administration!"

Campaign fatigue was settling in with the voters and the silly tit-for-tat media games were all the candidates could accomplish in the meantime. Everyone knew Bush would not agree to debate again until after the Republican convention. It had been several months now since Richardson had become the de facto Democratic nominee and the independent campaigns of Bloomberg and others had faded into historical election footnotes. For despite Perot's reform, money still ruled the campaign process, and Roger, though very proud of the distance he had run, remained disappointed in the system. He harbored thoughts of completing Perot's reform with free and equal air time for all candidates, more open debates and very tight contribution and spending limits. But he also worried that the people still would not demand more from their own electoral process, preferring to place their trust in Lady Fortuna to decide their collective destiny.

Finally, in early September, the Republicans held their convention in Dallas, Texas. After all the controversy generated by the selection of the Democratic running mate, Jeb's campaign kept a tight lid on their VP selection process, hoping to get some similar mystery and excitement, and a boost in the polls, in addition to the regular convention bounce.

A still youthful, but completely grayed, former President George W. Bush was greeted with loud cheers by his party faithful. He made an emotional tribute to his father, although he had passed away more than five years earlier, and then gave an unusually humble introduction of his brother, using the word, "proud" several times.

When Jeb finally introduced his Vice Presidential choice, former Kansas Senator Sam Brownback, to blaring trumpets and shooting streamers, the crowd erupted, probably due more to the festive atmosphere than the completely obvious choice of running mate, which was shocking only in its absolute expectedness. Although he'd been in the private sector for over five years, Brownback had been a popular Senator and occasional Presidential candidate who shared everything in common with Jeb Bush (except for his conversion from evangelicalism to the controversial Catholic Opus Dei sect, which he publicly denied), and coming from an important Midwest state, he was at the top of most pundits' list.

Bush and Richardson squared off in a lively, yet fairly predictable debate two weeks later in San Francisco. Bush defended his record as Vice President. Richardson challenged him to finally bring all our troops home from the Middle East. Bush painted Richardson as a "very able diplomat," but questioned his ability to stand firm when necessary, rather than always negotiate. Richardson attacked Bush's special interest ties. Bush warned that Richardson would break the budget with generous government programs...

...

WIRE REPORTS - Oct 10, 2016

8:39pm EST - There has been some kind of nuclear explosion or contamination in Pakistan, near the city of Quetta. 230 U.S. troops reported killed and 459 currently missing. It is still very early in the morning in Pakistan. Information is sketchy and these numbers are expected to climb.

9:07pm EST - Vice President Bush: There has been a nuclear explosion in Pakistan, but we have determined that it is NOT a terrorist attack. There has been a catastrophic accident at an ageing nuclear power facility ten miles south of the city of Quetta. I repeat - there is NO nuclear attack in Pakistan. Terrorism has been ruled out. Today is a day of mourning, but it is not a day of war, and I urge you not to panic. It appears that the worst nuclear reactor accident in history has taken place today, and we hold our American troops in the area and their families in our prayers, along with the Pakistani people. The President is aboard Air Force One and will speak as soon as he touches down at Andrews Air Force Base, which should be within the half hour.

9:13pm EST - 412 American troops now reported killed in the nuclear accident outside of Quetta, Pakistan, possibly thousands affected by radiation. Preliminary reports suggest that there may be thousands of Pakistani civilians dead. The entire southern side of the city is said to be destroyed and multiple fires continue to burn all over the city and its suburbs. According to Vice President Bush's brief statement, the nuclear reactor suffered an uncontained meltdown followed by fires, which led to enormous secondary explosions. As he says, this certainly would be the largest nuclear disaster in history. There's no doubt about that on this terrible tragic evening.

...

The campaign had just arrived in New York City when the news bulletins started coming through. Roger and Lenka stepped across the hall into the hotel suite set up as the campaign office for the next few days. They sat quietly on a beige couch, joining the dozen or so aides who were staring blankly at the television. Roger thought to himself that he had never seen any of these ambitious, Dockered young people sitting still for a moment, much less all of them together. They all seemed stunned. Lenka slid her arm around Roger. He turned to say something to her, but forgot what it was when he saw the tears welling up in her deep brown eyes. He closed his mouth, which was still hanging open to speak, and embraced Lenka quietly with both arms.

With just a month remaining before the November 8 General Election, an ageing nuclear weapons site near Quetta had suffered an uncontained meltdown and after fires broke out, major secondary explosions. Most of the country's systems had been in chaos for years in the aftermath of the U.S. invasion, although not as critically as in Iraq, for example, with its four hours a day of electricity and not much more than that for water. Not as critically, that is, until now.

The summer monsoons in that region, coincidentally, typically come to an end in early October and the jet stream slips into a calm southern route. This meant that the bulk of the nuclear fallout was swept slowly across Pakistan from west to east and then drifted over the entire southern half of its neighbor, India, highlighting the shared destiny of such close neighbors.

From the Richardson/Adams campaign, Oct 11:

As the skies loom darkly ashen from Quetta to Lahore, to Mumbai and Bangalore, the old "us vs. them" scenario has been removed from people's minds, for a time, anyway. Pakistanis and Indians are breathing the same nuclear fallout, through the same masks, are digging under the same soil for shelter, where they can. Both Republicans and Democrats are trying for endless, countless hours to make contact with their loved ones in uniform. Everyone is pulling together, as we humans do in times of tragedy, to aid the living and comfort the grieving. We stand united, all.

And slowly, here and there, anger began to bubble and rise through the sea of goodwill and compassion and Red Cross donations. Dismay turned to discontent. Uncertainty lingered and led to unanswered, and unanswerable, questions.

While most of the world was shaken by the human toll and the general fear, with humanitarian aid pouring in from all over the world, the dark corners of the internet teemed with frustration. There were furious accusations that India had been looking for an excuse to bomb Pakistan, that they'd actually secretly bombed the nuclear plant. Other conspiracy theories ran from Al Qaeda marking the sixth anniversary of the Triple Ten attacks, to the U.S. and India collaborating to wipe

Pakistan off the map, to the Americans dropping a nuke on Quetta to try and finally kill bin Laden and other top Al Qaeda leadership, no matter how many innocent lives went with him, or to send a message to various factions. Of course, the CIA knew well that Osama bin Laden and most of his top people had long ago fled to somewhere in the hopelessly lawless Horn of Africa anarcho-nation of Somalia. A total of just 17 special operations agents were sneaking around the area in civilian clothing on a seek and kill mission that had lasted longer than any other in American history.

The truth behind the nuclear disaster in Quetta was easier and more obvious. When worldwide oil production peaked in 2012 at 100 million barrels per day, at a price surging past $160 a barrel, every nation around the world was already rushing to fill the void with any alternative energies available to them. Although the Clinton administration had fast-forwarded new biofuel programs in the U.S., the demand for oil in developing countries, mainly China and India, had continued to grow exponentially, faster than any of the official predictions. Unfortunately, most of the oil producing nations, not to mention the oil companies, had inflated their numbers for decades, always hoping that some new pumping system or large field discovery would sustain the industry for another decade. In reality, none of the producers had been telling the truth. The fields had dried up, and there was just nowhere left to expand oil production without an astronomical investment, with no guarantee of profits on the other end. Gradually, over the course of the Spring of 2012, like a high-flying corporation with false receipts and tricky accounting, the oil house of cards came tumbling down, down to $24 per barrel, in fact.

Europe, and to a lesser extent, the U.S., had significantly reduced their oil consumption by that time. In Europe, the mix of wind, hydro, and second generation solar technologies (developed in 2010 and 10 times more efficient than earlier solar panels), combined with an EU-wide 90% recycling rate and hundreds of nuclear plants, which were now using enriched thorium, meant the bulk of the oil they were still using went for road and air transportation, not electricity. In America, the reverse was true. As soon as gas blew past $4.50 a gallon, Clinton pushed a huge biofuel bill through Congress, spending billions of dollars building new BioMix refineries, which were capable of producing fertilizers and highly efficient car and jet fuels, from fruits, grasses, recycled plastics, road kill (generally used in fertilizers), wood chips, just about anything that was ever remotely organic. They were also beginning to process synthetic glucoses, manufactured from scratch in the lab. The BioFuel Act of 2011 subsidized 1000 new BioMix pumps (two per station at just 500 gas stations), and car manufacturers quickly followed suit with BioMix engines. It also implemented another $2 per gallon in taxes on traditional gasoline to help pay for the pumps, making gasoline considerably more expensive than BioMix (although still only two-thirds the price of gas in Europe), and providing another incentive for people to make the switch. President Clinton often pointed to the BioFuel Act as a great accomplishment of her administration, but critics said she had actually dragged her Presidential heels on biofuel for the big oil lobby for two years, until she simply couldn't anymore, and they blasted the huge "European style" gas tax. Solar-powered homes soon became the norm. Although the energy crisis had dragged the U.S. into recession along with the ongoing credit and housing slowdowns, the more efficient solar panels were now seen as a critical investment, and prices dropped as the sector boomed.

China and India had instantly increased their coal production by 20%, while also investing in new nuclear plants. They had already been swamped in unbelievable levels of air and water pollution, and significant segments of China's population lived in areas that were quickly becoming totally uninhabitable.

Although Saudi Arabia and other Gulf states took a significant hit, the worst-affected were countries such as Russia and Venezuela, whose developing economies had been almost entirely dependent on the sale of high-priced oil, losing approximately half of their GDP. In most measureable ways, the world had abandoned the use of oil. No longer the grease in the world's wheels, production of oil collapsed almost overnight. In Pakistan, the energy crisis meant firing up every single nuclear facility they had, including older ones (which did not quite meet their *own* safety standards any more, much less western standards), and recycling their few nuclear missiles for fuel. By 2014, the U.S. had sold nearly half of its nuclear arsenal to nations around the world desperate for nuclear fuel. Russia was busy recycling its arsenal for its own energy use.

Iran's Ambassador to the UN had proudly announced that his nation had been alone in accurately anticipating the scope and immediacy of the looming oil crisis (although Europe had been pessimistic on oil for the better part of three decades), and that their controversial nuclear energy efforts had been well justified. They even announced they would be selling enriched uranium to their neighbors in the region. But no one could say whether this was just a bit of Iranian propaganda with the benefit of hindsight, or if they had had some extraordinary access to information from inside the oil industry.

12,000 American troops had been exposed to the radioactive fallout in Quetta. 439 had been close enough to the site to be killed by the actual explosions. With such enormous casualties suffered, President Lieberman had no choice but to begin a full scale military withdrawal in the aftermath of the disaster. The American public was unanimous in demanding the U.S. end its entire presence in Pakistan. The vast majority of the Americans with significant radiation exposure, whether military or contractor, were sent to U.S. military hospitals in Kabul, and the bulk of the troops redeployed to permanent American bases in Iraq and Afghanistan within the first week, although getting all 38,000 of them all the way back home would take several months.

An estimated 55,000 Pakistanis were killed in the first week of the disaster, with two million displaced and another half a million deaths in the following two years directly linked to the catastrophe.

...

The first, and only, Republican-Democratic Vice Presidential debate had been scheduled for October 15, just five days after the Quetta disaster. The nation, and the world, was in mourning. There was no appetite for debate in those dark, somber days. And there was little difference of opinion among the populace in the direct aftermath of the nuclear catastrophe, which had taken so many lives - American troops, Pakistani civilians, Indian and other populations, as the fallout cloud spun its way around the globe. President Lieberman had made several patriotic addresses to the nation, sounding brave yet depressed at the same time. Party forces attempted to reschedule unprecedented final week debates for both the Presidential and Vice Presidential candidates, but in the end, they could not make it happen. It was simply too soon.

Yet Election Day was drawing near. As life slowly

returned to normal, the two hour Quetta Disaster specials and telethons running less frequently, in this post-emergency atmosphere, the American public would register their phones or devices, and choose their next President. It felt like a more dangerously unpredictable world. The overriding sentiment was that we had far overreached our position in the world, that there was too much to do at home, and no satisfactory reason to be engaged so deeply in the internal political conflicts of other nations. In the aftermath of such a disaster, the people could find no answer to the questions, "Why are we even in these places? Why is it worth it?"

...

Roger leaned his lower back against the wall of the banquet hall, near the temporary stage entrance, his legs stretched out straight, forming a right triangle with the floor and the wall. Aides were scurrying like busy squirrels, even as supporters and donors filed in from the multiple sets of doors, gleefully chatting about their stock picks and scanning the tables of hors d'oeuvres, as if searching intently for a book they were sure they had just put down somewhere. He contemplated the gravity of where he was now, after this long crazy year, possibly just hours away from being elected Vice President of the United States. What an awesome responsibility he might now have to bear, and how slightly he had expected to actually be here. As larger numbers began to pour in, he was suddenly aware of how foolish he might appear to the party supporters, leaning against a wall by himself, encircled by Secret Service, and he quickly walked back to his green room. Over the last few months, he'd learned to ignore the rather alarming and constant presence of those uniform black suits with sunglasses and ear buds. He had to block them out, just to continue functioning. Lenka was not yet comfortable with them. She tried to chat with them to put herself at ease, but they always advised her coldly, that she was free to talk all she wanted, but they would risk losing concentration on her safety, should they, as they so pleasantly put it, "conversate."

Lenka and Roger were very well protected here, crammed into the back room of the official Democratic Party celebration with about five thousand Richardson campaign team members - at last count. They were in the Hyatt Tamaya outside of Albuquerque, a hotel as wide and brown as the bleak desert mountain range behind it. The room was swarming with Secret Service, as was the hallway, the bathroom, the roof, the entire building, probably half the state. Five televisions, three of them RealiVision and two TrueLifeDefs, buzzed with minute by minute updates as states processed their confirmations, district by district. (Despite the new technology, government always found a way to complicate the process, add redundancies, and introduce unforeseen errors.) Iowa had gone Democrat, no - it was too close to call again. The Carolinas were called for Bush on TrueLifeDef. Soon the whole slate of New England states was going to Richardson - New Hampshire, Connecticut, Massachusetts, Delaware, all the "spelling bee states," as some of the newer Internet-generation pundits called them. But the Richardson team expected those states. They were solid Democratic ground. And then Pennsylvania came in, with 64% for Richardson. That was the most lopsided victory yet, in a half-rural state too. Bill himself started clapping his hands like an enthusiastic baseball manager when Virginia went to Bush by only two percent. It wasn't just a signal of weakened support for Bush in the Republican states. This was a fantastic start to a popular vote election. Gone were the days of 25 votes for Florida and 33 for New York. Every voter would be counted, thanks to the Perot reform. New York now held 14 million votes, not 33. The state by state votes were still counted up for statistical indicators and demographic analysis, but as more states reported their numbers, the coverage shifted toward the cumulative popular vote and whatever trends the analysts could think up as the long night of reporting on a single topic wore on.

With the popular vote, the West Coast votes could not be so easily predicted, and so became the focus of every election's deciding hours. The candidates' home states of New Mexico and Oregon were well in hand for the Democrat and Independent team. Dusty put an arm over Roger's shoulder and said, "We've come a very, very long way my friend." They shared a hearty, tension-releasing laugh together. As California's heavily Hispanic 19 million votes came rolling in, the analysts began predicting what everyone in the room had been wishfully thinking all night - a Richardson/Adams victory.

Waves of cheers broke out with every trivial update. Roger and Lenka went back to their private green room. Lenka kept her arm around Roger's waist, which comforted them both as they walked down the stuffy hallway lined shoulder to shoulder with Secret Service.

They were both nearly hyperventilating from the electricity of the whole event, the constant noise, the hugeness of the crowd - and the shock. The whole campaign had been a daily grind, a mission to make a message heard. Neither Roger nor Lenka had allowed the Vice Presidency of the United States to take form in their consciousnesses. They had not actually expected it at any point along the way, although Lenka had allowed the feeling to creep up over the last few weeks.

"Ready to meet the happy crowds, honey?" Roger asked, feeling the heat of responsibility burn on his skin, and a sense of the surreal in the mindless celebrating, like a doctor performing open-heart surgery in the middle of a nine-year-old boy's backyard birthday party. "No, but that's the price we pay for changing the world, isn't it babe?" Lenka said in a smooth, reassuring voice. She spun around in her long, green silken dress.
"Are you going to the same party I am, honey? You look like you're going to the Oscars."
"I'm here just for you, sweetie," she said, smiling broadly now and locking eyes with him so fiercely he couldn't move until she let him go.

...

Lenka stood now at one side of the stage, clutching Roger's right hand. The crowd cheered constantly. She looked across to the other side of the stage where Bill and Barbara stood. She glanced down and noticed that the future first lady was gripping her husband's hand even tighter than she was, which calmed her nerves considerably. Before she knew it, they were walking out into the pandemonium. This crowd seemed twice as raucous as any rock concert that Lenka had ever been to. They met up with the Richardsons in the middle of the stage and they all waved their arms and smiled, Bill visibly sunbathing in the ecstatic once-in-a-lifetime attention being given him. Roger quickly realized this was an experience to appreciate while it lasts, and did a little basking of his own. He had felt satisfied with his accomplishments at several points during the campaign, and they all seemed to meld together in the endless enthusiasm of this final election night crowd. He turned to Lenka, genuinely smiling broadly now, and she began to laugh, shaking her head, unable to believe where they were.

Finally, Richardson stepped forward toward the microphone and waved his hands up and down, as if adrift upon the bobbing ocean and holding a plank, to quiet the crowd. At every other word, the crowd erupted all over again.

"We come here tonight... with a message...." He paused to let the supporters scream some more. "We have spoken with the American people... and you have spoken with us.... We may not see the same solutions to every need... but I believe we are in agreement, that we need a new way." The crowd went completely wild again, and the candidate took two steps back and a deep breath. "Everyone here tonight has given of their time and their hearts... to call for a new way in America. And when the voices of all America's voters have been heard..." Richardson began to push his voice up dramatically above the roar of the crowd now. "I believe, we will find, that they have collectively called... for that new way! Thanks to all of you... *together* with all of you, we declare victory tonight!" Richardson stepped back from the podium again and grabbed Roger's hand and lifted into the air. Roger's face was beaming. He was lost in the thrill.

Chapter 9
Hot Turns Cold

"We're keeping Schwarzenegger at Homeland Security and Domestic Surveillance? You can't be serious!"

"He's not hurting anybody over there. People like him. People even like working for him," Richardson answered calmly.

"Yeah, but..."

"Having a little sideshow in the executive branch can come in handy sometimes," he said with a wink. Roger wondered silently if he meant Arnold Schwarzenegger or Roger Adams. "And look, he knows how to listen to reason.... as long as he doesn't think you're talking down to him. That's more than I can say for a lot of the nasty old guys in this town."

Less than a week in the White House, and Roger was already feeling frustrated, partly because he'd only been less than a week in the White House, and he was already feeling frustrated. He felt sidelined. It'd been a lot of years since he'd had to sit by while someone else made decisions. He certainly had tasks and was being shown his due professional respect, but he began seriously contemplating whether his role would be more active if he didn't have the capital "I" in the parentheses after his name, not that he would consider joining the Democratic Party now. His reaction was, instead, to produce another acorn of anger at the whole system. He was now fully submerged in the top tier of a Democratic Party administration. Every hour of every day, the most ambitious and most faithful of the nation's young Democratic Party believers shuffled by him, collecting useless reports, mismanaging simple bureaucratic tasks and chattering incessantly into all kinds of phones as they whisked themselves from cubicle to office to cubicle, like some throbbing, buzzing, living honeycomb of inefficiency. "There must be a way to scrap this mess and build a regular business-like system for running the American government," he thought to himself. But he hadn't a clue where to begin.

A week later, Vice President Adams didn't have time to contemplate how active his role was. By Groundhog Day, he was buried in meetings with Senators to build support for the upcoming medical marijuana vote, hiring more support staff, running from meeting to meeting, hearing briefings on every troop movement. Once it started, the mail never stopped pouring in, both paper and electronic. He was amazed that so many people still sent paper mail. When he was younger, a handwritten letter had been considered more significant and worthy of reading than a typed one, but that attitude had died out a generation ago. At least, he thought it had. Roger was no "Milleniteen," but he had never been tied to old traditions either, and Washington seemed to him an enormous landfill of the nation's spent traditions. It made him feel a thousand years old.

He felt a little better when Richardson appointed General Honoré to head FEMA. He was exactly the kind of no-nonsense leader Roger wished everyone in government could be. Still, it was incredibly strange to see "The Ragin' Cajun" working for "The Homeland Securinator." The whole HSDS was filled with comic book characters.

General Russel Honoré had gained living legend status after overseeing the cleanup of Hurricane Gillian. After Houston suffered a repeat of New Orleans' Katrina disaster, again with communication links severed and FEMA overloaded and slow to respond, Honoré, the hero of New Orleans, was finally called in on the fourth day as the waters, twelve feet deep in some areas, began to drain away. His colorful style was captured for the nation any time a camera was around. Fox cameras were there when Honoré's National Guard troops converged on a shopping mall, which had become a makeshift shelter. Families were lined up outside, complaining of looting and violence inside. Cameras followed the troops inside, where more than a hundred people were running with arms full of boxes, screaming at each other, breaking windows - general mayhem. As the cameras panned around at the chaos, General Honoré lifted a bullhorn to his mouth and ordered everyone, "Sit down right where you are and don't move a finger. You're all under arrest by authority of the United States National Guard. If I see one of you goddamned hooligans even wink at me, I'll take you by the neck with my own bare fucking hands!" Fox managed to screen out the dirty words for the protection of the American people, of course. The mall went dead silent. When they saw the 400 military uniforms and the majorly pissed-off general, they put down all their boxes and sat on the ground. The culprits, mostly young black men, were being loaded onto a bus just behind the General while he gave a quick recap of the situation to the reporter, including how many arrests they'd made, when one of the men shouted, "I'm bein' mistreated cuz I'm black! I didn't do nothin'! Police brutality!" Honoré turned, took two steps toward the criminal and barked, "This ain't the police. Get your sorry ass on the bus!" Although he was facing away from the microphone, the General's voice was picked up loud and strong, and the kickass sound bite was replayed for weeks.

In 2014, Houston had taken a Category 4 hurricane head on, practically without evacuations, because the only reliable hurricane satellite the United States had, called QuikScat, had fallen out of the sky a year earlier, after continuing to function for five years past its expiration date. Without QuikScat, the potential landfall area was so wide, and the size of the storm so uncertain, that the warnings were ridiculously vague. Only about a thousand of the most paranoid of Houston's citizens fled north. America was outraged again at the government's ability to be oblivious. No one could believe we had only one hurricane satellite in the first place - one accurate enough to predict where evacuations would be needed, and that a new satellite hadn't even been planned, long after QuikScat was due to be replaced. Vice President Bush, because he had been known as a strong coordinator of hurricane relief efforts in his state of Florida, suffered a major drop in popularity, and many pundits said Gillian had stayed in voters' minds in 2016.

...

The honeymoon was visibly dying out in the media. The first hundred days of the Richardson administration were being diced up and given their funeral after the first month. Richardson was on the record saying his first hundred days would be devoted to bringing the troops home, decriminalizing medical marijuana, and fighting for a Presidential line-item veto. The troops had been coming home already - since the Quetta disaster - so his biggest headline goal was taken away from him by the press. One conservative web site called it a given, saying the troops had to come home at this point no matter who was President, and the rest of the networks took it as gospel and began their relentless preaching to their choirs, the American people. No one believed they had the votes for medical marijuana. With 40% of 12-year-olds reportedly now trying drugs, no one in Congress wanted to appear soft on drugs. The collective reply to the President's appeals for mercy on America's terminally ill was always, "Yeah but what if..."

Roger's well-established reformist reputation allowed him to go on CNN and lament that the United States was the last modernized nation in the world to still forbid marijuana for medicinal purposes. "Every western nation, and every developed nation, with the exception of the United States, treats marijuana as an effective painkiller for terminally ill patients. This is a health care issue, and we are preventing our doctors from providing the simple relief that citizens of 150 other nations have available when they need it. Should we send all our cancer patients to prison? Of course not, but we *are* effectively treating them like criminals, and that's not right. Look, this is not a federal program to hand out free drugs. We're talking about allowing the states to comply with federal law when they vote for medicinal marijuana. Forty states have medicinal marijuana provisions today, all voted for by the people, and then Washington has the nerve to tell the people that they have lost their say? Why should our federal government have the power to strike down laws that the people want?"

Roger's appearances drew good viewer ratings, but failed to garner votes where they were needed - in the Congress. Fox News began a daily "Countdown to Doing Something," calling Richardson's team helpless to accomplish any of its goals and harping on the arbitrary hundred day deadline. The line-item veto was even being called dead on arrival, despite still being six weeks away from its planned introduction in the House.

...

Roger got the nod from the President's secretary as he came down the hall and walked straight into the Oval Office. "You wanted to see me, Mr. President?"

"Good morning, Roger. Energy has a massive, five-year climate study coming out that looks at the last 20,000 years of cosmic radiation. It concludes that all our climate changes can be linked to the Sun's magnetic cycles, and we've got another mini Ice Age coming before the end of this administration. Those smaller studies weren't just campaign attacks on your background the last few years. They're looking more and more like good science."

"Bill, you may not believe this, but I never swallowed that whole Global Warming line, and I'm definitely not arrogant enough to take personal offense at the cycles of our Sun."

"I'm glad to hear you say that," Bill responded sarcastically.

"The Schwabe model makes a hell of a lot more sense to me than the Greenhouse Effect ever did, anyway. I mean, don't we *want* to have a warm atmosphere?"

"That we do, Roger. And that's beginning to be a problem, geologically *and* politically."

"Politically?"

"When this report comes out, Roger, you, and the White House, might get called hypocrites. We don't need that, certainly not in the first hundred days."

"So let me pitch the report," Roger offered.

"Pitch it? Mr. Solved-Global-Warming is gonna pitch Global Cooling?"

"That's a label that was pinned on me, Bill. My goal was to provide drinking water and energy. I never said we have to drain the world's oceans. I only said, if that's what you want to do, this system can do that too. I saw a way to combine three highly-desired products into one and then I built it."

"OK, I see where you're coming from, Roger. But how do you plan to explain that to Joe American?"

He spoke in a rapid, summary monotone. "Advances in science show that our Sun has overwhelmingly been the responsible factor in our climate changes, rather than human activities. Unfortunately, our Sun experiences 11-year cycles of peak and calm and we may need to actively manage our climate, now that we finally have an accurate picture of how it works. We've done a reasonable job of managing a warm cycle, and now we need to prepare for a cool cycle." He paused to let Richardson reflect on his words and then summarized, "The point is, it's not another end of the world scenario, it's just weather!"

"Don't ever say that again. Don't let them stick another label on you, Roger. If you use the words, 'It's just weather,' I guarantee you'll end up with your own personal, 'Trees cause pollution.'"

Roger thought for a second and then quickly agreed. "You're right. That's a bad phrase."

"The idea is good though. Go ahead and write up a speech. Sofia has a copy of the report for you."

"Thank you, Mr. President."

"We have a couple weeks before it goes out. I want to get this right. Talk to you later, Roger," he said, standing up from the arm of the couch and walking with Roger to the door of the oval office.

...

"My fellow Americans, I sit down with you tonight to address developments in scientific research certain to affect our nation, and our world. Five years of government-funded research have borne fruit and I wish to share these important results with you tonight, and to explain what it could mean for our shared future.

More than a century ago, the Industrial Revolution began spinning our great globe ever faster, while producing vast quantities of byproducts, all sorts of chemicals and pollutants, the consequences of which we did not foresee. Over time, we have identified and either effectively treated or removed many of these pollutants, and we have learned how to better manage both our resources and the systems which make use of them.

Within my own lifetime, I have seen vast improvements in the quality of the air and water in our great United States, and I have also seen various dire warnings, that our *human activities*, somehow meant to sound like something evil, will soon bring about the end of our very civilization and cause lasting, irreparable damage to the Earth which we call Home. Approximately thirty years ago, a new Ice Age was upon us. America was to be covered over by glaciers. A decade later, Global Warming threatened to permanently and irreversibly flood all of our coastal cities. I want to say tonight, that any kind of end-of-the-world scenario is dangerous and untrue. I consider it absolutely irresponsible for anyone to spread such unnecessary fear.

Climate change is indeed real, but it is a constant and natural change. Our universe functions in cycles. Our planet moves around the Sun once per year. The leaves change color in autumn and grow anew in the springtime. Change is a necessary part of life everywhere, and that includes our global climate.

With public funding approved under the Clinton administration five years ago, some of our nation's top scientists at MIT and the University of Florida, in cooperation with the U.S. Department of Energy and the Canadian government, have produced a compellingly thorough and groundbreaking report on the state of our global climate. Their research includes soil and ice samples as well as astronomical data dating back some 20,000 years. Building on smaller studies from the last ten years, they have been able to draw profoundly consistent conclusions.

The report that I have here draws a detailed picture of the cycles of our planet's climate, and shows in statistical depth, the process by which our global temperature is managed by the Universe and its intricate systems. Our Sun has a magnetic field, which experiences various cycles. The shortest and most visible cycle from our perspective, is the Schwabe cycle, a surprisingly regular 11-year cycle of higher and lower temperatures characterized by fluctuations in the number and intensity of solar storms, also known as sunspots. You may have heard of solar storms being blamed for increased background radiation and network interferences. Our Earth also experiences 11-year cycles of higher and lower temperatures, which line up extremely well with the timing of these Schwabe cycles on our Sun. In addition, the fluctuating intensity of the Sun's magnetic field, which causes the fluctuations in radiation storms on the Sun, also extends toward our planet and blocks or allows varying amounts of natural radiation from outer space coming toward our planet. These magnetic fluctuations have also been shown to occur at the same times that our planet has experienced corresponding higher and lower temperatures.

The truly exciting part of this report shows the process by which this natural radiation, from the other stars in our galaxy, reacts with the elements in our atmosphere to create clouds. The scientists working on this project have actually been able to create clouds in the laboratory for the first time. I won't try to explain the entire process here tonight, but using regular air from our own atmosphere, isolated in a laboratory, clouds can be created simply by introducing the same kind of radiation that comes to us from the stars in our galaxy. The particles in our air are stimulated to come together to form clouds in a very simple and reproducible way by these naturally-occurring rays. When more radiation comes through, more clouds are created, which causes global warming. When less radiation comes through, fewer clouds mean the heat escapes, and our planet cools.

Before we understood this amazing process, we tried to explain changes to our climate as byproducts of our modern technology, more pollutants. But we were never able to show, for example, how carbon dioxide traps heat, and it may have never been the original problem, although we did manage the effects of rising seas admirably. However, we can now show clearly how the Sun's magnetic field blocks natural radiation from reaching us, and also how that radiation causes clouds to form. And the most important part is, that we can reproduce this effect with simple, well-controlled and focused beams of light, or lasers.

The Sun's magnetic field is due for a large expansion a few years from now, which will greatly reduce the amount of radiation reaching our planet. That means fewer clouds will form, and our planet will cool significantly as a direct result. But with our now comprehensive knowledge of how the cycles of our climate function, we will be able to manage our climate, to keep it within the parameters acceptable for our Earth's civilization. I am happy to report, that for the first time in human history, should global cloud cover become significantly reduced, we have a tool available to respond appropriately and effectively. We will be able to add to the amount of cloud cover in our atmosphere, by simple and natural means, in response to any major cooling of our globe.

I invite you to read the entire report, which is available on the United States Department of Energy web page, and I look forward to further discussion in the scientific community of this important topic, which affects us all. I believe this is the beginning of a new era in climate management, with implications for better understanding of other natural events, such as Hurricane Gillian, which hit coastal Texas so hard a few years ago. With this knowledge, I believe we will be better able to maintain the stability of our civilization, and also to save many lives. Thank you, goodnight, and God bless America."

"It's very strong, Roger. A few things need to be changed though. Calling human activities *evil* is inflammatory. The leaves changing with the seasons is pretty corny. The point is good, it just sounds too damn condescending."

"You're right, Mr. President. We need to clean those up," Roger admitted, sounding a bit defeated.

"Don't sound so pissed off, Roger. It's really good. It's better than any of my junior speechwriters can do, and it's a perfect 20 minutes - I don't know how you did *that*. It's clear, simple, optimistic, and dodges the major bullets. I'll just have Dan go over those couple of rough spots and it's fine."

"So my team is done with this?" Roger asked, unsure of the process.

"Signed, sealed, delivered, my friend. You sure you've never worked as a speechwriter?"

"This is the first speech I've ever written that I haven't delivered myself."

"Hey, I'm still getting used to delivering speeches I haven't written," Richardson said empathetically.

...

Medicinal marijuana still didn't have the votes. Roger met with twenty Senators, each of them separately, in one week. Knowing the bill would fail, the Republicans pushed for a vote. The bill failed, 34-55.

The "Countdown to Doing Something" on Fox began to irritate the President. The troops still were not coming home quickly enough for the administration's taste. Most of the White House advisers suspected the Pentagon was purposely dragging its feet, hoping they wouldn't really have to leave their battlefields. Ten thousand troops were still in Iraq, seven in Lebanon, and two thousand in Afghanistan. The line-item veto bill wasn't looking good either.

Roger was getting hooked on coffee, he realized. "Jeezus, I'm all jittery," he remarked out loud, holding his shaky hand at arm's length, his light blue shirt sleeve folded nearly up to the elbow. He sat down at his desk, huffed out a sigh, and pushed a stack of documents to the edge of the desk so he could see his computer screen again.

An email address jumped out at him as his eyes darted up and down the list:

Sergey Brin, Google   Climate Management

Hello Roger,

I found the Climate Management speech very interesting. Did I hear some of your words in the speech? It is your area of expertise. A lot of technical development is going to be needed before any of that can actually be done, obviously. A few years is not a lot of time.

As you know, we've worked with NASA on a range of issues, not so much with DoE. Let me know if we can be involved in this.

Say Hi to Lenka.

Sincerely,

Sergey Brin

Google

"Jeane?" Roger called out.

"Yes sir!" she called, leaning out a door about five down, "I'll be right there."

The moment she walked in, Roger asked, "Are there still any executive openings in the Department of Energy?"

"I believe so, sir. Give me ten minutes?"

"Fine. Thank you. And let me know when the President can see me for five minutes."

Roger Adams   Re: Climate Management

Hi Sergey,

I did have a hand in the climate speech. I'm surprised you noticed.

You're very right about the technical development. I've spoken to the President and he agreed with me, that we need more talented people like yourself contributing to public service. We would be honored if you would bring your technical skills and leadership talents to the Department of Energy of the United States of America.

The Deputy Secretary of Energy position is yours if you'll take it. You'd be leading technical development on many important projects for the American people.

Are you available for lunch in Mountain View on Thursday?

My best to your family.
Roger Adams
Vice President of the United States of America

Brin accepted, nearly as warily as Adams had accepted the Vice Presidency. Roger assured him he would be able to make an important difference in Washington.

Six weeks passed, and the line-item veto was dead on arrival. After months of seeing so little progress on anything, Adams was beginning to crack.

"Roger, nothing, absolutely nothing in this town ever happens without some kind of compromise. Even though we're in the Executive, we have to be willing to bend," the President advised emphatically.

"Sure, I understand that. I can bend, but up to a certain point."

"I'm afraid you only *understand* that up to a certain point."

Roger stood with his arms crossed and looked down at the plush royal blue rug, contemplating the validity of the accusation.

"Look, maybe you never expected to actually end up getting locked into four years of this. I know you started as a message candidate, but that message brought you here, and now you have to do whatever you can to deliver as much of it as you can, and that means adjusting to the system in Washington."

"The message was that the whole system is wrong," Roger reminded.

"So work with the system to change the system. It's been done before. And don't take any votes for granted. A Democratic majority does not mean we get whatever we want automatically."

"How do we start winning some of these people over, Bill?"

"Remember that campaign you ran last year? You have to do that all over again, except your audience is a lot tougher now. You have to negotiate with everyone on that Hill and ask them what it takes to get their support.... without buying it from them, of course."

"Suddenly running for President sounds easy," Roger whined uncharacteristically, displaying just how out of his element he felt here.

"Just get one success first, and then build on it, as you always say."

Roger stood silent for a moment and then disclosed the ambitious idea that really had him nervous. "I've been working on a particular issue for many years actually, Bill, one that wasn't discussed much in the campaign. I was afraid it was too controversial to put on the agenda, when there was so much else going on, but

I think it could shift our entire domestic and foreign policy all at once."

"Well dear God, Roger, what is it?"

"Immigration."

He left a dramatic pause hanging in the air between them, and then began speaking excitedly.

"I was talking to an old friend of mine at UCLA, Professor Huckaby, when *he* brought it up. He told me he's got some brilliant kid there - you know, the kind that started college at 16 - who wrote a fantastic *term paper* on immigration."

"A term paper?"

"Yeah, exactly. It's called, 'The Win-Win Case for Mexico.' "

"Well that sounds awfully upbeat. Is he Mexican?"

"No. He's white... an average looking surfer dude, he says."

"A surfer?" the President asked, incredulous.

"Surfer... duuuuude," Adams said with a monster grin.

"Cowabunga," mumbled Richardson, unable to contain his sarcasm.

"Huckaby sent me the paper," Roger said, immediately back to business. "It's a 20 page history of Mexican-American relations and a list of reasons why we should offer full statehood to Mexico."

"Statehood?! Roger, I know you like the big ideas, but what exactly are you thinking about here?"

"I'm thinking about hiring this kid to help us draft a report that we can put out to the American people and get a conversation started, so maybe five years down the road, people might eventually support the idea. This kid's analyzed the economic, cultural, judicial and foreign policy impacts, as well as the effects of a new, 'spirit of cooperation' he calls it, on our image abroad."

"Look, I know how you operate Roger. I know that if you've been working on this for years, then there must be some overwhelming advantages that have been overlooked. But I don't see the public taking to this so much, no matter how you try to sell it to them."

"I know it's a challenge," Roger said quietly but firmly. Richardson's dropped his head toward the desk in deep thought, and then lifted his head excitedly. "Do you know how large Mexico is? My God, do you know how many Reps they'd have in the House?!"

"Yes sir, a helluva lot," Roger admitted. "That's in the term paper too, sir. He calls it a good balance considering they'd only have two votes in the Senate."

Richardson put down his reading glasses and leaned back in his chair pensively. Roger waited patiently. The President let out a heavy sigh and said, almost looking pissed off, "Let's try and get through the first hundred days without a disaster, and then we can talk about this again, alright? Go ahead and study it, but I'm gonna keep my distance from it for now. Everyone knows I grew up in Mexico, and it won't get anywhere if they think it's a pet project from my childhood."

"Understood. I'll keep it in my office."

"Roger..."

"Yeah?" he asked, turning around, the door already in his hand.

"If anyone asks, I say it's just something you're studying and I'm as curious to see it when it's done as anyone."

"Sounds good. Thank you, Mr. President."

The President shook his head doubtfully as soon as Roger was gone.

Chapter 10

The Win-Win Case for Mexico

The Win-Win Case for Mexico

Why Mexico Should Become Our 51st State

by Alexander Barth

Table of Contents

(page numbers from original Barth document)

Foreword

On May 1, 2006, nearly 2 million Mexicans, Mexican-Americans, high-school students, legal and illegal immigrants, and others left their jobs and schools and filled the streets of Los Angeles, Chicago, Miami, San Francisco, New York, Denver, Dallas, New Orleans, Phoenix and other cities across America to show their support for Mexicans and all immigrants in America. This was the culmination of months of huge protests, protests which have only grown larger over the last ten years, with estimates up to 12 million on May 1, 2015. They carry American flags, and signs reading, "We are Not Terrorists," and "We Build Your Homes." As factories, shops and schools close down ever year on, "A Day Without Immigrants," they demonstrate just how important they are to our economy and to our American society. The strength of their numbers and their solidarity in that pivotal 2006 protest brought their voice to the halls of the United States Congress, and a bill proposing that 12 million illegal immigrants be labeled felons quickly died under the glare of public opinion.

The debate over immigration in America was never louder, or more divided, than it was under President

George W. Bush. While past administrations have carried out limited reforms, Bush endorsed comprehensive immigration reform, centered on a controversial guest-worker program. Groups of citizens formed vigilante brigades to guard the border, trying to catch people walking across a wide open 2,000-mile border through daunting desert from Mexico without permission to enter the country. Foreign terrorists had demonstrated unprecedented desire and ability to launch attacks on our soil and our capitalist economy was becoming ever more dependent on opening new markets. Eventually, a guest worker program was initiated, with 4 million temporary visas in effect for Mexican workers today, but Bush's path to citizenship was never achieved, families remain torn apart, deportation raids carry on with no end in sight, and millions of Mexicans continue to cross the line in the sand, seeking a better life for themselves and their children.

While many have pointed out that support for the Mexican economy is the key to removing the incentive for desperate people trying to support their families, why hasn't anyone seriously considered completely opening the border and inviting the entire country of Mexico into our union as a new state? With a simple mutual agreement to join forces, we may be able to provide our neighbors the opportunity to pull themselves up by the bootstraps while boosting our own fortunes as well.

It may sound like a radical idea in today's highly-charged political atmosphere where the conventional wisdom frowns heavily on imaginative solutions and turns fearfully away from big changes or cooperation of any kind, but in its first 100 years, America was constantly expanding into new territories, resulting in tremendous growth and prosperity. Granted, we accomplished this growth mainly through conquest, but in the 21st century, expansion via globalization and free trade agreements is already well established. Expansion of free markets by mutual agreement is now commonplace, although unfortunately, half-hearted, mainly benefitting big business. A few more big clients for a few large multinationals is not going to help the people of Mexico raise their standard of living, nor will it address the roots or consequences of illegal immigration from Mexico to the United States. And allowing Mexicans work visas for a few years is akin to a summer job for a high-school student. But illegal immigrants aren't coming here to save up to buy a bicycle, and a temporary chunk of change is not the same as a lifetime of hope for advancement. Many wouldn't even have the funds to pay the fines and back taxes to join the citizenship program Bush proposed 10 years ago. Furthermore, the American economy receives few long-term benefits from bringing in temporary workers who do not contribute to the American economy once they leave. The only lasting way to solve this complex problem, which affects both of our nations in a multitude of intertwining ways, is to provide genuine hope and opportunity to our neighbors to the south - through full integration and cooperation. We can work together for our mutual benefit without sending jobs overseas or exploiting illegal workers. Shutting them out failed long, long ago. Let's face the facts and go with the rushing tide, rather than against it. Let's welcome the downtrodden economic refugees with open arms, just as our founding fathers did, to work hard, to pursue their dream of a better life.

If America is truly being invaded by our southern neighbor, as some people fear, then let's face the fact that a large segment of the Mexican people has already been organically absorbed into our nation, our economy and our culture, and let's finish the job. Integration is already well along. Several restaurant chains and markets across the whole southwest have a slot for Mexican pesos in their cash registers. California has extended health

244 \ America's Glasnost

insurance to all children, including illegal immigrants. No one believes it's possible to go back, so let's jump forward together. Let's raise the tide and lift both our boats. America today has more in common with our Mexican neighbors than we have differences. Some fear we cannot live together, or that the Mexican people will change America. But they already have. And there is no good reason why the UK must be the only nation with whom we share a special relationship, and there is no reason the millions of God-fearing, family-based, hard-working Mexican people shouldn't join us to build greater prosperity and security for all.

A Berlin wall in Texas is not a solution to anything. The crossing at California's southern border should be no different from the one at its northern border, where the only question they ask is, "You carrying any fruit with you today?" - designed to protect us only against agricultural disease. The middle-ages fortress mentality of the far right wing only adds to the hostility and fear between nations and among our own people, who have come to America from every part of the world. It is highly doubtful that everyone on either side of the border is currently psychologically prepared to accept the concept of fully integrating Mexico into the United States, but I predict it will eventually happen and to the benefit of both. The longer we wait, the longer we delay the numerous benefits and synergies, while needlessly prolonging the losses associated with the current system, which all parties admit, is fundamentally broken.

Let's invite Mexico to pledge allegiance to our Constitution and offer them statehood in our land of opportunity, the United States of America.

Chapter 1
Mexico's Presence in the U.S. Today

Of the 60 million Hispanics in the U.S. today, 40 million were born here, meaning more than 40 million Mexican-Americans are already American citizens.[1] Millions more have been naturalized. Less than 15% came here illegally, meaning that even if there wasn't an illegal immigration problem, there would still be millions of people of Mexican descent and other Hispanics working and living in the United States, learning English, raising their families, and living their lives just as the rest of us do.

"The Hispanic unemployment rate hit a low of 5% in 2006 and 3.5% in 2012. The gap between the seasonally-adjusted unemployment rates for Latinos and non-Latinos was just 0.4 percentage points--the smallest since 1973, when employment data on Latinos first became available. Wages for Latino workers have also been rising steadily since 2005, and at a faster rate than for other workers. These macroeconomic trends reflect significant

[1] *Source: Pew Hispanic Center tabulations of 2010 Census and 2015 American Community Survey*

improvement in the labor market for Latinos over the last decade and indicate that the jobs taken by Hispanic workers represent a significant economic indicator for the American economy overall.

The healthy job market for Latinos was driven mainly by the construction industry in the last decade. Construction added two million jobs between 2005 and 2008, the majority of them filled by foreign-born Latinos. Since the jobs recovery began in 2003, nearly 4 million Latinos have found jobs in construction, accounting for about one third of all new jobs gained by Hispanics."[2]

Not only do Latinos, mostly from Mexico, contribute nearly ten percent of our GDP, they are gaining and growing in every aspect of life in our United States. The longer they are here, the higher levels of education they reach, and the more their wages grow. In short, they are doing what they came here to do, to work hard and make their lives better, to achieve the American dream.

[2] *Source: Pew Hispanic Center Latino Labor Report 2014*

2 (Barth)

Just 12% of Hispanics born outside the U.S. are earning $50,000 or more per year. But nearly double that number, 23% of native-born Hispanics are making $50,000 or more per year. This says that given the same opportunities from childhood for quality education, nutrition and health care, Latinos are *outpacing* the earnings of African-Americans, 12% of whom are earning $50,000 or more.[3]

You don't need a phone survey to see that Mexican affluence in America is on the rise. A growing number of prominent and highly successful Latino Americans also point to Mexico's rising star.

Bill Richardson

"Bill Richardson served for 8 years as Governor of New Mexico and 15 years as New Mexico's Representative in the 3rd Congressional District. He served in 1997 as the U.S. Ambassador to the United Nations, and in 1998, he was unanimously confirmed by the U.S. Senate as Secretary of the U.S. Department of Energy. Governor Richardson has been nominated several times for the Nobel Peace Prize."[4]

[3] Source: Pew Hispanic Center tabulations of 2010 Census and 2015 American Community Survey
[4] Source: The Official Web Site of the State of New Mexico

He was a Presidential candidate in the 2008, and 2012 elections, and was on the short list for Vice President many times. He was born in the U.S. to a Mexican mother.

Alberto Gonzales

On the surface, they seem an odd couple. One, the son of migrant workers, grew up in a house without hot water or a telephone. The other is the scion of a rich and powerful political dynasty. But Alberto Gonzales and George W. Bush have joined in a largely successful effort to build a more muscular executive branch. Drawn to the quiet lawyer's up-by-his-bootstraps story, then-Governor Bush persuaded Gonzales to leave his lucrative law practice in Houston and become his general counsel in 1994. Bush later put Gonzales on the Texas Supreme Court, and when Bush moved north, he made Gonzales White House counsel and, in 2006, the nation's first Hispanic Attorney General.[5]

---

[5] *Source: Time, June 12, 2015 – The 25 Most Influential Hispanics in America*

Antonio Villaraigosa

Mayor of Los Angeles, Governor of California

Born in East Los Angeles to a Mexican immigrant father and native-born Mexican mother, Mayor Villaraigosa made a name for himself as a champion of civil rights and a leader of anti-war protests in the Vietnam era.

Jorge Ramos

CBS News anchor, former Univision anchor

Emigrated from Mexico City as a young journalist, has become a trusted voice not just to millions of Hispanic Americans, but to all Americans.

Chapter 2
The Process – How It Would Happen

The New Borders and Population of the United States

Mexico's southern border with Belize and Guatemala is less than one-third the size of America's current southern border.

From 1871 until 1973, Belize was a British colony called British Honduras and is still a member of the British Commonwealth. English is the official language of Belize, while Spanish is also widely spoken.

Guatemala was a Spanish colony and while there have been border disputes between Guatemala and Belize, they have never fought a war over them.

Following a quick bribery-based overthrow of Iran's democratically-elected government in 1953, the CIA repeated their wrong-headed strategy of destabilization and support for dictators the following year in Guatemala. In 1999, President Bill Clinton officially apologized for the decades of U.S. training and financial support of Guatemala's armed forces, who slaughtered approximately 200,000 civilians over the course of a thirty-year civil war.

Guatemala City is one of the most cosmopolitan cities in Central America. American relations with both Guatemala and Belize have been stable and productive for decades.

Mexico's southern border therefore, should it become our new southern border, would be far easier to defend against illegal immigration and terrorism. Not only is it three times shorter than the current border, it does not lie across empty desert, and the vast majority of current immigrants would no longer be immigrants, but American citizens. The INS would be free to concentrate its efforts on deporting criminals and the much smaller number of remaining illegal immigrants from other countries.

So who are these people we will be welcoming into our country? The estimated 2015 population of Mexico is 125 million. All 125 million would become full American citizens, as well as all Mexican citizens currently living in the United States, and anywhere else in the world. There are already approximately 60 million Hispanic people living in the United States, a large majority of them from Mexico and more than 12 million of those, illegal immigrants. The total U.S. population would expand to about 510 million, of which perhaps 180 million would be of Mexican origin, a little less than 1/3 of the total population.

The Referendum in the U.S.

"Should the United States government offer full statehood to Mexico and American citizenship to all Mexican citizens?" A nationwide referendum on this question will be necessary to ensure the success of Mexican integration into the United States. Popular opinion may not be overwhelming at first, but public support should build through frequent discussion in town hall-style meetings around the country with the President and members of Congress, as well as with officials from Mexico and Hispanic organizations in the U.S. When all the benefits become apparent, a clear majority should be in favor.

After a successful referendum, a 2/3 majority in both houses of Congress would ratify the official offer of statehood to Mexico.

The Referendum in Mexico

After a successful referendum, and a 2/3 vote in both the House and Senate, the United States Congress would authorize the President to invite Mexico to apply for full statehood. If Mexico accepts the invitation and applies for statehood, all Mexican citizens in Mexico and in the U.S., legally or illegally, would become U.S. citizens with all the rights and responsibilities that includes, paying federal and state taxes and enjoying full protection under the United States Constitution. If the process survives to this point, the referendum should pass fairly easily in Mexico, although certainly not without protest from some corners.

The Transfer of Citizenship

Every Mexican citizen in the U.S. would need to verify their Mexican citizenship in person with two forms of ID at a government office and trade in their Mexican identification papers for a new social security card. The Mexican government would distribute social security cards to all citizens within Mexico. The U.S. will likely insist that every Mexican in Mexico also go to a government office in person, but it's questionable whether the Mexican authorities will have the capacity to handle that many applications in such a short period of time.

Mexicans would be able to vote in the first U.S. General Election following the official acceptance of statehood.

In the event of a legal challenge to a future Mexican-born Presidential candidate, the Supreme Court would most likely rule that the law allows those born after the date of official statehood in the new state of Mexico to hold the office of President, but that it would not retroactively consider Mexico to have been a part of the United States before that time, and no constitutional amendment would be required.

A Year of Preparations

Once both referendums have been officially passed by the people and Congress in both the U.S. and in Mexico, a deadline of one year should be set for the full transfer of statehood to Mexico. Many processes of integration would begin at this point. The transfer of citizenship process described above would begin within weeks of final approval, and may very well take a year to complete. Both Mexican and American identification papers would be accepted as valid American identification for the duration of one year to allow everyone to switch over.

The Mexican peso would be phased out in favor of the American dollar. Market forces would certainly take care of this as soon as it becomes apparent that the peso has no future. The American and Mexican Treasury Departments would need to peg the peso to the dollar and cooperate on the transition. The phase-out may occur more slowly in the southern impoverished regions of Mexico.

Before joining the Union, the Mexican Congress would need to write and approve a state constitution modeled on other U.S. state constitutions or the current Mexican constitution, which they should be able to do within three to six months.

The President of Mexico would become the interim governor of the Mexican state until the first state elections. The entire Mexican voter rolls and electoral systems would need to be reformed to comply with the American voting system. The official date of entry into the Union should be set not less than one year prior to the next upcoming General Election, to ensure enough time for complex electoral reform to be completed throughout

Mexico.

Crucially, advisors from American police and justice organizations, (judges, lawyers, prison wardens) would need to get started immediately re-training the Mexican police and personnel at all levels of the Mexican justice system, to ensure they comport with American standards. Federal Government offices would also need to be set up in the new state of Mexico, retaining but retraining the local civil servants wherever possible.

The 51st State, or the Breakup of Mexico?

Mexico is three times larger than Texas and 10% larger than Alaska, but with a population of 125 million. By contrast, California is currently the most populous state, with 43 million. This means that the State of Mexico would be eligible for some 150 new seats in the House of Representatives, but only 2 Senators, barring some overhaul of our system of representation. Mexico may not be satisfied with such a disproportionately small voice in the Senate, and may prefer to act as a bloc of states with similar interests, rather than as one giant state, in the context of American politics.

For internal reasons as well, being a country of various regions with different ethnic mixes, economic classes, industries, and mixes of rural and urban populations, Mexico might very well consider it wise to apply for several statehoods, to become the 51st through 55th states, for example. Mexico is currently divided into 31 states. (Mexico's official name is actually the United Mexican States.) 31 new states within the United States of America would certainly be unwieldy and provide our new citizens with far more political power in Washington than any of our current citizens would consider fair. Any potential multiple-state solution should group current states together, preferably into 2 or 3 new states. However, Mexico's large urban centers are all in the central region of the country, and separation from Mexico's economic engine would only serve to further weaken its impoverished areas. For this reason, one large state of Mexico would be the best option.

Any attempt at semi-autonomy within the U.S. should, of course, be flatly and firmly denied. The only offer on the table should be standard, unadulterated statehood. On the other hand, there may be enough redistribution of the population to offset the extreme size of a single Mexican state. According to the Pew Hispanic Center, 6 of the 7 states with the highest rate of Hispanic population growth over the last twenty years were in the South, with the exception being Nevada:

North Carolina (365%)
Arkansas (342%)
Georgia (320%)
Tennessee (282%)
South Carolina (237%)
Alabama (195%)
Nevada (208%)

The report goes on to cite overall economic growth and strong population growth among all races in these same states.[6]

The point is that the people coming from Mexico are mobile and willing to go wherever the jobs are. After decades on the wane, the American South has been growing rapidly again in recent years, and according to these numbers, absorbing a significantly larger portion of the low-wage immigration influx than the rest of the nation. Mexican statehood may actually provide a real

[6] *Source: Pew Hispanic Center Report: The New Latino South, July 2005 and August 2015*

impetus to the repopulation and revitalization of the rural American South.

While some pundits have been announcing the last days of the United States (for the last hundred years or so), our nation is still young by historical standards and can certainly continue to grow and absorb new citizens, when the conditions are right. The European Union, for example, continues to expand without any disastrous consequences. Perhaps it's beyond recent memory for most, but it was just 56 years ago, in 1959, that Alaska and Hawaii were granted statehood, and 47 years before that when Arizona and New Mexico became states. The time now is not only ripe, the current economic and immigration conditions are practically begging for this change.

Chapter 3

The Economic Costs and Benefits for the U.S.

The government actually has quite a limited role to play in the development of a new Mexican state. Official statehood of course, must come from the federal government. With a few important steps, the government can set the stage for a successful expansion of the Union and then step back and let market forces do what they do best, to expand and grow in their own interests. Taxpayer money will be needed only to convert the justice, electoral and bureaucratic systems to conform to the American system and to bring Mexican systems into compliance with ours. Local and state taxes will be used to improve local infrastructures. The private sector will flood in to take advantage of the economic vacuum, quickly building up advantageous sectors and probably drawing many Mexicans home from the contiguous 48 to contribute to the growth of their home towns. This is not amnesty for criminals. This is a way to expand the middle class and thus, consumer base, in both the United States and Mexico, to create hundreds of new small and medium businesses and opportunities for everyone. Positive spending (investment in growth) is money far better spent than our current focus on negative spending (law enforcement and building useless walls). Others have proposed supporting Mexico's growing economy as a solution to illegal immigration, but in practice, not much has been done because our collective economic hands are still loosely tied. Statehood will mean it is in everyone's interest, in the economic interest of many U.S. businesses, of the U.S. and Mexico together as a whole, to grow and invest in Mexico, and everyone will be 100% free to make that investment and realize the full rewards of the investment we've been making since NAFTA.

Short-term Costs

The Cost of Labor

With the 12 million previously illegal Mexican immigrants holding United States citizenship, it would no longer be worth the risk of imprisonment to pay them less than minimum wage and the supply of illegally cheap labor for the unscrupulous American employers who have been exploiting illegal workers would be cut drastically, possibly producing a short-term economic ripple through the farming, meat-packing and construction industries, due to a sudden increase in their labor costs, however, those particular companies within those industries have been breaking the law to artificially contain their labor costs until now, and the law-abiding entities within those industries should place the blame squarely on their unscrupulous competitors for their criminal activities and take heart, that competition for labor in their industry will now see a level playing field for the first time in decades.

Bureaucratic Reform

The year-long preparations described in the previous chapter would require some upfront investment by the federal government in the Mexican federal system, including retraining government employees to adapt to the American system of justice, helping them to prepare and issue social security cards to all Mexican citizens, and to prepare American offices to integrate with the new offices in Mexico. Voter rolls and voting systems will need to be integrated into the American electoral system. Or perhaps Mexico should reform our chaotic electoral system! (In case history has been forgotten, voting irregularities led to huge scandals in our Presidential elections of 2000, 2004 and 2012.) According to pollster Warren Mitofsky, the Mexican electoral system is considerably superior. He states, "I would think the Mexican system with its strong election commission that is uniform across the country would be better than anything we are doing in the U.S. One of the problems with the U.S. is we don't have uniformity from county to county and state to state. Every county and state is making their own rules and they aren't making them consistently."[7] A cabinet-level transition team may even be required to filter out any corruption in the Mexican bureaucracy (and the American bureaucracy) and organize these tasks, given the scope of this venture.

The Justice System

Large numbers of police training personnel would be needed to ensure that the new Mexican state complies with American justice from top to bottom. Before entering the Union, every police officer in Mexico should be fully aware of the rights of every American citizen and the standard procedures and techniques of American police. Judges and courts will also require training from their American counterparts, and Mexico will be flooded with American lawyers, not only to try cases under American law, but also to guide Mexican lawyers in their preparation to take the American bar exam and become certified American lawyers.

[7] *Source: Newsweek Interview with Warren Mitofsky, December 12, 2012*

Short-term Benefits

Taxpayers

The most immediate impact will be seen on the tax rolls. With an official population jump of more than 135 million in just one year, millions of illegal immigrants in America now paying taxes, and Mexico's trillion-dollar economy, ranked 11th in the world, suddenly contributing to the American GDP, the tax rolls should see their largest year-on-year increase in American history. As a state, Mexico's economy would come in second only to California's, and since the brief politically-sparked peso devaluation crisis in 1994, Mexico has enjoyed a stable and steady overall growth rate, often better than America's standard three to four percent.

Oil

Mexico holds significant oil resources: 38 billion barrels of proven reserves, as compared to America's 16 billion barrels, according to the CIA World Fact Book. Mexican oil would become American oil, at cost, and American oil companies would move in to improve the infrastructure and transportation of the current oil production.

Water

Mexico currently has 1500 solar desalination turbines, providing 10% of their electricity and contributing to Mexico's healthy drinking water surplus.

Tourism

Mexico's tourism industry generates approximately $1.8 billion a month, 3/4 of which comes from visitors from the United States. It's not just Mexicans coming to the U.S.! Americans visit Mexico in the millions. Thousands of American students flock to the gorgeous resorts at Acapulco, Puerto Vallarta or Cancún for spring break every year. Ancient ruins of the Mayan civilization draw millions of visitors as well. Mexico boasts more than 12,000 hotels and continues to invest heavily in what has become their second largest industry. American tourism to Mexico would certainly increase even further if the passport requirement were removed and Americans who had not been to Mexico before go to explore our new Southwest.

Mexican Return

Tourism is not the only type of travel that would receive a big boost from Mexican statehood. Millions of Mexicans currently in America cannot visit their families, for fear that they would not be able to return. With statehood, the terrible obstacle separating illegal workers from the families they have risked everything to support, would fall, and millions of Mexicans would travel home to see their beloved wives and husbands and children and extended families. And large numbers of Mexicans in America, especially those who have flourished and prospered, will even move back to their home region on a permanent basis, eager to take advantage of the new economic hope in their home towns and help to build up their old neighborhoods.

Business Travel

Vast numbers of businesses, both large and small, would take advantage of the new internal market and would also travel to Mexico in the first year of statehood, eager to size up their new opportunities, to see what needs to be done, where to build new offices, to prepare to enter the market. Travel of all kinds would see huge short-term increases, on the road to more long-term investment.

Remittances

As mentioned above, tourism is Mexico's second largest industry. So what about the top source of Mexican income? Number one used to be oil until a few years ago, but now it's the $30 billion that Mexican workers in America send to their families each year. That's $30 billion that would immediately stop flying out of the country, and out of our economy every year. The simple fact is that together, the millions of Mexicans working in the American economy, constitute a huge segment of the Mexican economy which is constantly biting chunks out of the American economy and swallowing them into the Mexican economy. Like it or not, the Mexican economy already partially functions as a segment of the American economy, almost as a daughter economy, from which the American economy enjoys little reward. To detangle them now would be a disaster for both economies. To complete the integration in a spirit of cooperation would be to the enormous benefit of both.

Long-term Costs

Criminal Justice

Drug cartels and violent street gangs from Mexico have been increasingly over-running American inner cities for the last three decades. When we invite Mexico to become an equal partner in our United States, we will be inviting these violent criminals into the new federal prisons we will be building. While some critics may fear that Mexico is bursting at the seams with criminal gangs, the truth is that America is already bursting at the seams with criminal gangs from Mexico. What kind of pathetic drug lord would you be, if you weren't in the world's largest market for illegal drugs by now? The truth is, they have been among the most enterprising and well-connected, even profiting off the dreams of the poorest of their own fellow Mexicans, smuggling them into the United States by the most inhumane methods one might imagine, often costing impoverished immigrants their lives.

While all of the large Mexican criminal gangs operate in many American cities, they maintain bases of support in Mexico, thanks to corruption in the local and regional governments, as well as the simple fact of the tremendous power and influence their wealth brings them in more impoverished areas of the country. Bringing all of Mexico under the American system of justice, while not a quick fix, would finally give our local and federal law enforcement agencies, along with our criminal courts, the permission and ability to crush their operations at the root. These gangs have been able to flourish out of control for decades because we are powerless to stop them at their headquarters. All we can really do right now is ask Mexico again and again to please stop them for us, and the gangs ruling mercilessly over the streets of

American inner cities provide ample evidence of how effective that diplomatic pressure is. There may be some tough and drawn-out cases, and we may need to build several expensive prisons, but the streets will become safer, not only in Mexico, but in Los Angeles, Detroit, Chicago, Miami, in cities all across America, safer than is possible while these gangs operate from a foreign country.

Infrastructure

A necessary step toward the success of Mexican statehood, in order to provide the fullest opportunity for our new citizens and our new state, and to ensure future private sector development, is a long-term investment in the infrastructure of the less developed areas of Mexico – upgrading roads and lighting systems, bringing together smaller towns that may not be well connected to each other, making it possible for businesses to operate and grow in underdeveloped areas. Much of this should be done with local and regional taxes or bond measures, but some may need to be shouldered by the federal government, such as larger interstate and intrastate highways.

Environmental Restoration

Much of rural Mexico, especially in the southern regions, has suffered from a lack of land and water management. The federal government can bring its expertise to these regions and eventually restore depleted groundwater supplies, failing forests and over farmed land. These lands may also provide an opportunity to build sustainable alternative resources from the ground up. In developed areas, such as the enormous capital city, pollution and environmental destruction are also rampant. Mexico's urban areas will likely need 5-10 years to comply with EPA standards.

Education

Mexico's educational system, once first-rate, has, like the American educational system for that matter, been allowed to stagnate and decline over the last few decades. Of course, English will need to be taught as the primary language throughout Mexico, but teachers also need to be paid fairly for the important work that they do. It is often said that the children are our future. Yet we pay our teachers about as much as janitors. What does that say about what we are really willing to invest in our future, in our children? Mexican public schools will need to add English curriculum. But this also offers us the opportunity to improve all of our elementary schools. Pay our teachers a livable wage, and draw top-quality people into teaching. Make it a desirable occupation again, and watch how American education accelerates to match the academic achievement in Europe and East Asia.

Health Care

The health care system in Mexico is world-class, as advanced as American medicine, and some hospitals even feel like fancy hotels. That is, if you're in the lucky upper classes of the population. For the rural poor, just as in the United States, it's a different story. As with education, this is a sector of domestic policy that requires more investment today, right here in America, as well as in Mexico. Again, here's a chance to refocus our ongoing efforts and improve life for all, on both sides of the Rio Grande.

Over the last fifteen years, the Mexican government has gone a long way toward improving the efficiency and basic functioning of the bottom half of its public health care system. "In 2002, the government began working with A.T. Kearney to improve its faltering health-care system. The overall approach involved immediately shoring up the system's foundation and building a stronger infrastructure. There were short-term fixes, such as improving procurement processes, inventory, demand planning and regulation. And there were long-term solutions, such as a total restructuring of the medicine supply chain. The Ministry of Health also introduced a series of change-management initiatives to encourage a system-wide attitude adjustment. Already, the country is earning high marks for its innovative approach. In less than two years, the government improved its supply chain service levels—defined by the number of patients who received full prescriptions—from 70 percent to more than 90 percent, while reducing drug unit costs by 5 to 10 percent."[8]

Long-term Benefits

New Labor Pool

The large Mexican labor pool, which we've been increasingly exploiting over the last few decades is younger and healthier than the American work force. Many more taxpayers would be paying into the Social Security and Medicare programs, which are always on the brink of impending crisis, while drawing from them less, tilting the balance toward the positive and possibly adding decades to the viability of these systems.

[8] *Source: atkearney.com*

Birth Rate

Mexico enjoys a significantly higher fertility rate than the U.S., ensuring a full supply of labor for generations to come. The United States, like most industrialized and highly urbanized nations, suffers from a dwindling and ageing labor base, which can no longer expect to find a nest egg waiting for them after a lifetime of honest work. Industrialized nations around the world are panicking and struggling to care for their older citizens, while modern ambitious city dwellers put off having children until later in life and are satisfied with just one or two children, who economically, are more of a liability than an advantage, when there's no farm for them to work, no fields to plow. The higher birth rate of the Mexican population will compound the positive effect of the younger population mentioned above, filling vacant jobs and paying into the retirement system.

Border Control

As described in Chapter 2, the southern border of the United States would be three times smaller than it is today, and the vast majority of people presently trying to get in would already be legally inside the country. The INS and FBI would see huge savings both in terms of funding and manpower, freeing them up to devote their time and energies to other important matters, such as terrorism.

A Large New Market

The entire Mexican market would be 100% open to American development and reconstruction, as well as consumer sales - far more than the limited "free trade" provided by NAFTA. All types of American businesses would flourish, not chained down by bureaucracy. The travel, construction and service industries would grow significantly, and consumer spending – the lifeblood of the American economy - would follow close behind. Remember, while there is great poverty in parts of Mexico, the other half of the Mexican population lives in huge, wealthy cities – a fantastic market for American retailers. Legal services from American law firms would boom, given that all of Mexico would need American lawyers. Meat-packing firms and other companies that already employ Mexicans in large numbers could expand into Mexico, go to where their workers are, rather than waiting for their workers to come to them.

Education

It's no mistake that education is listed among both the long-term costs and the long-term benefits to the United

States. With a genuine investment in the education of Mexico's young people, we can turn out a talented and inventive generation of highly-skilled Mexican-Americans, capable of contributing to the prosperity and well-being of our nation as much as any other state in the Union. It's been demonstrated many times, anywhere in the world where there has been real long-term investment in education, the results have been tremendous. After the second world war, all of East Asia was struggling to rebuild. Today, thanks to top-notch competitive educational systems, the entire region is a stable economic powerhouse.

Creating Jobs, Not Losing Them

The most common fear of American protectionists is the howling complaint, "They'll steal our jobs!" The reality is that the American economy has been absorbing 15 million illegal immigrants over the last few decades while growing at an average of nearly 4% per year. NAFTA did not wreck the American economy. There are more jobs in the United States now than at any time since the dot-com boom of the late 1990s. Far more jobs will be added by completely opening up a large new market on our southern border to every American company. The unrestricted opportunity to invest in the development of an area 1/3 the size of the 48 contiguous states will be a new gold rush, comparable to the opening of the West in the late 19th century. Tens of thousands of new jobs will be created, lifting the local and national economies to levels not seen since World War II.

As mentioned in Chapter 1, almost 40% of all new jobs recently acquired by Hispanics in the U.S. are in the construction industry. This is precisely the kind of skilled labor that is needed not only here, but also in Mexico. This is a perfect example of how Mexican statehood provides the best incentives for everyone. The U.S. construction industry expands into Mexico to rebuild the ailing infrastructure, hiring Mexican construction workers who already possess the necessary skills, and many Mexicans in America return home to help rebuild their home regions. The red-hot construction sector of the American economy continues to grow while jobs are created and money is made on both sides of the old border, all while investing in future growth by building up poverty-stricken areas of Mexico.

Chapter 4

Wait! Why Will Mexico Want to Give Up Its Sovereignty?

Mexico has historically had reason to distrust the United States, but economic realities have brought us closer together in recent decades. With the world getting smaller and moving faster than ever before, it is inevitable that we bury old grievances and deepen our alliances, and even make new ones. In the context of international relations, enemies often become friends in less than a generation. Where would we be today without our bitterly hated WWII enemies, the nation once ruled by Hitler, and their allies, the kamikaze, "Japs," as they were referred to in every newspaper across the land? We even imprisoned our own citizens of Japanese ancestry. Yet the wartime propaganda moved on, and we moved on. Once demonized nations have become our best friends. Politics is predicated on the public having a short memory. Are the Mexicans our friends? Have they been our friends in the past? Here's a brief history, starting with the Mexican-American War:

The Mexican-American War (1846 – 1848)

The Lone Star State - practically a country within a country - there's no place on earth like Texas, a bastion of rugged individualism and liberty. But Texas was once a territory of Mexico. In the early 1820s, Mexico was more like a collection of Spanish colonies joined together in a coalition than the unified nation we know today. Texas was officially a member of that coalition, but began to pull away in 1824, when the President of Mexico threw out the constitution in an effort to consolidate power in Mexico City. Tensions reached a breaking point five years later, when Mexico officially abolished slavery in 1829. This was perceived as a direct threat to the economy and culture of Texas, and Texans began to openly rebel, and rebellion turned to war.

In 1836, the Republic of Texas defeated Mexico City's army and declared independence. They immediately turned to the United States for annexation (and for protection against the British and against Mexico, which publicly stated its intention to regroup and reclaim Texas from the rebels). However, the administration of Andrew Jackson actually rejected Texas' statehood ambitions, unwilling to provoke Mexico, and fearful of the internal political impact of adding another pro-slavery state to the Union.

In 1845, President James K. Polk changed a decade of American policy by finally accepting Texas into the Union and sent troops to the border to defend it from Mexico, which had still not accepted the independence of Texas, and officially considered it a breakaway region of their country. A Mexican cavalry brigade eventually decided to cross the Rio Grande and attack, killing a handful of U.S. soldiers, including an officer named Seth Thornton, in an attempt to reclaim their rebelling state.

When word of the skirmish reached the President, he called on Congress to declare war with the words, *"American blood has been shed on American soil."* While the vote was eventually lopsided in favor, critics from the opposing Whig party charged that the President had overrun the Constitution and pushed for war unnecessarily, and even that he had possibly lied about the facts, in order to start a war without the approval of Congress. There were anti-war protestors, such as author Henry David Thoreau, who refused to pay taxes to fund the war, and even the former President John Quincy Adams warned that an ulterior motive of the Mexican-

American War was to expand slavery in the United States. Even decades later, President and American Civil War hero Ulysses S. Grant commented that the American Civil War was a kind of karmic punishment for, and a direct result of, the Mexican-American War.

California, which had only been claimed by Mexico a few decades earlier in 1823, and was sparsely populated by a mix of Hispanics, Indian tribes, and a few white settlers, in the context of war, became a more strategic territory, which all sides feared would be occupied by someone else, including the British or French. The presence of gold in the California territory may also have been known to the American and Mexican governments by this time, with the famous gold rush just a few years off. In 1846, U.S. naval ships planted the American flag at ports at Monterey and Los Angeles. Relatively small, yet decisive battles won the territory of California for U.S. Captain John C. Fremont and the United States government. The Mexican general reluctantly signed a treaty, ending the war in California.

But the war continued in Mexico, on a larger and more punishing scale. In 1847, less than 5,000 U.S. troops laid siege to Monterrey, Mexico, in the face of 15,000 Mexican troops, although the Mexican force had inferior training, badly outdated equipment and weapons, and an exhausting trek to the scene of the battle. Heavy losses were incurred on both sides, but the Mexicans were eventually outgunned and they capitulated.

President Polk sent a second army by sea to besiege Veracruz, where the Mexicans were outnumbered 4 to 1. 12 days later, the demoralized Mexican army surrendered their city, but the health of the American troops was threatened by an outbreak of Yellow Fever, a horrific and potentially deadly mosquito-borne virus.

The healthy soldiers marched on toward the capital and took Mexico's second largest city, Puebla, without a fight on the way there, thanks to a population disgruntled with their own leader, the one who had tried to re-write the Mexican constitution to give himself more power.

Although Mexican troops were lying in wait for the American march to Mexico City, they gave themselves away by firing on a small forward team, and the American army was able to surround them and kill or capture a third of their troops. The American army occupied Mexico City before the end of 1847. A radical but vocal minority in the U.S. called for the annexation all Mexico, in line with the defining supremacist-expansionist philosophy of the American 19th century called Manifest Destiny, a set of holier-than-thou patriotic ambitions, centered around the re-education of natives, training them to adopt a European-style culture to overcome the supposed natural inferiority of non-anglo races, and the conquest of the entire North American continent for the God-blessed democracy experiment. However, even at the height of the popularity of the Manifest Destiny ideology, there were critics who argued that democracy and freedom should not and could not be imposed by force on any nation. These philosophical arguments, it seems, still have not been settled conclusively, even today.

Strangely enough, rather than rule over the entire Mexican territory, America used its resounding victory to offer Mexico a sum of 18 million dollars. In return for this sum, in the Treaty of Guadalupe Hidalgo, signed in 1848, the United States officially and undisputedly took control of Texas and California, as well as Arizona, Colorado, Nevada, and sections of today's New Mexico and Wyoming. Everyone living in these areas was given the choice to stay and become American citizens, or retreat to Mexican territory. Most remained and became Americans. Although they were officially U.S. citizens, they were not treated as equals. The land they had settled under Spanish rule was taken from them, and their mistreatment then, marked the beginning of an organized movement for fairness and equality that joined forces with the African-American civil rights movement in the 1960s and lives on today.

American troops in that time, as still holds true today, had the advantage of technologically superior firepower and advanced combat training. 90% of the 13,000 Americans killed in the Mexican-American War fell victim to disease, rather than the enemy.

Mexican-American Relations Since the War

The Mexican Revolution
When the incumbent President had his main rival jailed on Election Day in 1910, the seeds were sown for a revolution. Many Mexicans fled the instability and bloodshed, which continued for the next decade, and sought low-wage work in the United States, mainly agricultural work.

Mexican Repatriation
During the Great Depression of the early 1930s, the

United States experienced a wave of anti-immigration fears, blaming Mexicans for taking their jobs and calling them a drain on government social programs. The INS took the radical step of deporting half a million Latinos to Mexico, most of whom were **actually American citizens**, based purely on their ethnic appearance. This mass forced deportation of course did nothing to alleviate the economic crisis, which was not in any way caused by immigration, and only served to inflame tensions between the two countries and their peoples. Those who remained lived under curfews specifically targeted at Mexican-Americans. In 2005, the state of California issued an official apology for the unconstitutional removal of citizens and legal residents of Mexican descent.

Zoot Suit Riots
During World War II, in an atmosphere of fear sparked by exaggerated reporting and rumors of violence by Mexican-Americans, sailors, soldiers and marines, returning to the Port of Los Angeles fresh from the war, often went cruising downtown, or even into East Los Angeles, specifically looking for minority youths wearing the extravagant zoot suits favored by Mexican-Americans, and beat them, stripping off the suits and burning them in the street. The soldiers were rarely disciplined at all,

while the victims of the attacks were arrested for disturbing the peace. A zoot suit is a flamboyantly large, almost puffy, suit, requiring hand-tailoring and a lot of material, which was considered particularly rebellious during wartime rationing of many raw materials. To put a stop to the frequent fighting, the military's top brass eventually took the extreme step of banning all military personnel from Los Angeles.

Growing Trade Ties

While Mexico often stood up against the American position in international affairs in the Cold War era, refusing to cut ties with Cuba and criticizing disastrous U.S. military actions in Central America, the beginnings of a global economy brought the North American neighbors closer together. The shared border and shared history made the U.S. and Mexico natural trade partners, and official relations improved, mainly because we needed each other. Despite sharp disagreement over the United States' role in El Salvador in the 1980s, cooperation continued to grow, primarily in the attempt by both governments to gain some control over the increasingly powerful Mexican drug lords and drug trafficking across the border into America.

NAFTA

The North American Free Trade Agreement, an economic cooperation agreement signed by Canada, the U.S. and Mexico in 1993, while controversial for its supposedly radical opening of markets, was not able to deliver the kind of economic growth it promised because it was only a half-step into the market, not the truly free trade that its name would suggest. However, it did not suck millions of jobs out of the American economy as critics warned, and it succeeded in laying a groundwork of cooperation that all parties can now expand upon by opening a truly free and open market without borders between the US and Mexico.

A New Democratic Revolution

The election of Vicente Fox in 2000 was the first fully free democratic election in Mexican history, and it broke a seven-decade lock on one-party rule, going back to the time of the Mexican Revolution. Fox's politics were closely aligned to American policies, and when George W. Bush came to power in 2001, they excitedly discussed a deepening of economic cooperation to benefit both nations. This was always controversial. In fact, NAFTA had not ceased to be controversial, but the leaders pushed ahead with what was best for their economies until the terrorist attacks of September 11 made it impossible to do so. America slammed shut the gates at the borders in a nationwide hysteria. She locked herself in the bathroom, neurotically trying to asses if she could still trust anyone. When Germany and France balked at U.S. military aggression, they were labeled, "Old Europe," as if they were no longer our friends. Illegal immigration again became a lightning rod issue. The poor, desperate migrant worker might bring Middle East terrorists across the border with him, if they pay him two dollars – so went the illogical fear mongering.

The American military actions in the Middle East have long ago ceased to be a test of who is with us and who is against us. The cold light of day has made a nation drunk on fear squint into the unhappy realization that we did something last night that we now regret. The American people have come to realize that much of the world is as it was before, that many of our old friends never wanted to become our enemies, but we were just asking too much of them. Before Fox left office in Mexico, he tried again to push for tighter integration and fair treatment for Mexican workers in America. Bush proposed a guest worker program that would allow Mexicans to register to work in the U.S. for 3 years and provide eventual citizenship. With public opinion at 70% against him though, and his most conservative supporters disappointed at his unwillingness to follow them through every fire, nothing Bush proposed had much chance of being enacted. In his divisive final years, compromises between factions only watered down the proposals until they became rather useless shadows of their former bills.

In the meantime, Mexico has signed thirteen other free trade agreements, and is enjoying healthy economic growth, often better than our own GDP growth. Mexico is setting itself up for great success with partnerships around the world, yet it cannot seem to further strengthen ties with its closest neighbor, its most important trading partner, the United States.

So will Mexico trust us, when we ask them to join us in an equal partnership based on friendship and cooperation, despite the war in which we stole one third of their land? Yes, they will! They will, **IF** we extend them a true hand of friendship and cooperation. Remember, we held this nation's capital at the end of the war, yet we chose to purchase from them lands that were practically uninhabited, leaving their population largely undisturbed, and with a full right of return for anyone outside their

290 \ America's Glasnost

new borders. We have engaged in deeper mutual economic and cultural cooperation as our populations have become more blended over the last few decades, and most of all, America is still the only real melting pot of the entire world, built from the beginning by migrants from everywhere on earth, brought together by the common dreams of freedom and equality. Mexicans come from closer to home than most of the people who come to America to follow their dream. While that freedom and equality may not always have been fully realized, the dreams, the hope for those ideals remain at the core of the great American experiment, and they should so remain.

Just a generation after Martin Luther King, Jr. and others gave their lives for the equal rights and opportunities of everyone in our great nation, we are again confronted with a shameful, degrading quasi-neoslavery. We must end the illegal sub-minimum wage employment and myriad exploitations of millions of hard-working Mexicans in our country. And while it is degrading and punishing to a people who do jobs that no one else wants to do, the comparison is not entirely fair. African-American slaves were not paid anything when they were brought by force to do our farm work. Today's Mexican-Americans choose to come to America, fleeing the economic despair at home for whatever work they can find, and they are not collectively suffering beatings, lynchings or segregation, although there may be some individual cases. But Mexicans in America do often face discrimination and economic exploitation. Millions of Mexicans in America are paid illegally low wages and there have been numerous reports of Mexicans being housed in inhumane conditions and otherwise mistreated by unscrupulous employers. Yet they persevere, so they can send money home to feed their families and continue to dream of a better life. Anyone who is willing to give all they have for a chance at hope, deserves a genuine chance to reach it.

Chapter 5

The Economic Costs and Benefits for Mexico

Many of the costs and benefits for Mexico are, naturally, reflections of the same costs and benefits that the U.S. can expect to experience. In the interest of full analysis and also to illustrate that Mexico should enter this process as an equal partner, the pros and cons are here considered from the Mexican side.

Short-term Costs

Bureaucratic Reform

The year-long preparations described in previous chapters would require some upfront investment by the Mexican government as well, including retraining government employees to adapt to the American system of justice, distributing social security cards to all Mexican citizens, and integrating reformed offices of the federal government with the American system. Voter rolls and voting machines will need to be integrated into the American electoral system. A cabinet-level transition team may be required to coordinate the various tasks, given the scope of this venture.

The Justice System

Mexico will have to launch an all new drive to sweep as much corruption out of its justice system as possible before joining the Union. Mexico will have to share the financial burden of ensuring that every police officer understands and respects the rights of every American citizen and the standard procedures and techniques of American police. Judges and courts will also require training from their American counterparts, and Mexico should contribute to these costs as well.

Short-term Benefits

Oil

As mentioned earlier, Mexico holds significant oil resources: 38 billion barrels of proved reserves, as compared to America's 18 billion barrels, according to the CIA World Fact Book. The Mexican oil infrastructure is underdeveloped. American oil companies would move in to improve the infrastructure and transportation of the current oil production very quickly and within just a few years, Mexico's oil industry would see significant growth.

Tourism

Mexico's tourism industry generates approximately $1.8 billion a month, 3/4 of which comes from visitors from the United States. It's not just Mexicans coming to the U.S.! Americans visit Mexico in the millions. Thousands of American students flock to the gorgeous resorts at Acapulco, Puerto Vallarta or Cancún for spring break every year. Ancient ruins of the Mayan civilization draw millions of visitors as well. Mexico boasts more than 10,000 hotels and continues to invest heavily in what has become their second largest industry. American tourism to Mexico would certainly increase if the passport requirement were removed. International interest in Mexico's new future would of course draw even more tourists from further afield.

Mexican Return

Tourism is not the only type of travel that would receive a big boost from Mexican statehood. Millions of Mexicans currently in America cannot visit their families for fear that they would not be able to return. With statehood, the terrible obstacle separating illegal workers from the families they have risked everything to support, would fall, and millions of Mexicans would travel home to see their beloved wives and husbands and children and extended families. And large numbers of Mexicans in America, especially those who have flourished and prospered, will move back to their home region on a permanent basis, eager to take advantage of the new economic hope in their home towns and help to build up their old neighborhoods.

Business Travel

Vast numbers of businesses, both large and small, would take advantage of the new internal market and would also travel to Mexico in the first year of statehood, eager to size up their new opportunities, to see what needs to be done, where to build new offices, to prepare to enter the market. Travel of all kinds would see huge short-term increases, on the road to more long-term investment.

Long-term Costs

Loss of Sovereignty

While states do maintain certain rights and freedoms in our system of government, they are not the same as sovereign nations – they are beholden to the federal government in Washington, D.C. Fears of American imperialism are not new, but they have recently been heightened and controversial. On the other hand, a display of mutual cooperation could go a long way toward allaying those fears for the entire world, and the Mexican people, while losing absolute sovereignty, would gain a significant say in world affairs from within the American superpower, and an equal voice in Washington, a force which, like it or not, already holds real influence over their daily lives.

Long-term Benefits

Mexican Return
Again, the importance of reuniting millions of Mexican families can not be overemphasized. The societal impact of the good will created, and the economic impact of a society functioning primarily around the family unit are immeasurably positive and would be a true representation of the "family values" so often paraded by political campaigns of all stripes.

Millions of Mexicans currently in America cannot visit their families for fear that they would not be able to return. With statehood, the terrible obstacle separating illegal workers from the families they have risked everything to support, would fall, and millions of Mexicans would travel home to see their beloved wives and husbands and children and extended families. And large numbers of Mexicans in America, especially those who have flourished and prospered, will move back to their home region on a permanent basis, eager to take advantage of the new economic hope in their home towns and help to build up their old neighborhoods.

Criminal Justice

Drug cartels and violent street gangs from Mexico have been increasingly over-running American inner cities for the last three decades. But they are not loved by the Mexican people either. When we invite Mexico to become an equal partner in our United States, we will be inviting these violent criminals into the new federal prisons we will be building. They will no longer be smuggling the poorest of Mexico's people into the United States in airless trucks like simple cargo, which can end up costing immigrants their lives. They will no longer rule over their own poor villages and inner cities without mercy.

Although all of the large Mexican criminal gangs operate in many American cities, they maintain bases of support in Mexico, thanks to corruption in the local and regional governments, as well as the simple fact of the tremendous power and influence their wealth brings them in more impoverished areas of the country. When our justice system is able to crush their operations at the root, the streets will become safer, not only in cities all across America, but all across Mexico too.

Infrastructure

As the newest state in our Union, Mexico would see both government investment and private sector development. Long-term investment in the infrastructure of the less developed areas of Mexico – upgrading roads and lighting systems, bringing together smaller towns that may not be well connected to each other, making it possible for businesses to operate and grow in underdeveloped areas – will be a key to Mexico's continued growth. And with local growth, will come higher local tax revenues, which in turn, will contribute to even further development.

Environmental Restoration

Much of rural Mexico, especially the southern regions, has suffered from a lack of land and water management. The United States federal government can bring its expertise to these regions and eventually restore depleted groundwater supplies, failing forests and over farmed land. These lands may also provide an opportunity to build sustainable alternative resources from the ground up. In developed areas, such as the enormous capital city, pollution and environmental destruction are also rampant. Mexico's urban areas will likely need 5-10 years to comply with EPA standards, but eventually, all regions of Mexico should see improvements to their respective environmental problems.

Education

Mexico's educational system, once first-rate, has, like the American educational system for that matter, been allowed to stagnate and decline over the last few decades. Given that politicians are willing to follow through on serious reform (such as paying teachers a reasonable wage), the poor children in today's Mexico could be the doctors and engineers of tomorrow.

Health Care

This is another sector of domestic policy that requires more investment today, right here in America, as well as in Mexico. Again, here's a chance for life to improve for all, on both sides of the Rio Grande.

Raising the Standard of Living in Mexico

When American businesses have totally unfettered access to the entire Mexican market, they will move in or increase their existing presence without hesitation. It's a no-brainer. Furthermore, it will be in their own best interest to invest and develop where necessary. With the flood of new American business will come more jobs, not just in the large cities, expanding in every direction, but eventually to every corner of Mexico. Certainly, just as some areas of the United States remain impoverished, there will remains pockets of poverty in Mexico too, without major reform. But with an American minimum wage and thriving American businesses throughout the land, Mexico's standard of living will gradually, but surely, rise to American standards for many who are presently without hope of any kind. Any doubters can take a look at the middle classes of today's Eastern Europe and ask where those nations stood just twenty years ago.

Of course as Mexico grows, it would only contribute even more growth to the American economy as a whole, the rising tide that lifts all boats. And furthermore, the U.S. has not been simply somehow managing to sustain 16 million illegal immigrants – we NEED them, economically.

They are the cheap labor much of our success has been built upon, and before he left office, Mexican President Fox was predicting that in ten years time, we would be begging Mexico to send us workers, because Mexico's economic growth was already adding so many jobs. If he had been wrong, would we be adding 500,000 guest worker visas every other year?

Chapter 6
Mexico's Urban and Rural Regions

Mexico City

Mexico's capital city is a booming cosmopolitan megalopolis with large immigrant populations from all over the world, including more than half a million Americans. At about 21 million, its population is comparable to that of the New York City area. But in 1950, Mexico City was less than half the size of New York City. Today, the city is dotted with universities and skyscrapers, and is the center of commerce for all of Latin America. Like any quickly growing large city, Mexico City has its ongoing problems. With 11 million cars and 70,000 factories, it is also a center of pollution and poverty-driven petty crime. But the mean streets of New York City have never really been a day at the beach either. Mexico City is a federal district, rather than part of any state, an administrative designation duplicated from our own capital, Washington D.C. A large earthquake caused major destruction in 1985, but Mexico City bounced back quickly enough to host soccer's World Cup the following year.

Mexico City was founded on the ruins of Tenochtitlan, capital of the Aztec empire, by Spanish conquistador Hernán Cortéz after a three-month siege of the city. It was established by the Aztecs on a small island on a salty lake in a valley surrounded by plateaus and volcanoes. Freshwater rivers were dammed and aqueducts provided water to the population, until that is, Cortéz demolished them in his siege. The dams were never rebuilt, and recurring floods inundated the city regularly for centuries. After severe floods in the early 17th century, the lake was drained, causing major ecological damage to the entire valley and sinking the city below the level of the underground water table, so despite the lake being turned to desert, it continued to flood after every rainfall.

Mexico City's floods were not brought under control until long modern tunnels were built deep underground in 1967. Water management remains problematic for the city, as does its continued gradual sinking.

Guadalajara

Guadalajara, Mexico's second largest metropolitan area (about 5 million) is a world-class cultural center, the home of mariachi music and tequila, and a leader in industry and more recently, in the services sector.

Construction around the city is booming, and it boasts a world-famous Guggenheim museum. Architecture from diverse periods can be found throughout the city, with heavy French and Spanish influences.

Monterrey

In the 20th century, Monterrey transformed itself from a small outpost to a metropolis of over 4 million, boasting Mexico's highest per capita GDP and becoming a leader in Mexican and international business across a wide range of classic and modern sectors, now second only to Mexico City, while suffering far fewer of the common urban ills plaguing the capital. Monterrey enjoys one of the lowest crime rates in all of Latin America and is often mentioned in lists of top places to do business and in quality of life surveys. However, the climate is more extreme than other parts of Mexico, with very hot summers and freezing winters, more similar to the desert climate of Texas than Mexico's other, milder major cities.

Tijuana

Infamous for its strategic location across the troubled border from San Diego, Tijuana is a city of about 2 million people and is, like Guadalajara, a center for culture, tourism, and a haven for independent artists. Its reputation as a wild getaway for Americans in the Southwest began with the prohibition of alcohol in the U.S. in the 1920s, which forced Americans to run to Mexico if they wanted a drink. A spirit of economic cooperation between Mexico and the U.S. existed even then.

Today's work force in Tijuana boasts diverse skills and American companies of all kinds have moved into Tijuana and contributed greatly to its growth.

Cancún

With a $27 million loan, the Mexican government began building a tourist spot on an unused island less than 40 years ago. Today, Cancún ranks among the top tourist destinations in the world, covered in resort hotels and supporting a population of over 1 million. English is widely spoken and US dollars are common currency, although not the official one. There are two popular Mayan ruins in the area. In 2005, Hurricane Wilma stranded thousands of American tourists and almost completely destroyed the tourism infrastructure. Amazingly, most hotels were open for business again within a year.

Acapulco

Acapulco, a seaside town of 1.2 million, was, for more than 250 years, a major port connecting North America to Asia, thanks to the northern Pacific trade winds. It fell out of use at the beginning of the 20th century, but has gradually found fame as a tourist and spring break destination rivaling Cancún.

Rural Areas

Throughout the 1970s and 80s, Mexico's cities boomed with new manufacturing jobs, brought about by more favorable trade arrangements, such as lowered tariffs in the United States, and the people flocked from their villages to work in the cities, abandoning their agricultural lifestyle and agriculture, as a portion of the nation's economy, plummeted. The southernmost region of Mexico is populated mainly by indigenous peoples and suffers from diminishing forests. Deforestation has been a major problem, although hundreds of solar desalination turbines have provided desperately needed drinking water.

Perhaps surprisingly, thanks to wide scale government efforts, many rural communities have been using solar panel installations for nearly 15 years.

Chapter 7
Homeland Security

Safer Borders

As stated above, at about 700 miles from the Pacific Ocean to the Gulf of Mexico, Mexico's southern border is less than one-third the size of America's current southern border. And the vast majority of the people we're currently trying to catch coming into America, would become American citizens, whom we would no longer seek to "catch." In other words, the border would become infinitely easier to defend against actual enemies – terrorists and drug dealers from South America.

We are currently spending $20 billion to catch Mexicans coming into our country and then release them into our population. An unpopular $1.2 billion-dollar-fence was built, but it only managed to provoke fear and outrage on both sides. Ten thousand National Guard troops have been on a "temporary assignment" to assist the Border Patrol for more than ten years. Considering that 16 million people are already here and more than 2 million people cross the southern border every year by simply moseying across open desert, all this money is obviously being wasted. Bubble gum for orphans would be a better use of this money. Even when the government claims they have turned back a few million people, how many of those people are trying again and being counted 2 or more times?

Let's stop this futile battle against our own economic cooperation and free up our Border Patrol to actually defend a defensible border against real enemies. Then all the billions of dollars in new spending for border security can be invested in more effective control of the real threats out there, such as violent criminal gangs.

Controlling Gangs, Criminals and Drugs

As mentioned in Chapter 3, drug cartels and violent street gangs from Mexico have been increasingly over-running American inner cities for three decades. When we invite Mexico to become an equal partner in our United States, we will be inviting these violent criminals into the new federal prisons we will be building. While some critics may fear that Mexico is bursting at the seams with criminal gangs, the truth is, that they have all already come to America. They have been the most enterprising and well-connected, even profiting off the dreams of their fellow Mexicans, smuggling them into the United States by the most inhumane methods one might imagine, and often costing immigrants their lives.

While all of the large Mexican criminal gangs operate in many American cities, they maintain bases of support in Mexico, thanks to corruption in the local and regional governments, as well as the simple fact of the tremendous power and influence their wealth brings them in more impoverished areas of the country. Bringing all of Mexico under the American system of justice, while not a quick fix, would finally give our local and federal law enforcement agencies, along with our criminal courts, the permission and ability to crush their operations at the root. These gangs have been able to flourish out of control for decades because we are powerless to stop them at their headquarters. All we can do is ask Mexico again and again to please stop them for us, and the gangs ruling mercilessly over the streets of American inner cities provide ample evidence of how effective that diplomatic pressure is. The streets will become safer, not only in Mexico, but in Los Angeles, Detroit, Chicago, Miami, in cities all across America, safer than is possible while these gangs operate from a foreign country.

The Mexican Military

It's no secret that the American armed forces are stretched to the breaking point with deployments all across the troubled Middle East. Even field commanders within the Army describe it as broken. Although they would require some retraining, we would be gaining more than half a million volunteer armed forces, ¾ of them Army, well-trained and experienced with humanitarian missions. Mexican troops were even deployed to New Orleans to assist victims of Hurricane Katrina in 2005, and to Houston after Hurricane Gillian.

The Mexican Air Force is well equipped with a wide range of ships and airplanes. There are also several elite regiments based in Mexico City, including Special Forces, an elite Army Corps, and a Presidential Guard. Overall, the Mexican military is comparatively small, but highly professional. From 2006 to 2008, the Army was deployed to gang-controlled regions of western and southern Mexico, where they conducted field eradications and took several important crime bosses into custody, proving that they can be effective when they have political backing.

Chapter 8
The Cultural Impact

The Language Barrier

Contrary to popular belief, a great number of Mexicans in the United States have learned English and use it every day. And there could be no greater incentive for all Mexicans to learn English than genuine, unrestricted economic opportunity. Business dictates the use of languages. Given a real opportunity for economic integration into the U.S., just watch how many Mexicans run to sign up for new English classes.

The use of Spanish as a second language in the United States has been on the rise for years as well. Presidential candidates have spent millions of dollars on Spanish-language advertising since the 2000 election. Widespread use of the Spanish language is a reality in some states, yet contrary to fears, English continues to be used in every city, in every state in America. As anyone who's travelled abroad can tell you, English is spoken all over the world, and the death of English in America is not lurking around the corner by any means.

Private sector English literacy programs would become more popular, as Mexicans see genuine opportunity for full integration, while Americans moving to Mexico would increase the use of English among Mexicans through natural immersion and exposure to the language - just being around people speaking English.

"Among Hispanics under the age of 18, 92% of those that have been in the U.S. since before 2000 speak English only or speak English very well, and 81% of those that came to the U.S. between 1990 and 2005 speak English only or speak English very well."[9]

It is well known that younger people learn languages more readily and are also more adaptable to change. These statistics show that within a generation, we can expect a majority of Mexicans to be fluently speaking English, a remarkable feat of mass assimilation. Of course, Spanish would certainly become a more valuable second language than it already is too, which can only broaden our cultural understanding and contribute to the education of our own young people in our ever more connected modern world.

[9] Source: Pew Hispanic Center tabulations of 2015 American Community Survey

Mexican Opinions on Divisive Political Issues

Public opinion in Mexico on hot-button issues is generally comparable to that in America, once again demonstrating our similarities, and implying that statehood for Mexico would not significantly impact any special interest issue, beyond the obvious one, which is the equal rights long sought by the Chicano Movement in America.

Abortion Rights

In a public opinion survey taken in Mexico, "84% felt that abortion should be legal in some circumstances. A majority of participants believed that abortion should be legal when a woman's life is at risk (88%), a woman's health is in danger (84%), pregnancy results from rape (74%) or there is a risk of fetal impairment (65%). Far fewer respondents supported legal abortion when a woman is a minor (33%), for economic reasons (27%), when a woman is single (19%) or because of contraceptive failure (18%). In spite of the influence of the Church, most Mexican Catholics believed the Church and legislators' personal religious beliefs should not factor into abortion legislation, and most supported provision of abortions in public health services in cases when abortion is legal."[10]

[10] *Source: PubMed, Department of Health and Human Services, Nov. 2014*

314 \ America's Glasnost

Gay Marriage

In 2006, Mexico City legalized civil unions for homosexual couples, to much controversy. Civil unions became legal nationwide in 2013. The Democratic Revolution Party called it a victory for equality against homophobia, while religious groups were suitably outraged. The bill highlighted divisions and latent intolerance within the society.

Immigration

55% of Mexicans believe racism is the main reason for U.S. opposition to illegal immigration. 93% say the border fence has not had any effect whatsoever on illegal immigration.[11]

Bush and the UN

Bush's favorable rating in Mexican opinion polls was running 70% in the aftermath of the 9/11 attacks, similar to his numbers in America. Like everywhere else, his numbers declined steadily as the Iraq war dragged on. By early 2003, his favorable rating was 53%. And Americans are not the only ones sometimes distrustful of the United Nations. Just 49% of Mexicans today have a favorable view of the UN, while 22% have an unfavorable view.[12]

[11] Source: El Universal, April 2014
[12] Source: Reforma, March 2013

Religion and Tradition

Mexico is an overwhelmingly Roman Catholic nation, but bitter historical conflicts between church and state in Mexico have led them to adopt a close approximation of the separation of church and state to which we adhere today in America, although there are still controversies from time to time, just as there are in America on this topic.

Many Catholic rituals may seem excessively formal to Protestant eyes, but at their core, they are not so different from typical American celebrations, and Mexico celebrates many traditional Catholic saints' days as well as most of the same holidays we do, sometimes with the name of a saint attached, i.e., Labor Day doubles as the Day of St. Joseph.

Christmas

Mexico celebrates Christmas with religious observations from the Virgin of Guadalupe in early December, who according to legend, sought to have a temple built for her on the ruins of an Aztec temple in the 16th century, to children-led nativity reenactments through the middle of the month, to a celebratory meal on the Day of

Purification, or Epiphany, on February 2, which includes a ring-shaped cake with a figure of the baby Jesus hidden inside. Americans actually borrowed their traditional Christmas flower, the poinsettia, from Mexico, where it has been a symbol of new life for many centuries. Even the piñata, a favorite at children's birthday parties, originated as a Mexican Christmas tradition.

Day of the Dead

While Halloween is gaining in popularity, Mexico has its own unique holiday at this same time, the Day of the Dead. Huge numbers of monarch butterflies migrate back to Mexico from the north at this time of year, and ancient Aztec beliefs hold that the butterflies contain the souls of friends and family that have passed on. Like Halloween, costumes are a popular part of this celebration, but altars are also built with various foods and flowers (often bright marigolds) and photographs, and cemeteries are decorated with fresh flowers to honor the dead.

Easter

Mexicans celebrate the full two weeks of Easter, including a Lent sacrifice and dramatic full-featured reenactments of the crucifixion and resurrection of Christ. These are often elaborate and beautifully done productions which draw large crowds of tourists.

71 (Barth)

Chapter 9
The Impact on U.S. Foreign Policy

A Spirit of Cooperation

In a global poll by Mund Americas from 2002, the United States was described as "trying to dominate the world" by 77% of respondents, and only 22% agreed with the statement that the U.S. has a "constructive role in world politics". This was only one year after pro-American sentiment swept the world in the aftermath of 9/11. The rush to war in Iraq and the sure and steady descent into chaos in the ensuing years has cemented the American government's image as a go-it-alone imperialist power. Rhetoric from the Bush administration such as, "You're either with us or against us," placed our longstanding friends with disagreements into an enemy camp. A similar worldwide poll taken in 2013 showed little improvement in America's image abroad. More than 80% of respondents in various regions held the U.S. directly responsible for the decades of high level violence in the Middle East. Anti-American sentiment among the world's populations continues to run at fever pitch.

But how would these figures change if the United States government removed itself from those unwinnable wars and then offered a genuine opportunity for complete cooperation and development to the whole of Mexico? Impoverished Mexicans, hungry for jobs to feed their families, can see no reason other than racism, to explain why we would want to seal them off behind a Berlin Wall from Texas to California. But attitudes can change. The world sprang from their seats to stand behind America in the wake of the 9/11 attacks. Within a year, as is often said, the good will had been squandered. But administrations can change, and even administrations' attitudes can change when pressured by Congress, and world opinion can change too. The world could be seeing America in a whole new light this time next year – if our troops are finally coming home from the messes in Iraq, Afghanistan, Lebanon and Pakistan. Combine the relief of ending our bloody regional occupation with an offer for mutually beneficial and total cooperation with our neighbors in Mexico, and the entire international community could be standing with us once again, as they were just a few years ago.

There is obviously a lot more to foreign policy than one or two issues, but a proposal of such proportion, replacing an antagonistic isolationism with a deepening trust predicated upon mutual prosperity, could swing the momentum back in the other direction and symbolize a new spirit in our relations with all nations. Some exceptions will remain, of course, but at the least, our allies in Europe and Asia will not recoil defensively from every motion we put on the table. When we show we once again can reach out to people in need, our friends in the world will be more trusting of our aims, while our economic influence will continue to grow, in cooperation with the citizens of our new state. This could be the beginning of a new spirit of cooperation in American foreign policy.

Chapter 11

Scorched Rose Garden Diplomacy

A familiar sound lifted Roger's head from his work. It was the hollow clunking of his wife's favorite shoes. They came closer, and then she graced the doorway.

"Hey, I've missed you, honey." he said with an ever-widening smile, and then looked back down at his desk.

"Me too, tiger." Lenka said warmly.

"How was Toronto?" he asked, glancing up at her.

"It was good," she said liltingly. "There was this one little Vietnamese girl there. Her name was Bonnie Sue..."

Roger arched his back and then leaned backwards into his chair. "Bonnie Sue?" he asked skeptically. "I thought you said she was Vietnamese."

"Yeah. I asked about that. Her real name is Bahn-li su, but everyone calls her Bonnie Sue," she explained dryly. Then her voice rose in schoolgirlish glee. "Honey, if you could have seen her... she was the *cutest* little thing! I wanted to just pick her up and take her home."

"Lenka, we agreed," Roger interrupted sternly.

"I know, but..."

"No adoptions until I have the time to devote to it," he said with real exasperation in his voice.

"Don't worry, honey, I know. She was cute, that's all," Lenka said resignedly.

"You said you wanted to take her home."

"It's a figure of speech, Roger," she huffed.

"So what's new around here?" she suddenly asked cheerfully, consciously trying not to allow Roger's stress level to affect her.

"You mean in the last twenty seconds?" Roger mumbled, looking really frazzled.

"Is it that bad?" she asked, sitting down in the only chair with no papers on it.

"It's not good," he replied, speaking in a sigh and moving papers around.

He stopped and looked up at Lenka, gazing directly into her eyes for several seconds. He didn't exactly smile - his mouth moved in that way that Lenka knew well, but could never describe. It was something between a smirk and a knowing look, but Roger's eyes always appeared a little shinier when that expression visited his face. It was one of the things that would forever intrigue her about Roger, one of his unique mysteries that kept her so unquestionably in love with him.

"The President's not too impressed with the Mexico plan, and we've got five different smaller things going, just to try and get something done before the hundred day mark to get the press off our back," he said, falling quickly back into the rapid diction of the West Wing he'd recently acquired.

Lenka thought for a second whether he desired a response, and then responded anyway. "I don't know if you've had time to notice, but the climate change controversy is not all negative. You've got almost half the country talking more rationally about it, at least."

"The Democratic half?" Roger asked.

"The rational half, I think," she answered. She watched him open and shut several manila folders, rearranging them in various pile formations. "When did you get so absorbed in the media circus, Roger? You know the fucking corporate media doesn't represent the voice of the American people. That's *your* job, remember?"

Roger stopped moving folders and sat back in his chair again. "What? Fucking the corporate media?" She glared at him, unamused. Then Roger let out a snicker. "That's a joke, honey. OK, c'mon, I know you're right," he said. "We have four years here. I can't forget that.

There's just so much going on every day. It's really frantic. It seems like four years will be over in no time."

His secretary Jeane buzzed past the door and yelped, "Representative Sheldon on line three!"

"Thank you...." he yelled, and then whispered "...Jeane," realizing she was already far down the hall. He picked up the phone and said, "Hello Madame Representative, what can I do for you?" His eyebrows went up and his chin went down in surprise. "Really," he intoned. "I'll be happy to sit down with you... let's see... tomorrow at 7:30. Fine. I'm looking forward to it, Jessica. Thank you."

He put down the phone and said to Lenka with quiet astonishment, "A bi-partisan group in the House wants to push for a line-item veto."

"You see, you're not so alone up here as you thought."

"It'll never pass the Senate, but it *is* the first encouragement I've had in weeks. We'll see how far it goes."

"Just push it as far as you can, honey. That's what got you this far."

...

"What do you have, Roger?"

"A bi-partisan group of Reps is putting together a line item veto. They say they've been catching total hell back home to do something about wasteful spending and they think they can get the votes to pass it."

"That's what I like to hear," Richardson beamed.

"These always die in the Senate though, don't they, sir?" Roger asked, surprised at the President's optimism.

"Any good news we can put out to people, Roger. It always makes everything run more smoothly."

"Understood. I gave them my ideas this morning. They say they'll have something written by the start of next week."

"Good. I'll start talking about it to the press tomorrow. As soon as the Senate gives us a vote on that, we'll start up the immigration dialogue," Richardson said calmly.

Roger's eyes shifted sideways, as if not sure he'd heard correctly.

"I've been thinking it over, Roger, and I decided it's a good idea. It might take twenty years to do it, but it's a good idea. Emma's working on a major rewrite. I want to pare it down to the economic impact and how interdependent we already are, with the foreign policy impact as an added benefit. In general, we need to control the tempo more, set a new tone. I'm going to be talking more about cooperation and showing the

American people that we're going to be putting out bold initiatives. We need a positive vote on the Hill first though, to get some damn momentum going."

"Yes sir, Mr. President. I'd like to get that damn momentum going too," he said, sounding determined.

Richardson turned to the Joint Chiefs. "General, how many troops are coming home this week?"

...

Roger walked at breakneck pace down the hall with Senator Frisch.

"It may not hit the news until tonight, but we've got huge levels of public outcry against the opposing Senators. The line-item is definitely coming back, most likely without the foreign earnings tax. We're gonna have to break them down and do one at a time,"

"What do you think of a bill swapping the death tax for the foreign earnings tax in one go?" Roger suggested, practically out of breath.

"That could be a good strategy. I'll see what Obama says about that. But let's get that veto first!"

...

A week after signing part of a piecemeal line-item veto into law, the President gave an immigration speech in primetime. Roger's arms rested on stacks of policy and his Adam's apple felt like a whole pear stuck in his throat. Watching the televised speech from his West Wing office, he momentarily felt a surreal sense of infinite power, as when realizing in a dream that one can fly by simply stepping off from the ground. He watched in amazement as the President of the United States laid out a long-term path to Mexican statehood, read a list of the economic and cultural benefits of doing so, and promised, "as our troops come home from the Middle East, to gradually replace American militarism with a new spirit of global cooperation, not just with words, but with actions. Our nearest neighbors, and our allies around the world, will once again enjoy a firm friendship with the United States based on mutual respect, and our great democracy will again be hailed by all, as an example to the world. Thank you, good night, and God bless America."

"He's really going to end the wars," Roger mumbled out loud in his darkened office, his parted lips moving only slightly while the colors from the television flickered across his face. The sound of the President invoking the word *"militarism"* rang through his head, bouncing from one side of his brain to the other, at varying volumes. It was this word, the barbaric images it brought to mind, uttered probably for the first time by a President directly to the American people, that convinced him that Richardson was intent on defusing all the ongoing wars and bringing us peace. The UN Ambassador, the lifetime diplomat - he realized suddenly, that Bill Richardson's legacy was going to be to make America a nation of peace and freedom for at least a generation. Roger saw clearly now, that he did indeed belong to this White House. He was not just working with one of the good guys among politicians. Here was one of the few people on Earth actually capable of pulling the whole globe back from the precipice of a third World War, and as President, he was in a position to do so. Roger had always known Bill was a great guy and one of the few honest politicians he'd ever met, which is why he'd felt comfortable joining his ticket, but now he didn't see him just as the kind of man he could work with to try and get some of his reforms enacted. He didn't even see Bill as a Democrat anymore. He only thought of him as the man who would create a real and lasting peace.

...

That same week, Roger Adams was on Meet the Press to discuss the President's plan to bring 80% of American troops home from the Middle East within six months. Republican Senator Lindsey Graham sat next to him.

Senator Lindsey Graham: "The Middle East is a very dangerous part of the world. If we pull out *all* of our troops now, we could see the whole region fall under Iranian influence. Look, we've already pulled out of Pakistan, and we're still seeing instability and violence there. Turning and running the other way is not the answer. We have got to stick it out, or we're just going to have greater problems down the road."

VP Roger Adams (speaking directly to the host): "We've been *sticking our feet in it* for more than a decade, and the violence is spreading, not being contained. Tim, I am convinced that most Americans realize the gravity of the situation we face today. We have lived with wars for too long. And I can tell you that these wars are growing larger, more difficult and more intertwined. There is real disaster brewing in the Middle East, and in a disaster of this magnitude, I assure you, making more threats and dropping more bombs will not bring us any closer to peace, nor victory of any kind. Bringing our troops home is an important first step, but most of all, in Bill Richardson, we have a President who will actively seek out peace and cooperation, a President willing to be the one who raises a hand to halt the fighting and the devastation, a President strong enough to rescue us from mutual destruction."

Senator Lindsey Graham: "With all due respect, our presence is not the cause of the violence in the region, Mr. Vice President. On the contrary, we're the only ones who have been able to hold it together this long."

VP Roger Adams: "Hold it together? I absolutely disagree. How can you call giving guns to everybody, 'holding it together?' Look, in Iraq, we started with an easy military defeat of the guy the CIA installed to hold the place together the last time, and then we removed the government entirely. As that nation slowly slid into chaos, we gave weapons and our support to one faction, and then the next, and then the next, practically begging them to start a civil war. In the end, we chose to pay many of the militias off to join a tightly-controlled centralized Sunni government, the same faction that Saddam came from, and so what I want to know is, what is so different in Iraq today, compared to where it was at the end of World War II? - same political situation, but a lot more lives lost, billions of American taxpayer dollars spent, and a lot more rebuilding to do. We haven't even accomplished anything in the 13 years we've been there. If anything, we're going backwards. American governments have tried to democratize foreign nations for the last century, and only very rarely have they succeeded. In most cases, we gave up on democracy and supported dictators who the CIA deemed effective. You may point to elections as a symbol of democracy, but a symbol amounts to far less than a free democratic republic. We staged elections in Iraq just as their civil war was breaking out, and eventually we supported a new Sunni dictator. Now who would call that democracy in action?

Any schoolchild can tell you that violence leads to more violence. But Martin Luther King, Jr. put it more eloquently when he said, '...violence multiplies violence, and toughness multiplies toughness in a descending spiral of destruction.... The chain reaction of evil — hate begetting hate, wars producing more wars — must be broken, or we shall be plunged into the dark abyss of annihilation.' This is what the American people are facing today – a spiral of more and more wars."

Senator Lindsey Graham: "Martin Luther King, Jr. was talking about Vietnam."

VP Roger Adams: "He was talking about peace."

Tim Russert: "We have to go to commercial. We'll be right back."

...

Tim Russert: "The President laid out a shockingly radical proposal this week for Mexican statehood. This has brought immigration screaming back to the front pages in a way I haven't seen in years! One of the other networks has even said this is Mexico's plan to finally take us over and the Mexican President Richardson should be hanged as a foreign invader!"

Senator Lindsey Graham: "This is why we have a Congress, Tim - so the White House can't just go and enact dangerous plans like this one without some oversight. We don't want to bring all these criminal gangs and drug runners into our country as legal citizens! It's just crazy. We have a good relationship with Mexico, but let's let the Mexican government deal with the rampant poverty and corruption in their country and we'll just continue to keep a good watch on the border."

VP Roger Adams: "We do have a good relationship with Mexico, and we share a long history together too. For the last few decades, we've also have been building our economy, and our houses, on the backs of cheap Mexican laborers, and then we deport them, and that's not right. It's time to think about a more equitable relationship with our hardworking neighbors.

Mexico's gangs and drug runners came to America a long time ago. Welcome to the 21st century, Senator. If we had jurisdiction, we might finally be able to reach them at their bases of operations, unhindered by Mexican corruption. Concerning poverty, some remains, that's true, but we're also talking about an economy that's now larger than California's. If Mexico does become our 51st state, it will have the largest economy of any state in the nation. Maybe Mexico should be worried about carrying South Carolina's slumping economy, Senator."

Senator Lindsey Graham: "South Carolina is a strong

state sir, with a large immigrant population, but Mexican laborers have been coming across the border illegally for decades. That's a felony - millions of felonies. And you want to grant amnesty to the entire nation, to come and take the rest of the American jobs that they don't have yet? It's just incredibly bad thinking."

VP Roger Adams: "You might just see a lot of Mexicans return home, if they have the same great opportunities there, in a new American state. Don't you think these people would like to see their families again? And millions of Mexicans could not have possibly come to America and built lives here, if American businesses had not needed those workers and employed those workers. If American businesses had complied with the law and not hired any illegal workers, then no illegal workers would have had an opportunity to come to America in the first place. They came for the jobs. Talk about bad thinking! How can you look at millions of people who risked their lives and worked for pennies on the dollar to provide food and shelter for the families and then call them criminals? The criminals are the businesses that hired illegal workers and paid them illegally low wages. Why don't you go after those thousands of American businesses, if the labor at the heart of the American economy is so criminal, Senator? You can't because they vote for you. Unfortunately, it's easier to put the blame on foreigners who don't vote."

The lights came down and the microphones came off. Roger thanked the host and jumped off the stage. Senator Graham dashed toward the doorway after him. "Mr. Vice President," he called out as six-foot-two-plus Secret Service agents closed a circle around Adams, making him nearly invisible.

"We just had our discussion, Senator," Roger called over his shoulder, not even turning to face Graham. "Anything I have to say to you, I'll say it in public."

Graham fumed. Roger ignored the grumbling he heard behind him and walked with his seven agents out the door to a waiting limo. When the door swung open, the sunlight swooshed in directly onto Lenka's long, tan legs and Roger nearly swooned as he put his head down to step in and was greeted by his wife's glamorous smile.

"How was it?" she asked, leaning back lazily in the plush limo seat.

"Everything you'd expect," Roger said hastily, trying to put behind him the unpleasant face-off with Senator

Graham. "So what do you think about our first Rose Garden today, honey?"

"I'm a little nervous. What are we supposed to do? Just smile the whole time?"

"Didn't you get briefed yet?" Roger asked urgently.

She sat upright. "No. Do I need a briefing? Is it that complicated?" Lenka asked, now becoming really concerned.

As genuine doubt leaked from her confident facade, Roger began to snicker, and Lenka's expression quickly moved from worried to playfully disgruntled. "Don't do that!" she said loudly, accentuated with a slap across the shoulder, which drew a craned neck from the Secret Service.

"I'll brief you, honey," Roger said, still trying to suppress laughter.

"Not tonight you won't," she stated coldly.

"No seriously. Listen. Bill comes back from his Middle East trip at noon. We're at the Rose Garden by 4:45 and at five o'clock we step outside to greet the Ukrainian President and her husband. They speak English, but translators will be there too. Yulia Timoshenko is very sweet; I know you'll like her."

"When did you meet the President of Ukraine already?"

"She used to run the gas business in Ukraine. I talked to

her several times on the phone, er, she talked to me - about how much I *didn't* want to sell turbines to any of Ukraine's monopoly clients." Roger looked at her sideways and then broke the stony silence with his hands out defensively, "OK, I know - she's cute. But don't get jealous," he implored her snidely. "She's a foreign head of state, alright?"

"Ukraine is run by privatization oligarchs too? I thought Timoshenko was one of the reformers in the revolution," Lenka asked inquisitively, slyly pretending she didn't even hear Roger's defense of allegations unmade.

"Ukraine's experiences were very similar to Russia's before the revolution. No one got into politics without being in gas or oil first. Of course, you know they had trouble forming a stable coalition government until 2010. It was so chaotic; the EU didn't even want to touch accession talks until two years ago."

"So what's the occasion today? Just that she won re-election?" Lenka asked.

"We're congratulating their country on another successful democratic election and encouraging movement toward the West. And privately, we're congratulating Yulia on personally being a stabilizing force in the region through the years."

"OK, and what's Yulia's husband's name?"

"Oleksandr. Like Alexander, but OLEK-sandr," he said slowly. "I imagine he might be pissed if we call him Alexander. He's a bit stodgy, from what I'm told."

"So I won't tell him any of my dirty jokes?" Lenka teased.

"No you won't, dear," Roger said dryly, the commanding voice, which he never used with her, causing Lenka to giggle.

...

Yulia was *devastatingly* sweet in person, more so than Roger had let on, Lenka thought to herself while the six of them - the Presidents, their spouses, and Roger and Lenka, chatted frankly in the Oval Office. The Ukrainian President wore a stark, shimmering dark blue dress and her trademark crown-of-braids hairstyle. Lenka admired Yulia within two minutes of kissing her on the cheek and struggled to fight off the temptation to imagine that a kiss on the cheek could slide toward the mouth, their long thin arms suddenly but smoothly wrapping around each other's tightly belted waistlines.

Richardson was having no luck explaining to Timoshenko the benefits of softening her rhetoric against the Russian President, Dmitry Medvedev. Yulia pressed Bill's hand between hers firmly and declared to him that Russia was not the only country in need of a stronger self-image. "For the health of our nation," she explained, "we must boast of our nation's accomplishments from time to time, and we must have something on which to boast." He glanced down as she clasped his hand and said to her knowingly, "I understand." Roger had convinced Oleksandr to recount some of the adventures from his two years in hiding, and he was obviously riveted by the man who was not nearly so stodgy as had been rumored. He leaned over slightly in order to listen to both Timoshenkos simultaneously. Since coming to Washington, he had developed the ability to listen to one conversation while eavesdropping on another. Although he wasn't expert at it yet, he did notice an awkward silence from Richardson after Yulia stated flatly, "The American people, like most people, are actually totally willing to give blood for oil, Mr. President. They just get very pissed off when they don't end up getting any oil."

The group gathered at the door to the Rose Garden and when Oleksandr concluded the story of his taxi chase through the suburbs of Vienna, Richardson asked cheerfully, "Everybody ready?" And they stepped into the sunny afternoon garden together.

The Rose Garden was filled with reporters, including several Ukrainians. Richardson spoke for less than a minute, offering his congratulations on a peaceful election and thanking Timoshenko for her efforts toward democracy and describing her leadership as, "good for the people of Ukraine."

Just as soon as Timoshenko stepped forward and said with a big smile, "Thank you, Mr. President," an enormous BOOM shook the sky and everyone jumped. "Was that a sonic boom?" Richardson asked immediately with a nervous laugh. But as he spoke, large flaming chunks of plastic and fiberglass began raining down, and the Secret Service swarmed the leaders. Several agents began shouting as loud as they could, "INCOMING! Everybody GET DOWN! TAKE COVER!" Six agents jumped on the President and within seconds, ran into the Oval Office. Three agents pulled Lenka into the bushes under the nearest tree, and she disappeared from view, buried under a tent of black suits. Roger stretched himself in her direction in vain, for he was fighting six agents himself, who were literally carrying him into the West Wing by his arms and legs.

"LENKAAAA!!" he screamed, with an absolute viciousness he did not even recognize from himself.

"LENKAAAA!!" he howled helplessly, over and over again. He didn't even feel himself screaming until they were back inside the building. Just a few seconds had passed, but seconds that felt like days. "Get me back to my wife, NOW!" he ordered, fully red in the face.

"STATUS on Chicken!" the agent called through the mess of yelling. Roger could hear the frantic shouting of ten different voices on the agent's earpiece now, all overlapping. There was shouting everywhere, an impenetrable wall of noise. "EAGLE is in the NEST. EAGLE IN the NEST! STATUS on Chicken! CHICKEN HAWK in the NEST! ... PUMA COVERED in the FIELD. Still IN THE FIELD... Request STATUS on Chicken! I NEED a 20 on CHICKEN!"

"Take me to Lenka! GET ME THERE NOW!" Roger screamed, the desperation in his voice echoing off the walls of the hallway in his own ears.

And then a huge ball of flame tore right through the ceiling and the top of the wall with an ear-splitting screeching sound, and another piece right behind it, landing in two huge, nearly simultaneous crashes, and buffets of black smoke poured from the Oval Office. Two of Roger's Secret Service agents dashed down the short hallway and into the Oval Office, but the President had already been moved to the basement. Four agents still held Roger where he was, halfway down the hall between the Oval Office and the Rose Garden.

"Our primary obligation is to your safety... and hers. We'll have to wait here, sir. Please," the agent begged as professionally as he could of the Vice President, feeling the stress of disobeying an order.

"You saved me, Jonathon. I'm extremely grateful," Roger said angrily through clenched teeth, and then yelled again in total, uncontrolled rage, "NOW LET ME FIND MY GODDAMN WIFE!"

Through Roger's screaming, the earpiece still screamed, "PUMA IN the NEST!" And then, "CHICKEN MOVING TO the NEST! CHICKEN ON THE MOVE!"

"We go to meet them now, or you're all going to SIBERIA! That's a PROMISE," Roger barked.

"Yes sir," he relented, with the news that Lenka was on her way in. "Let's move," the agent said. The four men still holding him down let go of Roger and the whole group sprinted back toward the Rose Garden. At the door, which was white, but now with a black-ringed hole the size of a baseball burned into it, they ran straight into four agents, who were carrying Lenka by the arms, seemingly also against her will as she floated on the sea of agents. Twigs stuck to Lenka's head scratched Roger's head as she plunged into his arms from those of the Secret Service. Lenka's whole body quivered and Roger felt tears dripping down his cheeks. He struggled to whisper, his voice shaking, "Are you OK?"

"Yeah," she squeaked. "Just scared...." Roger pulled up the short sleeve of her dress and put his lips to her bare shoulder.

"...and filthy," she added, briefly shaking a crying laughter from the tension.

Only now did Roger look up through the window, still holding Lenka tightly and lifting her up on her toes, to see the grasses of the Rose Garden all black, and a small fire burning in one corner. "What the fuck is happening?" he asked out loud, his mind slowly clearing from the hyperfocus on Lenka and his sense of reality returning to him. "Steven?"

"We don't know yet sir. But from what I saw, I'd say something exploded in the sky and then fell on us, probably an aircraft. Sir, the President is safely downstairs. We need to take you to a bunker ASAP."

"What about the Ukrainian President?" Roger asked,

suddenly fearing a serious diplomatic incident.

"The entire Ukrainian team are downstairs with the President."

"Downstairs?!" Roger asked urgently. "In which room?"

"Nothing too sensitive, Mr. Vice President. They're with the President and 18 of our men. They are secured. Please, let's go to one of the bunkers, now, Mr. Vice President."

"OK." Roger eased his grip on Lenka and looked down into her watery eyes. "Are you OK to head out to a bunker, honey?" he asked gently.

"Yeah. I'm OK," she said bravely.

"Are we sure there's nothing else coming at us up there, Steven?"

"The Air Force just gave us an all clear, sir. And we'll be taking the Arlington tunnel just to be sure."

"Is there a phone in the tunnel?"

"Yes sir."

"Good. Let's go."

...

"Mr. President."

"Roger, Steven tells me you and Lenka are OK?"

"We're a little scared, Mr. President. How are you?"

"I got a chunk of something below the knee, nothing serious," Richardson said, sounding totally calm. "Our guests are frazzled, making a lot of phone calls home, but no serious injuries. It sounds like everyone got out with just a few scrapes. Listen, Roger, the Air Force shot down a small plane which they now believe was packed with explosives."

"They shot it down?"

"They shot after it turned toward us at the last minute. They didn't have much time, obviously, but if the plane had exploded in the garden instead of in the air, we'd be picking up dead journalists right now, maybe dead Presidents. Now listen to me, Roger. Don't assume the Russians did this. This isn't their style."

"Are you sure, Bill?"

"I'll meet you at your UDL in 90 minutes and we'll talk."

"Yes sir." Roger forced himself to return to a normal manner of speech, to restore some professional demeanor. "Thank you, Mr. President."

...

"Hi Roger. Hi Lenka." The President spoke with confidence in his voice, as if it was just another stressful day and walked into the plain white office of the Vice

President's UDL, the UnDisclosed Location buried several stories below the Army and Navy Country Club just across the Virginia border. The air tasted stale like chemicals, typical for installations so deep underground, due to the extensive air filtration systems.

"Mr. President," they said together.

"Lenka, you look rattled. Are you alright?" Bill asked warmly and squeezed her arm. Her cheeks were still red.

"I am rattled. But I'll be alright. I just need some time."

"That's understandable," Bill said. "Roger, how are you doing?"

"I'll be OK, Bill. I admit though, I lost it when the agents separated me from Lenka. I think I re-assigned some of my guys to Siberia during the chaos."

"I'll get them re-assigned back to the White House, don't worry," Bill said without laughing. "Now listen, the media will be blaming Russia for this, probably within the hour."

"Isn't that a possibility?" Roger asked.

"I don't think so. They're not that sloppy and they're not that aggressive. Right now, I think it looks more like a lone nut scenario. Besides, the Russians are ten years into the Condor. They don't want to start all that over again."

"The Condor?" Roger asked.

"You haven't been briefed on the Condor Statute yet?"

"I'm afraid I haven't. What's the Condor Statute?"

"The Condor Statute is longstanding White House policy - unwritten, but well understood by heads of state throughout the world. Any foreign government linked to an assassination attempt against an American President or any other high-ranking member of the federal government is punished with a minimum of 20 years without normalized relations with the White House. A sort of 'separation from God,' if you will."

Lenka and Roger both listened intently.

"Russia's more than halfway through theirs."

The small room was silent. Roger zoned out as he thought back to the early 2000s, and then it came to him.

"Are you saying the FSB threw the grenade at George W. in Tblisi?"

"Absolutely. You see, here's the thing about the Condor. Just like any political tool, it can backfire or be used by the opponent in a clever new way. In this case, we're talking about Vladimir Putin, former KGB agent and a very shrewd Russian. Do you know Putin's grandfather was personal chef to both Lenin and Stalin? He's not your average egotistical politician. He grew up in the inner circle of the Soviet party system. He *believes* in a greater Russia, like some kind of Manifest Destiny."

"So how did he manipulate the Condor?" asked Lenka, mildly surprising Roger with how intrigued she was.

"The KGB always made use of mafia methods. Primarily, they believed, and Putin still believes, that using a brutal method once sets an example to everyone else. They considered it more efficient, and some say more humane, than chipping away at a larger group with small punishments on everyone. Of course, we call that ruling by fear. But the grenade in Tblisi was a message. It was to tell us that they felt so strongly about keeping Georgia and the other former Soviet states on their borders within their sphere, that they were so critical to Russia's future and domestic stability in their view, that they were willing to take a Condor. You have to understand, that there's so much big talk in international diplomacy, that heads of state rarely take anything other leaders say seriously. They all draw their own conclusions about what other nations are really thinking, how far they're really willing to go, what weapons they're really building. Often, the only way to show you're serious is to actually take action. Of course, the poor Armenian kid they hired had no idea they'd given him a deactivated grenade. He thought he was creating a diversion for a team of FSB snipers to assassinate two Presidents - George W. and Saakashvili. We knew he'd had some training when he shot up the special forces that came to arrest him and snuck off into the woods. They only caught up to him later because he was wounded. Cheney was on the phone to Putin the next day saying the CIA had the Armenian kid linked to the FSB, and Putin basically said, 'Make of that what you will.' The fact that the old Soviet grenade wasn't live is a pretty basic indicator anyway, that someone's sending a message. No one accidentally mixes up their live grenades with their empty antiques. The CIA also believes the FSB set the Armenian free soon after the pro-Moscow coup in Georgia in 2010."

"Why are the Russians so threatened by those little countries around their borders?" Lenka mused.

"They're not threatened by them," Bill explained, "just as we're not scared of Haiti. But these are not just little states around their borders. Some of these struggling new nations were once among the most important and prosperous regions of the Soviet Empire. Remember when I said Putin's grandfather was Stalin's chef? Stalin was from Georgia. So they don't see those little states the way we see Haiti, it's more like if we lost New Hampshire, Massachusetts and Connecticut. We wouldn't just say, 'OK, see you later,' would we? Putin takes a longer view, and he considers it crucial to their national identity."

"No, I see what you're saying," Lenka said, feeling like an eighth-grader finally connecting to a history lesson. "And Putin is still in charge behind the scenes, even now?"

"Absolutely. He extended the term of office to six years precisely so he could hide behind his loyal soldier Medvedev for a minimum of twelve years," Bill explained. "He'll probably be kicking around in the halls of the Kremlin until he dies or goes senile." Bill thought for a second and then added, "Let's hope he doesn't go senile."

"So that's why we have all those missiles aimed at Russia again, and it also explains why Cheney was so hell-bent on taking down Saddam Hussein," Roger realized. "After the attempt on Bush Sr. in 1993, we were forbidden to negotiate with Iraq on anything until 2013."

"Yes, but that was another calculated risk. Saddam didn't think the U.S. would have the guts or the backing to really go after him. And for many years, we didn't. We contained him. Of course, Saddam didn't see 9/11 coming and even after 9/11, he never did believe the

U.S. could gather enough support to invade. But it's true, that was one of the reasons Cheney was so aggressive on regime change in Iraq - it wasn't just the embarrassment of supporting Saddam for so long, it was that Saddam had purposely removed any chance of dealing with him with the blatant assassination attempt, while other countries from France to China to Russia were taking full advantage for years, entrenching themselves in Middle East oil, and we were losing out on account of our own policies.

Everyone knew Saddam was using U.S. support for his own purposes from the beginning. What dictator wants to be a colonial puppet all their life? He wanted Iraq and its oil to himself, and he thought he'd cut off the U.S. for 20 years by taking a Condor as soon as a Democrat came into the White House. And when they did go in, they never expected Saddam to be that tough or that bold. They only saw his crippled military power and figured he had nothing to bluff with. Because the entire population never successfully rose up against Saddam, Cheney and his team truly did believe the Iraqi people were sedate enough to accept any government handed to them, especially if it was less oppressive than Saddam's. Of course, they didn't foresee Al Qaeda's depth and breadth either. They really thought they'd simply disbanded a small group of criminals in Afghanistan and that job was done."

"How could they think that?" Roger asked in all seriousness.

"Because bin Laden's jobs had been pretty small in the years before that, and they figured it was the same kind of isolated, regional band of disorganized criminals you get with 99% of these terrorist groups. They never saw the strength of the anti-Western message being taken up, and the internet's ability to spread their message, until it was too late, of course. And the ability of Al Qaeda to ignite other conflicts from the outside didn't develop until after two years in Iraq. The irony is that in their public comments, Cheney's team constantly tried to link Al Qaeda and Iraq. But there never was any link until we created it."

"Bill, how many times has the Condor Statute gone into effect?"

"There's two others that I know of. There's Cuba - that's a different case entirely of course, because they succeeded in their attempt."

"So that puts them on our regime change list forever," Roger supposed.

"Yes sir. Exactly."

"And Oswald was, what, picked up by Cuban agents

after Moscow rejected him?"

"Moscow regularly kept Castro's team informed about potential spying activities in the U.S., generally throwing them the bones from the table to let Castro pick them clean. After Castro lost his secret missiles, being that Moscow was the island's only lifeline, he was desperate to prove his worth to his Soviet masters. And in addition, Kennedy was trying to overthrow Castro from his first day in office. It was kill or be killed for Castro. Bobby Kennedy, of course, presented an even greater threat to Castro, as he would surely have used the Presidency to follow the same policy, plus seek revenge for the death of his brother. Incidentally, no one knows who the second shooter was, but he was on the grassy knoll."

"Wow," Lenka blurted. Richardson grinned.

"You said there were *two* others, Bill," Roger reminded.

"Three weeks after China entered the Korean War," he continued professorially, "there was a multiple-shooter ambush at Truman's residence. The White House police took out the assassins and subsequent FBI investigations found that the PRC had been secretly funding the Puerto Rican Nationalists, which is the group that the assassins were connected with.

As soon as the twenty years were up, Nixon started making connections in China, and by '72, he was shaking Chairman Mao's hand and grinning for the cameras more comfortably than he had with Elvis. The American people may have been surprised because his reputation was so aggressively anti-communist, but he'd been itching to get in there for years. He probably even built up the rep in part so he'd have the credibility to go there. Nixon secretly admired the ability of the Chinese system to keep a billion people pretty well squelched and under control, and he couldn't wait to open the Chinese market to American business - but he had to, because of the Condor Statute.

Now this was a case where the Chinese considered us enemies after World War II anyway. They didn't give a damn about the Condor Statute. They thought Truman was about to nuke them after we marched up North Korea to the Chinese border. In fact, it could very possibly have been the right decision for them, because General MacArthur has since been widely quoted as saying we should actually - and I'm quoting - nuke China, eastern Russia, and everything else. He was later fired for his overly aggressive stance, but I'm not convinced Truman didn't consider it for a time. He was always buried under criticism for losing China and not standing up to Stalin. Truman also definitely believed at the beginning that Korea could lead to World War III. The assassination attempt may have actually changed his mind."

"Unbelievable," Lenka cooed.

"But Truman didn't devise the Condor Statute, did he? It must go back further."

"Indeed it does, Roger. It goes all the way back to Old Hickory - Andrew Jackson," Bill said slowly, the mysteries of the White House's long secret history sending a shiver through both Lenka and Roger.

"And how long has this creepy underground bunker been here?" Lenka inquired softly, looking around at the musty, bare walls.

"About 3 years," Bill answered non-chalantly, leaning back on the desk, arms crossed and holding his elbows.

"Oh," Lenka muttered, looking a little confused.

"Jackson had seen plenty of war," the President continued, "and had especially learned the brutality of the Europeans - the British and the French in particular. France had more than one bloody revolution in Jackson's lifetime. He was a pretty nasty General in combat himself, responsible for the massacre of thousands of

Indians and the winner of more than a hundred duels. He was not the economic sanctions guru that Jefferson was. One day, a man walked up to Jackson at the Capitol and fired two pistols at him. If they hadn't both misfired, he likely would have been killed."

"Who was the assassin?" Lenka asked.

"He was just some poor soul who it turns out had been diagnosed with schizophrenia," Bill answered. "He shouted something at Jackson about not making him King of England. Now this particular guy was not a foreign threat, but the President recognized that it would be just that easy for the British, who had lost New Orleans and their top General to him and knew well that he despised them, or the Spanish, from whom he'd seized Florida by might, to weaken America's position or change American foreign policy by sending a single man to walk up and shoot him. Seeing the need to discourage foreign nations from attempting to influence America through assassinations, he unofficially enacted the Condor Statute by informing his cabinet and sending messages to the leaders of Europe, and it's been passed down from President to President ever since. Although assassinations aren't as easy as walking up the Capitol steps with a pistol anymore, the statute is obviously more useful today than it's ever been in protecting

American policy and the American President."

The phone rang once and the President reached across the desk and picked it up and said, "Richardson." After a few seconds, he switched on the speaker and put down the receiver.

"...ding to Director Kim's information so far, it looks like the pilot was acting alone, a white male, age 43, ex-Army Ranger from Midland, Texas named Randall Howe, no family. The plane was an old Skyraider out of Manassas. He flew under radar for about eight minutes, popped up due north, several miles from Washington, until as you know, he swerved east on a direct line for the White House, which is when we knew he wasn't a lost pleasure pilot. There's more. FBI found a DVD manifesto at his residence - a lot of vitriol against Mexican immigrants. Director Kim will be here in half an hour to show you a copy. Also, Prime Minister Balls has scheduled another call for eleven o'clock tonight." Bill picked up the phone and said, "Thank you, Kathy. I'll be there in twenty minutes."

"You were right, Mr. President," Lenka said. "It wasn't the Russians."

"I have a feeling this'll be worse than anything Putin

ever does," Bill said pessimistically and then stood up to leave.

Roger stood up as Richardson approached the door. "Mr. President, I'd like to go home and spend some time with Lenka for a few days, if you don't need me right now."

Bill looked at Roger's face and then Lenka's. They both looked stressed and shaky. "Come back on Monday," he said warmly. "Take care, you two," he added and walked out the door smiling in admiration of their obviously close relationship.

"Thank you, Mr. President," Roger said.

"Thank you, Mr. President," Lenka echoed, almost forgetting to say it.

"We can go home?" Lenka asked weirdly, sounding worried.

"You heard the briefing, honey. He was acting alone, and the President and the White House were most likely the only targets. Remember, not everyone knows I wrote the statehood speech. The President was the one who delivered it. Let's go home and put our toes in the ocean sand for a few days, huh?"

"You think we can relax after today?"

"We have to try," Roger said, laughing slightly at the thought of never relaxing again for the rest of his life.

"You're right, Roger. I love it when you're wise," she said, cracking a small smile. "Do I get a rubdown tonight?"

"Yeah, for starters...," he said on the rim of her ear, then put his arms around her for a quick romantic kiss on her soft mouth on their way out of the bunker.

Chapter 12
The Israel Strategy

At the last minute, Roger stepped out of his office and caught the President coming crisply down the hall on his way out of the White House. Richardson walked quickly, encircled by his Secret Service agents, and he appeared distracted, with his head down as he sifted through a few papers. "Mr. President," Roger called out, "Have a good trip."

"Thank you, Roger," he said, lifting his head just in time to see the yellow notepad paper that Roger held out toward him, folded in half. He opened it, read it, and closed it without slowing his step. Scribbled in pencil, the note read, "Equalize aid $$ to Israel and Pal.??" With the double question marks, Roger signaled that this was a new thought, a brainstorm for consideration, rather than a firm endorsement. Richardson decided before even settling into his seat in the Presidential limo, that correcting the imbalance in foreign aid to Israel and Palestine would be one of the strongest symbols he could present to the world to prove he was serious about peace, and he decided to do it.

President Richardson allowed his domestic policy decisions to filter down through the networks of capable people, whom he'd trusted enough to have in the White House for just such a purpose. But he remained a leading hands-on diplomat on the international stage, and he met with the Israeli and Palestinian leaders every week, usually over secure videonets, but also very often in person. He took a four or five day trip to the region nearly every other month. He included quick stopovers in Iraq and Afghanistan as well, but only long enough to make his presence felt. His mission was to solve the Arab-Israeli problems.

Richardson's first unofficial summit was hosted by King Abdullah II in Amman, Jordan. He was to sit down for informal discussions with Prime Minister of Israel Avigdor Lieberman, Prime Minister of the Palestinian Territories Ismail Haniyah and British PM Ed Balls, who had worked nearly his whole career with Gordon Brown and had recently succeeded him at No. 10 Downing Street. UK newspapers were still ringing with moronic quasi-humorous headlines like, "England's Got Balls."

President Richardson began speaking as soon as

everyone had settled in their seats. "To begin with, gentlemen, I want everyone to understand clearly the American background on the larger picture, so we all understand the ground on which I stand. This will not be quite the same as your prior experiences with American-led negotiations.

American policymakers had come to view our mighty Cold War enemy, the Soviet Union, as our one great obstacle in every situation worldwide. Washington was filled with strategists who had been extraordinarily focused on the Soviet Empire for their entire careers, and to them, the removal of the Soviet Union from the fields of power seemed to leave an open frontier. Political academics and ideological writers could see little difference, on paper, between the removal of oppression from eastern Europe's peoples, and the potential removal of oppression from the peoples of the Middle East. They saw only a weakening of the forces they had opposed in all global conflicts, and momentum to plant democracies spreading eastward, from Prague to Kiev to Tblisi, on across to Kabul and Baghdad and Teheran. They saw only political equations, not clashes of cultures and resources. Because the threat of nuclear war with the Soviet Union had been the only deterrent to Israeli expansion of hostilities for decades, and because their professional perspectives had been limited to only these equations, they could no longer see any material obstacle to, nor any reason why, Israel, and the United States, should not simply conquer and administer these lands where in their view, a new vacuum of regional power provided instability which promised to be filled by a less agreeable entity, if not by our own. Although it may seem dim from your positions, gentlemen, it was clear to our academics, that save for enlightened American dominance and interest in the region, every government and people of the Middle East was highly vulnerable to a sweeping revolution of either Sunni or Shiite islamofascism, neither of which we wanted to see, for many reasons, including of course, restricted access to global markets, rising oil prices, and most of all, the rise of a new stalemated global conflict, on par with the U.S.-Soviet Cold War. As strange as it sounds, our people saw an opportunity, via limited military actions, to pre-empt and prevent a slightly different kind of chaos than the one we eventually created ourselves. They honestly believed that with that Soviet barrier removed, nothing stood between the people of the Middle East and their own democratic uprisings but their ruthless puppet governments. They calculated their equations, and convinced themselves, that as they removed governments one by one, the citizens would shake our hands with gratitude and immediately get to the business of happily establishing their healthy democracies and bustling free trade economies and building out their middle class suburbs with backyard swimming pools, because as Reagan said, that's all the *Russians* ever really wanted, and that must be what everyone truly desires. And although we claimed publicly that Al Qaeda was linked to Iraq, our policy-makers never dreamed that Al Qaeda was actually capable of making a dent in Iraq. They thought Al Qaeda could be scuttled like any local terror group. We never realized we were feeding a global anti-Western propaganda agenda until it was far too late to turn back. The fighting was supposed to be easy, and indeed it was at the start. But the people, as a whole, were expected to innately know what to do with their new opportunities, to spontaneously establish their own colonial-style governments for themselves, and this is where the academics were surprised.

Unfortunately, none of us can go back in time and make what has happened unhappen. Israelis and Palestinians are living side by side, and that will not be changed. We must come together and declare that we prefer peace, no matter what claims we have held in the past. In my personal opinion, the most dangerous path for everyone is the path of continued wars. We have proven, historically, that when Israel and her neighbors agree to make peace, peace can be made. Jordan, Egypt, Iraq - all these countries have made peace with Israel. When the people most harshly and directly affected by Israel's recent history, the 5 million refugees of the Palestinian territories, are able to make peace with Israel, the rest of the Arab world will join that peace, and the entire region will be free to prosper and grow, with whatever form of government each nation wishes.

Our goal then is peace, and I believe the way to peace begins with both sides acknowledging that the other must be allowed to live in peace. Israel must accept that there will be a viable, contiguous Palestinian state, and the Palestinians must accept that Israel cannot be made to disappear, and in turn, they also must accept their neighbors. Commitment to this peace must mean that when a skirmish occurs, the other side will not use it as political cover to instigate a new war. Commitment to this peace must mean that the Palestinian people will be free to govern themselves and their movements and their economy, just as the Israeli people are free to do. Commitment to this peace must mean that you speak to your people constructively about leaving the destruction of the past in the past."

PM Liberman: "I do not wish to interrupt your excellent speech, Mr. President, but the destruction is not only in the past. We are living under great threats to our existence right now."

President Richardson: "Now Prime Minister Liberman, I know you have spoken publicly for many years about the need to bomb Iran's nuclear facilities. I do hope you don't take your recent election victory as a mandate to make war against anyone, including Iran."

PM Liberman: "I am surprised that you would mention this here today, Mr. President." Richardson had purposely brought up the subject for the first time while Palestinian and other Arab diplomats were in the room. He knew the new Prime Minister would be both intimidated and insulted by the lack of warning.

President Richardson: "I intend to speak openly and clearly the same words to everyone, both publicly and privately. I am here to help everyone come to a peace agreement, Mr. Prime Minister, and I am serious about it."

PM Liberman: "We have good information that Iran has continued its nuclear weapons program, even without Ahmedinejad's threats. Just because Iran has gone quiet, doesn't mean the threat is reduced."

President Richardson: "Then the threat is balanced. Once a bomb is dropped, a threat becomes war, and that is what I am here to avoid."

PM Liberman: "War is sometimes unavoidable, Mr. President," Liberman stuttered uneasily, his eyes quickly searching the reactions of the others at the oak table.

President Richardson: "If you must have war, then I cannot stop you, Mr. Prime Minister, but I will make all assurances to the Iranian Supreme Council, along with every other government, that the United States will not be entering any more wars in the Middle East. We will not re-fuel anyone's airplanes, we will not sell any bombs, and we will no longer prop up unsustainable governments unsupported by their citizens."

PM Liberman: "Surely you will come to our aid when we

are attacked?!" the Prime Minister howled. "Will you stand here today and give every Arab nation a green light to destroy Israel?!" he asked, horrified by Richardson's suggestion.

President Richardson: "Mr. Prime Minister, you have your aggressive reputation, your well-trained military and your nuclear weapons. I consider these significant red lights for any nation wishing to attack Israel." The Israeli leader turned toward British PM Ed Balls in total astonishment.

PM Balls: "I've spoken at length to the President, and I do believe he means what he says," he advised in his calm British manner.

President Richardson: "This is what I mean when I say I have come here to create peace. The United States will not participate in making war under any circumstances. We have suffered enough from our mistakes in this region, and I believe every nation represented here today has suffered more than enough as well. I will say it again, to everyone. I am here to foster peace, and the United States will not participate in making war under any circumstances. If any nation here attacks Israel, know that she will likely unleash her fury unabated, and the United States will probably not have the power to reduce the enormity of that retaliation for anyone. Likewise, Israel, if you should attack Lebanon or Palestine or Iran or Syria, you will not receive American bombs nor troops nor airplanes, and they may very well unite to defeat you. I believe the British will also advise, publicly and privately, that should you make war, you bring war upon yourselves."

PM Balls: "Absolutely, Bill. I believe the unwavering support of the West has made the nations of this region to quick to take up arms. We can't have half the world dependent on the other half. You'll all have to realize the consequences of your own actions. We'll not absorb them from you any longer." Clearly, Richardson and Balls had discussed the strategy in advance.

PM Liberman: "A new Prime Minister and a freshly-elected President think they're going to change the world overnight, is that it? I have news for you, Bill. Anyone who's ever tampered with Israel in American politics has come down hard and come down fast. Just because you're a happy new President doesn't mean you'll be any different."

President Richardson: "Mr. Prime Minister, you can use all the political lobbies you wish. I will explain my position to my people and to the world in the same clear terms I have used here today. But I understand that the Israel lobby is powerful. You might stir up a lot of trouble and noise, that's true. You may even tarnish my reputation or prevent my re-election. But that's four years away yet, and I promise you that in these next four years, the United States will not be persuaded, pushed nor provoked into supporting any war between the nations represented here today. You can spew as much propaganda as you like, but even if the American Congress were to bow to your wishes, even if they were to make a declaration of war, they cannot deploy a single soldier or give a go to a single fighter jet without the word of one man, and that one man is me."

PM Liberman: "You expect me to just stand here and accept these grave threats to the nation of Israel?!" the ultra-hawk scowled at the Western leaders.

PM Balls: "Certainly not, Avi. We expect you to make peace with your neighbors, expand your economy and provide the opportunity for a better life for your children. That's what a nation is supposed to be about, and we are here to support you toward those goals."

President Richardson: "America has traditionally stood with the Israelis through all manner of horrors. I do not consider this unfailing loyalty wise nor reasonable. I am not on the Israeli side and I am not on the Palestinian side. My aim here is to create peace for both sides in equal measure."

The Palestinians could not quite believe their ears. All of them were thinking at this point, that perhaps it was some kind of rouse cooked up by the Americans and Israelis to destroy the talks before they begin.

PM Liberman: "You will regret this day, and very soon, Mr. President. You will not be allowed to abandon Israel."

President Richardson: "America will be an ally to Israel, and also to Palestine, and when we stop making war, we will all have the peace we have sought for sixty years. I believe that Prime Minister Haniyah and Hamas would prefer to govern their people than send them all to their deaths. Am I right, Prime Minister?"

PM Haniyah: "Yes, I agree. We fight because we are

occupied and oppressed. We will fight occupation and oppression until the end of time if we must, but of course, I would prefer our nation was not occupied and not oppressed. If we can end the ruin of our nation, we will not seek war again."

President Richardson: "Prime Minister Liberman, when you respect the democratic elections of the Palestinian people and remove the motivation for them to attack you, they will focus on rebuilding their nation and the lives of their people. Once the conditions of occupation are removed, they will have no reason to attack."

PM Liberman: "Palestinian people will never be content in Israel. We must be separated. Israel is a Jewish nation. We have no trust between our peoples."

President Richardson: "Israel is your nation, you can kick out anyone you please according to your internal laws. We'll consider that a domestic issue for the time being."

PM Haniyah: "I think it unwise to create more refugee groups. Where will those people go?"

President Richardson: "Let's not get too far ahead here. There are no new refugee groups. I don't want to start talking about hypothetical situations until we get some real results first."

PM Haniyah (agitated): "The Israeli Prime Minister has just promised to create a new group of Palestinian refugees. I do not consider this hypothetical."

President Richardson: "Please, Mr. Prime Minister, we need to focus on one thing at a time. Israel will not remove anyone from their territory immediately, correct Prime Minister?"

PM Liberman: "Not immediately, no."

President Richardson: "So let's work with the immediate situation first, agreed?"

PM Haniyah: "Agreed," he huffed reluctantly.

"Israel has nothing more to discuss here today," Liberman announced angrily, his eyes full of suspicion as he jumped up to leave.
"I have one more thing to tell you, Mr. Prime Minister,"

Richardson said quietly.

"You must tell me while I walk out," Liberman snapped as he headed toward the door.

"As a demonstration of our impartiality in the peace process, United States foreign aid to Israel will be set at one billion dollars for this year, and our Palestinian aid will be in the exact same amount."

Haniyah's jaw dropped open, unwittingly drawing Liberman's furious eyes. The Israeli Prime Minister looked as though he wanted to unleash a profane river of vitriol at the American President, but thought better of it, stepped through the door and slammed it as hard as he could, causing a monstrous thunderclap in the room, the solid oak walls seeming to shudder under the force, and the air pressure in the underground facility jumped palpably.

After watching Liberman walk out, Richardson turned back toward the table and sat pensively. Palestinian Prime Minister Haniyah lifted his head up high and looked across the table, down his nose into the President's eyes and spoke slowly and dramatically in Arabic, looking almost like a native American tribal chief speaking for generations of his people. Richardson felt that he was witnessing an important moment and his heart sped up. The translator waited for Haniyah to finish and then said, "My people will know today that there is a new American President, a man who is serious about peace."

"Thank you," Richardson said simply, and bowed his head slightly to show respect.

"I suppose today's meeting is over, since the Israeli delegation has departed," Jordan's King suggested.

"Yes. But I believe we have seen a great first step forward," Balls said triumphantly.

Haniyah nodded in agreement and stood up from his chair.

As they all got up to leave, King Abdullah put his hand on Richardson's shoulder and said, "Bill, this is the first progress we've seen since you were at the UN. We were close then. If you can stick with this plan and get Israel to pull back to the 67 borders, we will finally have a real peace."

"That's exactly what I want. And Americans have had enough. I think Israel's desperate political screaming in the U.S. might just backfire. If the American people know anything, it's the sound of desperation and the sound of asking for money. I think the hardest part of the whole process though, will be sharing Jerusalem and the holy sites. I'm gonna need your help on that, your majesty."

"We'll keep working on it. Thank you again, Mr. President. It's always nice to see you."

"Thank you. Always nice to see you too. We'll talk soon."

...

"How'd they react?" Roger inquired anxiously.

"About how you'd expect, from Liberman," Richardson said. "The others I would describe as happily stunned."

Roger smirked and Bill noticed. "Don't get too excited Roger. Wait 'til you see the backlash here at home. We'll be called everything from a dog's leftovers to Hitler's cousins."

Chapter 13

The Transparent Road to Prosperity

Brin came screaming into Roger's office just two hours after the President had returned from the Middle East, "How can you guys do this? How can you completely abandon Israel? You've just sent an invitation to Iran via global television to clear them off the map!"

Lenka looked up at Sergey from her seat near the door. "Oh hello, Lenka. I'm sorry, I didn't see you there," he said to her humbly. "Hi Sergey," she said with a bubbly wink. "Go ahead and scream at him. I've had my chance at him today," she grinned. Sergey wasn't sure what to say for a moment. Roger, sitting at his desk, looked like he hadn't slept at all, but he said to Sergey slowly, wearily, "Sergey, I know this is an emotional and personal issue for you, but listen, we have to level the field a little if we're going to make peace. Don't get confused here, Sergey. We all want what's best for the Israeli people. Bill and I believe the extreme imbalance of power is fundamentally perpetuating the violence. I know you want peace as much as anyone, Sergey, but fairness toward all the participants, true impartiality, will create the best chance for long-term peace. The entire Palestinian population has been suffocated for nearly a century, almost exterminated. Every time Israel presses on them harder, it only makes life worse for everybody."

"Roger, with all due respect, you and the President are making a fatal error in judgment. Israel is surrounded on all sides by forces supplied by Iran. It's an Islamic revolution, remember? You're not going to make them happy by saying, 'let's all share' like we're in kindergarten! You're only giving them the weakness they've been waiting for to overrun Israel, to join together and destroy Israel!" Tears began welling up in Sergey's eyes.

"Please, Sergey, I can see that you're upset, but have some faith in Bill's diplomatic experience. He's been involved with this for decades. Certainly you don't think he's going to oversee the destruction of Israel? Think it over for a while. Look, Hamas is in government. They've been elected three times. That's actually the best place for them because it's the only incentive for them to stop the violence. They're also the best organized and the most effective administrators in the territories. They entered government because they want to lead Palestine, not because they long to be Iran's puppets. When Palestine is given the opportunity to establish its own nation again and life finally becomes livable there again, Haniyah will not only want to maintain peace, his people will demand it from him. Under circumstances like that, when life is getting better for everyone, Iran won't be able to convince anyone to attack Israel for them."

"You're just hoping the people will all become happy faster than Iran can launch attacks. That's crazy! You're dooming Israel!"

"I'm sorry. I just disagree, Sergey. Long-term collective punishment of an entire people offers some short-term political gain, but it makes those punished feel dehumanized, angry and desperate. The Germans tried to teach us that with two world wars. Fascism doesn't just come out of nowhere, Sergey. It arises with popular support when a nation sees no other choice. There will always be a few mentally disturbed people, in every nation, who harbor the darkly grand ambitions of fascism. The catastrophes come when we create the untenable conditions that force a nation to call upon them as a last resort to save them from certain destruction."

Sergey stepped closer to Roger's desk and said in a voice low and full of doubt, "I've scheduled a meeting with the President for tomorrow afternoon. I was hoping you might come with me and ask him to moderate his position in some way at least."

"I won't," came Roger's simple reply, and Sergey walked away in pained silence.

...

There was similar outrage in the media :

No longer addicted to Middle East oil, U.S. sells out Israel to Iran

President invites Iran and Hamas to destroy Israel

U.S. and Israel: Friends No More

Richardson's Final Solution for the Middle East

...

The next night, Roger was writing away at his desk when he heard a beep and then another beep, and the beeping grew louder. He found a watch under a CIA briefing folder and remembered he'd set the alarm for 6pm. He stood up, turned off the desk lamp and rubbed his right eye, although a mechanical thought jumped like a bunny from the grass to the front of his mind as he did – "Don't rub your eyes." His eyes had become redder and unbearably itchy recently, and he knew that his own subconscious reflexes were partly to blame.

He had been so worn out when he woke up that morning, that he'd promised himself a relaxing early night with Lenka. Hence, the alarm. He opened the second desk drawer on the right hand side and dropped the watch into it from shoulder height. The pile of papers in the drawer cushioned its fall, but he didn't care if the old Casio timekeeper broke either. He never liked watches, and he never wore them on his wrist. Even from childhood, he'd always thought they seemed ridiculously unnatural, like a first primitive step toward turning people into robots. Now people were getting their digital car keys injected under their skin at the wrist. Roger just couldn't imagine why anyone would want to do that (nor how to go about borrowing the car).

After the five minute drive up Massachusetts Avenue to the Vice Presidential residence, Roger stepped out of the limo to find Lenka sitting on the quaint porch of the old Queen Anne home. She stood up, smiling.

"Congratulations on taking a half day off, tiger," she beamed.

"Thanks," he replied, half sarcastic, half serious.

"Sit down. Let me rub your shoulders a little bit."

Lenka's neck rub was so relaxing and so overdue, Roger nearly fell asleep. He started, blinked and then stood up.

"I'm going to cook you some dinner, honey," he offered, "What do you want? Italian?"

"Ooohhh..." she said, turning to look him seductively in the eyes as he followed her into the house. "I'll have the veal scaloppini with your famous apple green beans and,"

"Whoa. This isn't Olive Garden missy," he said firmly and turned her around, grabbing her by both arms. He pulled her body up against his. "You give me a genre. But I'm cooking up the menu here," Roger said, asserting himself in the kitchen as he liked to do.

"Well then," Lenka said, precociously taken aback and releasing herself from his grip just as it seemed they would kiss. "Italian," she said, waving her nose in the air.

"Fine. Italian. Hmmm," Roger said, pursing his lips in melodramatic contemplation as the taste of the dish Lenka had requested forced its way into his taste bud imagination. Hoping he'd tick her off a little, Roger pretended it was his own idea. "I think we'll go with a succulent veal scaloppini accentuated by a sweet apple green bean concoction..."

"Oh you think you're dashing, don't you, Roger?" Lenka said viciously, tilting her head down and squinting at him disdainfully.

"You wouldn't love me if I didn't try to be," he countered.

Lenka lifted her head and giggled sweetly. Roger leaned against the counter and watched her admiringly. Then they chopped and sautéed and had a beautiful dinner together. They were both firm believers in the axiom that everything tastes better when you make it yourself.

After dinner they went for a walk around the observatory gardens, trying not to notice the Secret Service agents sneaking around them just a few yards off in every direction. She put her hand in his and with her other hand, held Roger's arm romantically. He noticed that his breathing felt deeper and more relaxed. Perhaps he was finally adjusting to life in Washington.

Before bed, as he did every night since taking office, Roger unfolded and flipped open the large collapsible notebook on the nightstand to read his email. Among the 25 new emails in the last hour, one looked important:

Sergey Brin, Dept. of Energy   Resignation

Dear Roger,

It is with deep anguish and great sorrow that I inform you that I cannot remain in the position you were so gracious to offer me at the Department of Energy. I have given the President my resignation and explained to him that I will not abide this administration's dangerous new policy in the Middle East, which I believe opens our great ally Israel to certain aggressive military action from Iran, as we have discussed already. As you know, I come from a Russian Jewish family and Israel is of extraordinary personal importance to me and to my family.

I wish you great success in all your policies, and I hope you and the President are able to modify your Israel policy before we are met with any tragic consequences.

I remain your friend and I send my greetings to Lenka.
Sincerely,
Sergey Brin

"That's fucking wrong," he mumbled with emphatic disappointment. "Shit," he added a few seconds later.

"What's wrong, Roger?" Lenka's voice echoed from the bathroom.

"Sergey resigned."

"He resigned?" she asked, not sure if she'd heard right.

"Yeah, he quit!" Roger said, raising his voice to be heard, but also snapping a bit.

Wrapped in her bathrobe, Lenka walked around to her side of the bed and leaned in toward Roger. Coming down on her stomach, she put out her elbows and propped her head up by the chin, and her feet sailed automatically into the air, pointed like a ballerina's. Her hair was wet and Roger inhaled the peachy scent of her shampoo.

"Why did he quit?" Lenka asked, "Because of the Israel thing the other day?"

"That was yesterday. Yeah."

"Oh yesterday? Um..." Lenka often lost track of the day.

"So he left under protest?"

"I guess you could say that, yeah."

"That's too bad, tiger. I'm sorry."

"He said to say hi to you though."

"He did? In his resignation?" Lenka said, confused.

"He resigned to the President, honey. He wrote me an

email to let me know why he resigned and thanking me, you know, because I originally suggested him for the job, and at the end he said, 'I remain your friend,' and he sends you his greetings too."

"Well it sounds like he's not holding it against you personally. That's good."

"I hope so. I don't think he would do that. But it could just be that Russian politeness too. I've seen a lot of eastern Europeans that were just raised to act polite regardless of the situation."

"Roger, Sergey's not like that," she said, mildly scolding.

"I hope not, honey. I said I hope not."

"Trust your friends a little bit, baby."

"Honey, we're in Washington."

"But Sergey's not from Washington, Roger. Don't do that to him."

"OK," Roger said, exasperated. "I'll give him the benefit of the doubt. It's hard to tell though, when someone's so emotional."

She sensed that he was himself emotional – one of his few friends that he'd brought from his business world into the Washington world had made him feel like he'd been changed, maybe too much, by it all. "Just give it some time. When your policy works out OK for a few months, maybe he'll cool off."

"Yeah, maybe."

"Come here, tiger," Lenka cooed, climbing halfway on top of him and snuggling her nose in tight behind his right ear.

"Mmmmm..." Roger hummed contentedly as he tried to release the troubles of another day and slipped gradually toward sleep.

...

"What the fucker!?" Lenka heard Roger yelling in the other room. She was still groggy, but she had no doubt that he was seriously agitated.

"What is it, babe?" she asked, pushing her hair from her face and squinting against the dawn sun.

He put his hand on the bedroom doorframe and leaned in, his half-tied necktie dangling in front of him. "Remember Shauna Jenkins from Florida?" he asked angrily.

"She was our state campaign manager, wasn't she?" she asked, blurring her sleepy words just a bit.

"Yeah. She's all over television spreading scandalous lies this morning."

"What?!" Lenka said, now fully awake and totally surprised.

"She's claiming she has an ongoing long-term affair with me!"

"Oh my god," Lenka said wearily.

"What the hell is she thinking?" Roger boomed, turning back into the other room so he wouldn't be yelling at Lenka.

Lenka tumbled out of bed and into the other room. She leaned against Roger and watched a few minutes of Jenkins' press conference replay through still bleary eyes. Then she squinted and sighed.

"Look at that tacky yellow business suit," she mumbled to herself. "She probably thinks she'll become a celebrity or something," Lenka suggested as she walked back into the bedroom.

"Or she OD'ed on crazy pills," he theorized loudly. "Goddamn Florida. When do we hack them off of the continent and float them away already? Jeezus Churist."

...

"I'll leave it to the experts in the media to speculate on her motivation, but Ms. Jenkins is lying, that is clear. My wife and I share a very close and happy relationship. Lenka knows that I am not capable of cheating on her, and I have never cheated on her."

The White House press room erupted in a flurry of waving hands and shouting.

"Bob?" Roger said with fatigue in his voice, pointing at the ABC reporter.

"Mr. Vice President, there were some photos that surfaced during last year's campaign that appeared to show you entering an adult club with a woman under your arm."

"Right, the strip club photo. I didn't bother responding to this trash during the campaign, so why would I respond to it now?"

Lenka cupped her hand over Roger's ear while the press room erupted in another round of noise. Roger nodded his agreement, and Lenka stepped in front of him. The room quickly went quiet. Lenka spoke with calm confidence.

"If the photos had been better, you might have discovered that the woman going into the strip club with Roger several years ago was his wife."

The press stood silent for half a second and then broke into total screaming chaos. As Lenka opened her mouth to speak, the shouting died down but one question rang out.

"Are you trying to cover up your husband's infidelities?"

"There are no infidelities to cover, and it's brash of you to ask, Erin," she scolded. "For the record, I dragged Roger out for some fun on his birthday. We can do that if we want to. We're grown-ups. No one got hurt. Well, Roger maybe suffered a bit of whiplash," she said, laying her fingertips at the top of his ear and running them down across his neck, "but otherwise, no one got hurt," she smirked.

Now the reporters were completely quiet. Had they been on a Hollywood beat, this might have been standard fare, but this was the Vice President of the United States. Finally, a Sky Wall Street Journal reporter returned to the original accusations, determined not to be distracted by the Second Lady's startling revelations. "Mrs. Adams, if you enjoy adult entertainment together, how can you be sure the Vice President doesn't also enjoy such activities without you?"

"I don't know where you reporters get the nerve to form such deeply insulting questions," Lenka said, now starting to tremble with anger. Roger put his hand on her shoulder to pull her back from the mic, but she pushed his hand off and continued. "This really digs deep into our personal lives now. But since you can't leave us our privacy, I'll explain it to you. I hope you're taking good notes. About two months ago, as I'm sure you all remember, there was a frightening attack on the White House. Roger and I were in the Rose Garden that day and when the fireballs began to come down on us, Roger and I were pulled in different directions by our brave Secret Service agents. I was not hurt, but Roger was separated from me in this moment of danger, and I have never even told him this, but I did hear his screams above all the noise. I heard him screaming my name in the most disturbing howls of distress I have ever heard in my life, and I knew he could not imagine being separated from me in that moment. The President went back to work within the hour that day, but Roger took me home to Oregon and held me tight for hours on end and cooked dinner for me and didn't let me out of his sight all week. This is a man whose greatest pleasure in life is sharing his time with me. If this man is a lying womanizer, than I am the world's greatest fool, because I would sooner buy a bridge from the hobo who sleeps beneath it, than buy the notion that Roger Adams would ever do anything to hurt me."

Everyone stared at Lenka, mouths gaping. Roger leaned forward sheepishly and said, "It's true, I did order my Secret Service team to return me to Lenka's location during the Rose Garden bombing. I believe I temporarily reassigned some of my agents to Siberia in a moment of duress, as well," he added, hoping to replace the humbling feeling of being totally exposed with a bit of dignified humor.

The rushing pushing of pens across paper and the clickity clack of various handheld typing devices combined to form a loud, strange urban background noise in the press room. Most of the seasoned White House reporters were suddenly busy working out the dynamic hidden love story of the Vice President and the Second Lady. Sensing that they had their stories, Roger chose not to mill around waiting for another round of questions. He put his arm around Lenka, whispered to her "Let's go," and already halfway to the door, yelled, "Thank you" over his shoulder to the White House press corps. "Mr. Vice President!" a few called out, but he was already gone.

Back in his office, Roger whined, "That was very embarrassing."

"Don't be embarrassed, tiger, it's the truth, and now you won't get any more invented mistress stories," Lenka offered proudly.

"Of course I'm not embarrassed of the truth or of you, absolutely not. But whatever happened to the decorum of the White House? The nation's capital can't become a tabloid."

Lenka snickered. "What rock have you been living under for the last two and a half centuries? Do you want me to name them? Let's see - Monica Lewinsky, Iran-Contra, Watergate, Marilyn Monroe, Teapot Dome, Jefferson's slave mistress..."

"OK honey, OK," Roger capitulated, putting his head down in his hands, feeling so exhausted he could cry.

"I'm sorry, tiger," she said consolingly.

"That's not the legacy I'm hoping to join," he muttered through his hands.

"I know," she said slowly and stretched her arm over his broad shoulders.

Lenka didn't realize how far she had opened up Roger's vulnerable side in front of the eat-you-for-breakfast White House press corps. He hadn't realized either, that she would go that far when he agreed to let her talk about the strip club photo, which honestly was exactly what she said it was - she had dragged him out on his birthday, even though none of the reporters actually believed it.

"I need some sleep," Roger mumbled.

...

Nearly all the sites, and several major papers too, much to the surprise of everyone in the White House, wrote gushing, soft-lit love stories about Roger and Lenka Adams. The overwhelmingly negative rants on immigration and Middle East policy were actually pushed below the fold for a few days in favor of things like:

Veep Enjoys Steamy Married Life

Ad(d)ams Family Live Up to the Name - Eccentric and Adorable.

Everything seemed to smooth over after that. The fringes of the nets were still screaming, as they did every day, but the public generally tired of the major controversies and the news moved on, allowing the Richardson administration to continue its work under less public pressure. Roger managed to rally congressional support for a repeal of domestic drone surveillance flights, which over the last few years had become a highly invasive and widespread new toy for law enforcement agencies at all levels. Federal agencies still had high-powered satellites at their disposal, but at least small remote control aircraft were no longer chasing citizens around U.S. cities for no good reason. Troops were coming home in large numbers. President Richardson had already been able to cut billions of dollars of overspending with his new Presidential line-item veto and each successive bill that came across his desk came in with fewer pork barrel items to cut. The Foreign Earnings Tax Break was still in place, but the Majority Leader promised it would come before the Senate again when the timing was right. The teacher's minimum wage was coming up later in the year, and it looked like it was going to have the votes needed to pass.

Charges of anti-Semitism against Richardson were widely disparaged as extreme rhetoric against the seasoned diplomat who was himself a member of a minority. It didn't even have the sound of truth to it and the powerful Israeli lobby lost face, just as Richardson had predicted. Some pundits surmised that either the Chinese or the Saudis would soon overtake them as the most powerful lobby in Washington. The Israeli people were nearly in a frenzy. Feeling the loss of unconditional American backing, they demanded overwhelmingly that Liberman return to peace negotiations. Only the most militant hardliners were opposed. The concept of a

Palestinian right of return had fallen away years earlier, but otherwise, little had changed in the matters up for discussion. Israel was to return to its pre-1967 borders and return all Palestinian prisoners to Palestine and Palestine would halt all attacks. It was agreed that Jerusalem would be shared, but would never be the capital of either nation. The difference now was mainly that no party felt they could afford to walk away from the table. The Palestinians finally began to believe they would have their independent state, which allowed them to unite under Hamas, for Hamas was able to proclaim victory in their fight for Palestinian independence and shift their focus away from Israel and toward a maelstrom of domestic problems. The Israelis were simply not in a position to take on the entire region alone. As months of negotiations passed, they gradually recognized that there had been very few Palestinian attacks in recent months, that Hamas had transformed its position, even promising to recognize Israel as a final step of the peace process, and peace, so distant for so long, felt possible.

...

By Christmas time, the White House was running

smoothly and Richardson and Adams' reforms were beginning to show promise before their first year in office was up. The Washington establishment looked like an amazingly different set of people decked out in tuxedos and gowns for the White House Christmas Ball.

"How you feeling these days, Roger?"

"Optimistic, Mr. President."

"Good," he said cheerfully. "I knew you'd get settled in."

"I'm not used to taking such small steps, but now I'm starting to see how it can come together," Roger opined.

Richardson laughed. "It's a 240-year-old pile of molasses here in Washington. I'd say we're moving it about as fast as it goes."

"Some people can't slow down for it, I'm afraid," Roger said, reflecting on the recent departure of one of his few friends in Washington.

"I wanted to talk to you two about that actually," Bill said, looking directly at Lenka. She just waited, having no idea what he was about to say. "Lenka, I'd like you to consider taking over the Rainmaker Project at the Department of Energy."

"I'm honored, Mr. President," she said, catching her breath but not one to stumble on etiquette. "I must admit, I'm a little surprised as well."

Roger appeared equally surprised.

"You worked as a geologist before taking the helm at Women and Girls Assistance, didn't you, Lenka?" Richardson asked.

"For about ten years, yes."

"I can pull some strings to get your White House security clearance through," Bill said, jabbing her lightly with his elbow like a clown.

Lenka giggled, not knowing how else to react to the President's silly humor at this most formal of events.

"I'll take it under serious consideration, Bill. Thank you," she said, her voice still floating on a bed of repressed laughter.

Bill gave her a small nod and then looked across the room for a moment.

"Mr. President?"

"Yes, Lenka?" he answered her, leaning forward with a smile.

"I was always optimistic."

FINE .

www.ingramcontent.com/pod-product-compliance
Lightning Source LLC
LaVergne PA
LVHW0252030726
800001B/172